DISCOVERING THE MARQUESS

Courting a Curious Lady, Book 4

Lexi Post

ARE YOU SIGNED UP FOR DRAGONBLADE'S BLOG?

You'll get the latest news and information on exclusive giveaways, exclusive excerpts, coming releases, sales, free books, cover reveals and more.

Check out our complete list of authors, too!

No spam, no junk. That's a promise!

Sign Up Here

www.dragonbladepublishing.com

Dearest Reader;

Thank you for your support of a small press. At Dragonblade Publishing, we strive to bring you the highest quality Historical Romance from some of the best authors in the business. Without your support, there is no 'us', so we sincerely hope you adore these stories and find some new favorite authors along the way.

Happy Reading!

CEO, Dragonblade Publishing

Additional Dragonblade books by Author Lexi Post

Courting a Curious Lady Series
Uncovering the Lord (Book 1)
Confounding the Earl (Book 2)
Disarming the Baron (Book 3)
Discovering the Marquess (Book 4)

Marrying a Mabry Series
Stealing the Duke (Book 1)
Painting the Earl (Book 2)
Revealing the Viscount (Book 3)
Once Upon a Haunted Haven (Novella)

Acknowledgments

For my husband Bob Fabich, who showed me that who I am, faults, quirks, and all, is "perfect" for him. I'm so lucky to have found my perfect match.

For my sister Paige, who read this story in short order and had excellent suggestions for helping my readers understand the hero better.

I also need to thank Marie Patrick, who was with me every step of the way, reading chapters as soon as I finished them and giving me the encouragement I needed.

My Lexi's Legends came through again, making this writing journey so much more fun. In particular I'm grateful to Patricia Way, Carey Naylor Sullivan, Bette Read, and Eileen Saunders McCall for their wonderful name suggestions. A special thank you to Debra Keath Bernucho for giving me some great ideas for winning over a reluctant child. I am truly lucky to have all my Legends supporting me and I appreciate every one of you.

Author's Note

The Courting a Curious Ladies series was inspired by two of my three favorite books of all time—Louisa May Alcott's novels, *Little Men* and *Jo's Boys*, published in 1871 and 1886 respectively. These were the next two books after *Little Women*, and I fell in love with Jo's school for boys. In Alcott's novels, there are a dozen boys as well as a few girls, all of whom go through the trials and tribulations of growing into adults. In *Stealing the Duke*, Lady Joanna sets up a school for ladies of the peerage modeled after Oxford and Cambridge. It's called the Belinda School for Curious Ladies.

Discovering the Marquess is specifically inspired by the character Thomas from Alcott's books. He was good natured, but rather enthusiastic and accident prone. Eleanor shares many of his characteristics. She is good natured, loud, clumsy, and mothers everyone. While Tom has unruly curls, Ellie has bright-red hair. And though Tom's love interest is more a friend that he does anything for, so too does Ellie try to be what other ladies in her school are and looks out for them. But just as Tom moves on and finds his true love, so must Ellie. Unfortunately, Ellie's journey has a few more bumps in the road, some expected and some completely unexpected.

CHAPTER ONE

Late November, 1817

SINCE MEETING HER husband two hours ago, Eleanor Compton of Dulac, now Marchioness Ferncroft, had made three observations. He was very handsome, he was exceedingly formal, and he was unusually grateful. It was the last that had her curious.

Lissa, the Baroness of Bellamore and her dear friend, tapped her on the arm as the vicar reverently pulled out the register from a locked cabinet. She whispered, "Are you pleased?"

Pleased? Ellie was still in awe. "I'm far beyond that. For once my mother has been singing my praises because I was going to marry a marquess. His children are darlings and are so well behaved, I'm not sure I can believe it. And he is far younger and more handsome than any man I've spoken to in two Seasons."

"Shh, Ellie." Lissa put her finger to her lips.

Drat. Her excitement had raised her voice again, and now Lord Ferncroft looked at her inquiringly.

She gave him a small smile and a nod before turning back to Lissa. "Did you notice I didn't trip or bump into anything? Maybe getting married will mean I won't have any future mishaps."

Lissa squeezed her arm. "It doesn't matter. You are a wonderful person with a big heart, and I just know that your husband and his children are going to benefit greatly from having you in their lives."

Ellie risked another look toward her new spouse as he spoke

in low tones with the vicar. She still felt as if she were in a dream. Until now, the only men interested in her at the ripe age of a score and four had been men her father's age. Lord Ferncroft was no more than ten years older than her and had absolutely no white hair. Her pulse tended to speed up every time he looked at her. She turned back to Lissa, who, with her husband, the marquess's brother, had instigated the match. "Thank you. You are the best of friends." She squeezed Lissa's arm to make clear her sincerity.

"You were there for me when I needed help. It's only fair. In fact, I even slipped the book into your chest. You'd forgotten it."

At Lissa's statement, Ellie frowned. "No, I'm quite sure I packed *On the Construction of the Heavens* by Herschel. I would never leave that behind."

"Ellie, not *that* book. The one that will help you gift the marquess with another son."

She'd purposely left that particular book in her armoire back at the Belinda School for Curious Ladies, since she'd had no time to read it before leaving. She'd planned to let Sophie know where to find it. Sophie loved reading. Knowing *the book* was in one of her chests for a maid to find had heat filling her face. "Oh."

Lissa patted her hand. "Don't worry. I wrapped it in paper."

Relieved yet still rattled, Ellie looked about just to be sure no one overheard them.

"Lady Ferncroft, if you would?" The vicar, a kind older man whose white hair was noticeably missing on his pate, held his hand toward the register.

"Of course." She quickly moved to the table where the book lay and stood next to her new husband.

"My lord?" The vicar nodded as if telling them it was time to sign.

Darius Taylour, the Marquess of Ferncroft, lifted the quill and dipped it into the inkwell before confidently affixing a sprawling and elegant signature in the register. When he finished, he handed her the quill.

Not trusting her voice as her heart fluttered at his attentiveness, she gave him a short nod before leaning over to set the quill in the inkwell for additional ink. Somehow, though she wasn't quite sure how—whether it was the fluttering of her heart or the bird shadow that flew by the small vestry window—she missed the opening and accidently pushed the inkwell, which sent it skidding across the table, only to overturn, splatter black ink upon the vicar's vestments, and fall to the floor. "Oh no! I do apologize."

The vicar appeared to be in shock as he stared down at his black-spotted white surplice, his mouth open.

Her heart sank, partly because she'd thought that possibly, by being married, her penchant for being clumsy had miraculously disappeared, and partly because she was quite mortified at what she'd managed to do. "Maybe I can help."

As she started to turn, the marquess grasped her wrist. "I'm sure the good vicar will be fine with acquiring a new surplice, which I will be pleased to purchase for him. I think it best that you sign the register."

Feeling her face heat with embarrassment, she acquiesced. "Of course."

Thankfully, the marquess took the quill, which she hadn't realized she still held, from her hand. He then calmly walked around the table, crouched down to dip the quill in a puddle of ink on the stone floor, and brought it back to her.

As she looked up at him to thank him, feeling more gratitude than perhaps the situation warranted, he placed the quill in her hand. "Will you sign?"

She nodded, caught in his mysterious gray gaze.

"On the register?"

Blinking to stop staring, she forced herself to face the book on the table and scrawled her name, not nearly as elegant as her husband's but clearly legible. At the realization it was the very last time she would be known as Eleanor Compton of Dulac, a surge of happiness filled her, and she dropped the quill on the book to turn and smile at the marquess.

He, however, wasn't looking at her. In fact, he reached across her and grabbed up the quill.

She looked down to find a black spot of ink three lines below growing larger and closer to her signature.

"Anthony, I believe we need you now as our witness?" The marquess turned to his brother.

Though the vicar frowned at her, Lord Bellamore grinned and, copying his brother, crouched down and dipped the quill in the spilled ink before pulling the register toward him and signing it next to the black spot.

"I believe I'm next." Lissa walked behind the vicar and took the quill from Anthony, quickly bending over for ink and signing the book on the other side of the spot. "Now it's official."

Ellie sensed her new husband's relief, which had her studying him as he gave a smile to Lissa and Anthony. She couldn't fathom why anyone would be relieved to have married her, especially a man of such wealth, refinement, and handsomeness.

As Anthony stepped forward to pat the marquess on the back, Lissa came over and gave her a hug. "I'm exceedingly happy for you, Ellie."

When Lissa released her, she opened her mouth to question her, but Lissa linked their arms. "Now you must come out to the church proper, because the other Curious Ladies wish to say goodbye."

For the first time that day, Ellie's enthusiasm waned. In all the excitement of marrying the marquess, she'd forgotten that it meant not seeing her friends daily anymore. She would worry about them without her being at Silver Meadows.

As soon as she stepped into the almost empty church, Sophie ran down the aisle toward her, tears already gathering in her pretty green eyes. "Ellie."

Ellie gave her dear, quiet friend a strong hug, her own eyes misting a bit. Then she set her back. "Now *you* must take care of the new ladies in the school, since I'm not going to be there to do it. And you must send me weekly reports on how everyone is faring."

"I will. I promise." Sophie nodded even as she dabbed at her cheeks with a lace handkerchief.

"I will also want to know all about how your literature studies are going with Mrs. Kingman. And when outings are offered, no staying behind just because I'm not there."

Sophie's eyes rounded, but then she took a deep breath and nodded solemnly. "I promise."

"And I promise not to let her." Georgie, who was never still for long, clasped Sophie by the shoulder so they stood side by side. "She will be by my side at every outing. And who knows, maybe one of us will be following in your footsteps soon enough."

Ellie smiled widely at Georgie, whose greatest passions in life were birds and dancing. "I do hope that is true. And when the Season starts, I'll even be able to play chaperone now."

Both ladies' eyes widened at the realization.

"A role you were born to play." Rose strode forward, a smile playing about her mouth. "I do hope they don't both marry and go off leaving me all by myself."

Ellie held her hands out, well aware that Rose's prospects were better than any of theirs, if she'd stop playing pranks long enough to talk to a few men. "Of course they won't leave you alone. You'll just have to marry in the same Season, which I'm sure won't be a problem."

Georgie stepped up next to Rose. "It won't be if we can pull her away from her studies long enough to attend a gathering or two."

The three women chuckled, and the sound had Ellie feeling a bit more confident that they would be fine. They had each other, and more ladies were coming to the school every day. Her own marriage to a marquess would assure the duchess of even more scholarly students soon.

Then, before she could truly accept the significant change in her life, her friends had each kissed her on the cheek and filed out of the church to continue their old lives.

"Ah, here is where they got off to."

At Lord Bellamore's announcement, she turned around to find him and his brother standing in the archway.

A small tingle of excitement started again in Ellie's belly as she gazed at her husband. He and Lord Bellamore were a *study in contrasts*, as Lady Sommerset, her art history instructor, would say. The marquess was taller and leaner, with short black hair and gray eyes, while his youngest brother was broader, a little shorter, with fashionable-length blond hair and blue eyes. Ellie far preferred the more distinguished look of her husband. She quite believed that discovering the marquess would be as exciting as discovering a new star cluster!

Lissa spoke for them. "Don't worry. We wouldn't wander too far from such exceptional husbands."

Anthony strode forward, laughing. "That, my dear elderly brother, means she wants something."

Lissa gave Anthony an innocent look. "Now, why would you make such an assumption?"

"Because I know you well."

Lissa turned to Ellie. "This is what comes of knowing each other for years. I can't surprise him very often. You have so much to look forward to."

The marquess approached. "As do I. Lady Ferncroft, shall we travel to Hawthorne Park for our wedding breakfast, where our families await?"

Her new name was far too formal for her, but she would wait to discuss how they addressed each other in private until…well, they were in private. "Yes, my lord."

He offered his arm, and she took it, grateful for his strength, which should keep her from any more mishaps. As they exited the church, a shower of seeds greeted them from her wonderful friends and the villagers of her husband's estate.

She could almost feel his pride, and looked at him to find the marquess smiling at those around them. It was the first time she'd seen him smile, which was a relief. She had started to wonder if maybe he was always serious and stiff. She certainly hadn't wanted to be married to a lord "stiffboard," as Lissa called some of the aristocracy.

He led her through the shower of seeds to his waiting coach. The Ferncroft crest decorated the door, and the footman were all at their posts. He handed her up into the empty coach then joined her, taking the seat opposite.

Surprised to find them alone, she addressed her immediate concern. "Where are the children?"

The upturn of his lips lingered still, even rising a bit more. "I sent them ahead home with their nursemaid. They behaved very well, and I didn't wish them to have to be so for too long."

Pleased by his thoughtfulness and caring, she relaxed. "I was very impressed with Maggie and Peter. You must be proud of them."

"I am." He continued to gaze at her.

Was something amiss? She patted her hair to be sure it was all still in place. Then again, he could simply be staring at its bright red color. Surely Lissa and her husband had told the marquess about her "unfortunate fiery locks," as her father termed them. As her new husband opened his mouth, she prepared for his disappointment.

"I hope you will find Hawthorne Park to your liking. There are parts of the house, I will admit, that are not my favorite, so if there are any areas you would like to change, please confer with me. Except for my study, I'm open to suggestions."

Nonplussed by the lack of criticism, she didn't speak at once as she tried to refocus on his actual words. "That is very generous, my lord."

He waved his hand as if it were nothing. "My late wife found fault with much of the house and fully enjoyed changing it over, some rooms more than once."

She raised her brows at that. Her husband must have quite a

bit of wealth for that to be so. Her own father kept her mother regulated to one room every two years. That meant Lord Ferncroft was situated well, as well as quite handsome. Which again raised the question, why had he married her?

"Now, as to the nursery, you may need to confer with my children. In fact, I have no doubt they would enjoy a different scene than what is presently there. It is a meadow with a lake with swans, though my daughter insists they are geese, which Pete will then immediately pretend to hunt." Again, his lips lifted.

That he would allow his children of five and seven to have a say in the nursery décor was quite remarkable, and not a little out of character for the formal marquess, from what she could see. Her curiosity, now completely roused, needed answers. "Why did you marry me, my lord?"

He blinked before cocking his head. "Why? I had thought I made it quite clear that I wished for a mother for my children."

Despite his obvious affront—though whether it was to her bluntness or ignorance, she knew not—she'd been taught to logically argue, and so she would. "Yes, I was made aware of that. What I meant by my question is why me, specifically? There are dozens of younger women who would be quite open to your attentions. And why an arranged marriage without ever meeting me? Were you not worried I would not do?" *She* certainly had worried about that, and still did.

His brows drew together in obvious puzzlement. "I knew you were a woman of the peerage and, according to my brother, one who would welcome being a mother to my children. And as to your age, my lady, I *specifically* didn't want a younger woman. I am thirty-six and far too old for a simpering miss straight out of the schoolroom. In addition, not only did my brother recommend you, but the Duchess of Northwick sang your praises most readily. She was quite insistent that you had a good intellect and would manage my family well. Lastly, you were available and possibly open to an arranged marriage. Since your attributes met all of my requirements, I did not see a reason for us to meet.

Would you have preferred I interview you like a high-level servant?"

She shook her head, a bit stunned at his revelations. He obviously did not want a wife for himself, but for the management of his home and the caring of his children. Illogically hurt by his explanation, while at the same time grateful for the kindness of Lord Bellamore and the Duchess of Northwick, Ellie lapsed into silence—not a common occurrence for her.

It appeared it wasn't so much that the marquess had sought her out specifically, but had a list of criteria and she happened to meet them all. It washed away the cloud she'd floated upon for the last month while the banns were read and the settlements were finalized. Though he said he didn't interview her like a common servant, he had done far less.

She folded her arms as much to comfort herself as to stay warm. On the other hand, no matter how she found herself a marchioness, she was. And a mother of two. She had never hoped for the first and had craved the second since she was a child of five years and insisted on giving her dolls cocoa. If she were able to follow the Duke of Northwick's teachings in logic, she was indeed in very good circumstances. That was somewhat of a consolation. But the fact that it wasn't enough had her feeling guilty for expecting something more.

"Lady Ferncroft, I do need to make something very clear in regard to my children."

At her husband's voice, she pulled her gaze from the lap of her best blue dress to his face. "Yes. I hope we will always be clear with each other. What about your children?"

"I chose you specifically because of your skill in mothering others. I do not want my children to have a mother they see every other day to inspect their dress and who only parades them before guests. I'm sure you will be having guests for tea, and my children are not to be used as gossip fodder. I wish you to be the kind of mother who is involved in their lives on a daily basis so they know they can depend upon you and will wish to seek you out when they are afraid or hurt. Anthony and I had a rare but satisfying childhood because our parents were involved with us. They did not hand us off to tutors and governesses. Though we had both, it was our parents who actually raised us."

The marquess raised his hand. "Yes, I understand it's quite unorthodox, and I can only lay that blame at my mother's door, as I assure you, my father, the Duke of Roxburgh, did not have such an upbringing. However, having experienced it firsthand, I believe it the best way to raise children to take on the responsibilities they will inherit in adulthood. So, I ask you—am I correct in believing that you can provide this type of childhood for Peter and Maggie?"

As he spoke, her unrest dissipated, giving way to the joy of his request. It was her secret dream to be involved in her offspring's childhood, and one she was anxious to pursue. Lissa had been absolutely correct. Lord Ferncroft *needed* her.

She held back her smile, curbing her enthusiasm, which was no easy task. Lissa had cautioned her not to reveal too much, too soon. "You are correct. I can provide such an upbringing. Though I would ask one boon of you in return."

The man stiffened from the tip of his angular nose to the straightening of his shoulders. "What boon would you ask beyond marriage?"

She gave him a soft smile. "That in private and with the children, we address each other by our given names. I believe it will help Maggie and Peter to accept me. Losing their mother had to be a terrible loss if this was their type of childhood."

As her husband looked away, she worried that he might not acquiesce to her request.

Finally, he returned his gaze to her, his gray eyes not giving away how he felt. "My late wife did not agree with my views on children. Therefore, it was incumbent upon me to make myself available to them, but I'm sure that you can understand how difficult that is with all my responsibilities. By adding you to my family, I believe we can now accomplish my goal in regards to my children. To that end, I agree to your request and will address you as Eleanor in private, specifically before my children."

That her simple boon had revealed so much more information about her husband had her spirits lifting. He was obviously a reasonable man and gave much thought to everything he did. Though some ladies may be uncomfortable with such a man, she felt much better that her mate for life had strengths she didn't, and most likely vice versa.

More than pleased with their mutual understanding, she smiled. "Thank you, Darius. I am quite pleased to be able to be of assistance."

Though he did take a sudden breath when she called him by name, he gave her a regal nod. "I am most grateful."

And there it was, the answer to her unspoken question. She now understood why he was grateful to have married her. She would do all in her power to fulfill his expectations.

CHAPTER TWO

DARIUS CLASPED HIS hands together on his desk as he contemplated his response to the nursemaid. He truly did not wish to dismiss her, but he also couldn't have her coming to him to counter his wife's orders. On the other hand, his wife's plan did seem to be beyond the norm. "And have you brought your concerns to the marchioness?"

Anna nodded. "I have, sir, but she insists that she knows far more about reading, writing, and history than any governess and that under no such circumstances will she hire one. But there is more, sir."

He closed his eyes briefly. Of course there was. He opened his eyes and glanced at the small clock on his desk. It had been barely fifty-eight hours since he'd brought his bride home and a mere four hours since his parents departed, and already his housekeeper, butler, a maid, and the nursemaid had come to him with concerns about the new Lady Ferncroft. How could his life have seemed so normal just the day before last and now be something he didn't recognize? "Do continue."

The nursemaid clasped her hands together. "Peter doesn't like the new marchioness. He's been refusing to do anything she says and insists that if she does not leave, he will starve himself!"

That his son would even think to refuse eating had concern rising hard in Darius's chest. Peter had been born too soon and was too small for his age as it was. The last thing Darius needed was for his son to starve himself.

"Would you like me to fetch my lady?"

There was something in the nursemaid's tone of voice that had him thinking again upon his response. It was as if she'd expected to be the final straw against his wife. Was his staff more opposed to Lady Ferncroft than his children?

His housekeeper, in her complaints, had mentioned the lady's red hair as if that made her have a temper. The maid mentioned that a teacup had been overturned as if on purpose, and the butler had been unhappy when Lady Ferncroft refused to take a footman with her into the garden. And now it was his wife's refusal to hire a governess. It was time he investigated the truth of the matter.

He returned his gaze to the nursemaid. "No need. Go to the kitchen and tell Cook to sit you down with a cup of tea and prepare some Shrewsbury cakes." He rose from his chair. "I will search out my wife."

The nursemaid rose as well. "She's in the nursery with Peter and Maggie."

He had surmised as much, since the nursemaid was with him. "Thank you. Now go see Mrs. Clark."

"Yes, my lord." The nursemaid rose, gave a brief nod, then exited his study.

He pulled down his waistcoat. His new wife, despite her hair, had seemed very calm, even appearing quite pleased when he'd informed her the night before that they could postpone their wedding night until they knew each other better. In fact, she seemed relieved, which he had expected. He did still need another son, but he hoped to engender his wife's loyalty and empathy.

Though she was unaware of his black moods—a situation he wished to keep—her connection with his children was essential to their lives. His bouts of strong melancholia brought about not only unreasonable anger but harsh words that if inflicted on others could completely change the future of any relationship, which was why he sequestered himself for days on end. He could not control his actions at such times, so to keep everyone safe and his authority and image intact, it was necessary to remove his presence from others.

Having a wife his children could depend upon during his absences was of the utmost importance to him. It was also quite possible that one day he would follow in his uncle's footsteps, and if that unfortunate event were to happen, it was imperative that his wife be able to provide love and comfort to Peter and Maggie. He would sacrifice everything to ensure they were well cared for and protected.

He started out of his study and headed upstairs toward the nursery. His mother had taken an instant liking to his new wife, and even his father, the duke, approved. All seemed to be progressing according to his well-thought-out parameters. He could see no reason for the upheaval his staff seemed to be experiencing.

At the top of the stairs, he paused. Childish laughter came from the left where the nursery was situated. *Magpie.* His chest filled with warmth to hear his daughter's laughter again. That sound alone had him anxious to discover the reason.

He strode down the corridor past his wife's suite of rooms, past her private parlor to the final room before the building took a right toward the guest rooms.

A squeal of laughter penetrated the door as he approached, followed by a lovely, full-bodied laugh that could have only come from his new wife. Not wishing to make too much of a disturbance, he quietly opened the door.

The scene he walked in upon had him halting. Lady Ferncroft had a napkin draped over her head and what appeared to be hot cocoa above her lip like a mustache as she sat at the table facing his daughter, who had a blanket wrapped about her like a cloak. Both had smiles on their faces, but his son, who sat next to Maggie, had rolled his lips in as if trying not to grin, his arms crossed over his chest. A bowl of melted ice cream sat nearby, while the bowls before his daughter and his new wife were empty. Ice cream was one of his son's favorite sweets, so for him not to be eating any was serious indeed. It was the last that had Darius's contentment evaporating. "What goes on here?"

"Father!" Maggie jumped off her chair and ran over to him, then gave a curtsey like a lady. "You must join us, sir. We are learning about the flowers that bloom at night. Did you know there are flowers that bloom in the dark?" Her pretty blue eyes rounded.

"I did." He strode forward.

"Darius, you must join us. We are having hot cocoa with ice cream, though I fear you are too late for the latter. Learning is more palatable with a sweet, don't you agree?" Lady Ferncroft smiled up at him as if her idea was the most logical of ideas, her chocolate mustache now gone.

Her use of his name caught him off guard. Only his mother called him that. However, it did remind him of his agreement. "Eleanor, why do you wear a napkin on your head? Why is my daughter traipsing about in a quilt? And why is my son not allowed to eat?"

His wife's smile disappeared and her brow furrowed. "Is it not obvious? I am the Sheriff of Nottingham and Maggie is Maid Marian. We invited Peter to be Robin Hood, but he refused. I assume he didn't wish to eat the caramel ice cream because he wanted to give it to the poor."

It was his turn to be puzzled. "And what does Robin Hood have to do with night-blooming flowers?"

Maggie sat down next to his wife. "Father, isn't it obvious? We are learning about Nottingham catchfly flowers. Did you know they bloom for three nights? Could we have some planted in the garden?"

"I don't want any flowers." Peter scowled. "I don't want anything."

Lady Ferncroft took the napkin from her head. "Surely you want something."

"I want you to go away."

If he hadn't been watching his wife, Darius would have missed her tiny flinch at his son's words. Not happy with such rudeness, he opened his mouth to reprimand him, but she spoke first.

"Is that all you wish for? Then, Peter, I will be happy to leave." She rose. "After all, I have many duties to ensure the house is run efficiently, and having fun with you and Maggie truly is not on my list. I'm so glad you let me know. I will happily remove myself so you may enjoy your day."

"Please don't go." Maggie grabbed her hand. "You didn't finish teaching us about the flowers."

Crouching down, the lady of the house put herself on an equal level with Maggie. "Perhaps that lesson is best saved for spring. I promise to talk to the gardener about having the various night-blooming flowers planted so that in the spring we can venture forth at night and see them bloom. Would you like that?"

"Yes. I would. Will you come back tomorrow and teach us something different then?"

Lady Ferncroft looked over at Peter. "Would you like me to come back tomorrow?"

"No."

The lady sighed as she rose. "I'm in a quandary now. You wish me to return, and Peter wishes that I don't. Perhaps you two could discuss it and let me know?"

"We can do that." Maggie gave her brother a serious look.

"Now, I best get back to my duties. Darius, did you wish to have cocoa? There's plenty here."

He did indeed, as he wished to talk to his children, but he also wished to talk to his wife. "As much as I would like to partake, I also have duties to attend to. But I promise to attend another ice cream and cocoa lesson in the future."

He didn't miss the pout on his son's face, nor the disappointment in his daughter's eyes. He steeled himself against it. It was his responsibility to be sure his new wife and his staff were in accord before he could enjoy any time with his children. It was critical that everything fell into place before he needed to leave again. He held his arm out for his wife. "I would be happy to escort you."

"Thank you, Darius." She strode toward him. She did not glide or stroll. It was another characteristic he had noticed about her. Wrapping her arm around his, she looked at him expectantly. "Shall we?"

He led her from the room and back downstairs directly into his study. He released her and closed the doors behind them. "May we talk?"

"Oh, we must." She strode to his desk and leaned her backside against it. "I'm concerned about Peter. He really needs to eat more. I have never met a little boy who didn't eat ice cream. He seems small for his age. Does he have health issues? Because the Duchess of Northwick is quite knowledgeable in that field and might be able to help."

"My son was born too soon and has always been small, but I assure you he does eat ice cream, particularly caramel ice cream." He hesitated to tell her why, remembering her reaction to Peter's demand that she leave, but it was imperative that they all move into a new routine sooner rather than later. "His nursemaid says Peter refuses to eat because you are here."

"Oh." The light in her blue eyes seemed to fade. "I suppose he still misses his mother."

Darius strode across the room and took a seat in his chair. "She passed away almost eight months ago, but he is young." He fully expected his wife to move to one of the wingback chairs and take a seat. She did not.

Instead, she remained on his desk and turned her head to look at him. "First, he loses his mother. Then he has only you for eight months. Then he's told I'm his new mother without a by-your-leave. You *did* tell your children you were marrying, correct?"

"I did. I had hoped to give them something to look forward to."

Lady Ferncroft hopped off his desk and strode toward the window.

Unfortunately, her hip hit the lantern on the corner, and he jumped up just in time to keep it from toppling over. He set it closer to himself and resumed his seat as she turned to address him.

"Perhaps I was overanxious. I wished to offer Maggie and Peter my friendship as well as my wisdom. Oh yes, I almost forgot. There will be no need to hire a governess. Your nursemaid was expecting her cousin to be hired for that purpose, something I believe was arranged by your late wife. But I believe I know what's best to teach them. I've had a far better education than a governess, and I'm more than willing to spend the time with such lovely children."

Now that explained why the nursemaid had complained. "If you feel you would like to take on my children's education until Peter is old enough for a tutor, then I am willing to support you in this." He couldn't see her reaction because the light streamed in behind her, causing her red hair to appear on fire. It was a startling illusion. Still, he could tell that she had tensed simply by her lack of movement, though he had no idea why.

"Darius, you do know about the Belinda School for Curious Ladies, do you not?"

"I know that it is a school for ladies of the peerage run by the Duke and Duchess of Northwick and from which my sister-in-law, Lady Bellamore, came."

"And do you know what it teaches?"

He found her question odd. He sat back in his chair and waved his hand. "I'm sure it is the usual painting, music, history, etc."

His wife let out a rather loud sigh before striding back to his desk, this time placing her behind upon the side.

He moved the lantern to the opposite side as a precautionary measure.

"Darius, the Belinda School does not teach painting, or music, or dancing. It does, however, teach philosophy, geology, literature, and, my personal favorite, astronomy, among other subjects. It is a school for ladies set up to mirror Oxford or Cambridge." Her voice rose until the final word was quite close to a yell.

Her volume and content had him stiffening. "You're telling me you've studied the likes of Plato, Hutton, Swift, and Galileo?"

"Yes." She clapped her hands. "I'm so pleased you know them. We shall have such lovely dinners discussing their ideas. I only point out my education so that you understand I do not take the education of your children lightly. However, I am also their mother now." She hopped off the desk, this time without knocking anything about before she strode back to the window. "It is this second role that is equally important and more difficult to navigate."

She strode forward, this time walking past his desk to the bookcases on the opposite wall. She stopped and stared at the books for a moment before turning to face him. "Unfortunately, there are no great tomes to be found on becoming a mother to growing children after their mother has passed. Poor things. So I will endeavor to do my best." She held her hand up. "That's not to say I won't make mistakes, but we learn far more from our mistakes than our successes, and I'm sure the children at such young ages are resilient. In fact, I was just telling my maid this morning—Oh, I hope you won't mind buying her a new dress. I fear in my excitement at spending time with Peter and Maggie that I waved my hand a bit too close to my teacup and it spilled, staining her pretty dress quite terribly. You see, I take tea in my room long before many are awake."

He gave a nod, happy to note it was not a purposeful act after all, but still reeling over the new information about her schooling.

"She really is a lovely young woman. But back to my purpose. Children are resilient, and I'm sure that eventually we will all enjoy a happy comfort with each other once we get over a few missteps here and there. Don't you agree?"

Unfortunately, she had pondered the subject of her relationship with his children far more ardently than he had. "I believe you are correct."

Her smile was instantaneous, and her face practically glowed. He had noticed how pale and soft her skin looked at the church, as there were a few freckles along the length of her straight nose and three on top of it at the end. It was a small nose, and he wouldn't have thought much about it except they had stood close to each other during the ceremony, and he'd become quite mesmerized by the light brown dots. When she smiled, as she did now, she was really rather pretty.

She leaned back against the bookcase, causing the bronze bust of Plato himself to move precariously closer to the edge. "Wonderful. Now, I do have a question about the safety of bringing the children into the garden." She pushed away from the bookcase and started forward, causing the bust to teeter on the edge.

He rose from his chair and approached, hoping to save his wife from an embarrassing moment, and she halted in front of him.

"I wandered into the garden outside the parlor shortly after your parents left, as your mother had told me how beautiful it was in the summer. I was not going to stay long outside, as all I had was my shawl, but one of the footmen insisted on accompanying me. I told him his services were not required, and he did balk quite a bit. From what I gathered, your late wife always took a footman, so either she was not as robust as myself or it's dangerous to walk about in the garden due to brigands of some sort."

Despite his concern about the bust, she captured his attention with that. "I assure you, there is no danger in walking through the gardens."

She laid her hand on her ample bosom. "I am very relieved to hear that, as that was exactly what I told the footmen. Now, in the woods about the property, I'm sure there are poachers and highwaymen on occasion."

"My lady, allow me to put to rest any concerns you have about the safety of Hawthrone Park. I vow that anywhere on the property you will be completely safe, even the woods."

"I am so pleased to know that, as I enjoy viewing the stars at night."

Too late he realized his mistake. He would have to think of a reason to keep her from the northern wood. Then again, viewing the stars from the garden would be much more rewarding, so there was no need for her to walk any of the wooded areas.

"And Darius." She laid her hand on his arm. "No need for formality between us. Remember, you can call me Eleanor, or even Ellie, as my dear friends call me. After all, I do think we will be quite good friends."

At such close proximity, her tiny freckles were noticeable, yet none were sprinkled along her neck or chest. He found his gaze dropping to where her pale-blue day dress covered her rather large bosom, and a strong curiosity about those bountiful globes started in the back of his head.

"I'm so pleased we had this talk. I'm truly looking forward to our conversation at dinner." With that, she patted his arm before striding to the doors, where she stopped and looked back at him and smiled. "I have to say, you have put so many of my worries about marrying to rest in such a short time. Thank you."

His wife then opened the door and closed it heartily. A bang sounded to the side of him. He started at the sound and looked over toward the bookcase to find the bust missing. The illustrious Plato was on the floor. Walking over to it, he crouched down and lifted it up. Plato had sustained no injuries; however, the same could not be said for the floor. Two large gouges had been made by the corners of the bust.

He rose and placed the bust back on the shelf. At least he had resolved all the servants' complaints to his own satisfaction. Now to take action. Most of his servants had been with him since he first came to Hawthorne Park directly from Oxford. There were only a few his late wife had hired on, like the nursemaid just before Maggie was born, so there shouldn't be too much resistance once all was explained. He walked to his desk and rang for his butler.

It was mere moments before the man walked in. "Yes, sir?"

Darius stood behind his desk to address the man who knew more than anyone in the house, including himself, most likely. "Beacham, I would like a word with you and Mrs. Torbett."

"I shall have her fetched immediately." The tall butler strode out and was back within seconds. "She will be here posthaste. May I inquire as to what will be the topic of our discussion, sir?"

Not wishing to have any prejudgments made, Darius shook his head. "No."

Beacham's eyes rounded for a mere second before he controlled his reaction. "Very good, sir."

Darius appreciated Beacham's formality in everything but also understood the man's surprise. There had been more than one time when he'd had to take his butler into his confidence. In fact, this would be another time, but for a completely different reason.

Mrs. Torbett bustled in. The housekeeper's cap had allowed a few strands of salt-and-pepper hair to escape, most likely from the exertion of her duties. "My lord. I came as quick as I could."

The woman's round cheeks were a bit red from her rush, as she was not thin, though not heavy either—and rather strong, from what he'd been told. He waved to one of the chairs before his desk. "Please, Mrs. Torbett. Have a seat. You too, Beacham." Darius remained standing. "I have called you both here to take you into my confidence so that you might better assist me."

"I be happy to help, my lord." Mrs. Torbett leaned forward in her chair.

Beacham quickly chimed in. "I am at your disposal, sir."

"Very good. It appears that my new wife has not made the best impression upon some of the servants."

"My lord, she did spill tea upon the maid."

At Mrs. Torbett's reply, he raised his right eyebrow at her before turning his gaze to Beacham, who pursed his lips. He moved his gaze back to the housekeeper. "Yes, so she told me. She waved her hand as she spoke and inadvertently knocked the tea over." He held up his hand as Mrs. Torbett opened her mouth, forestalling another interruption. "And I tell you more in the strictest of confidence. While she was in here talking with me, she almost pushed the lantern off the desk and did, in fact, succeed in knocking the bust of Plato off the shelf, though she didn't realize it."

The two immediately turned their heads toward the bookcase where Plato sat, far back from the edge.

"I returned the bust to the shelf, but the floor did not remain unscathed."

Mrs. Torbett turned back to look at him. "Oh, my poor lady."

Surprised, he cocked his head, interested in his housekeeper's sudden change of heart. "Mrs. Torbett?"

"I mean the poor dear. To be so clumsy with her status. I'm sure she's been plagued by this her whole life. No wonder she's so excited to have a family. She probably never expected to marry. I mean, with that hair and her knocking things over, I can't imagine any upstanding lord finding her appropriate. But you, my lord—your kind heart has not only given the children a new mother but my lady a family she probably never expected to have."

As Mrs. Torbett took out a handkerchief and dabbed at her teary eyes, Darius stood dumfounded. Again, he didn't understand what Lady Ferncroft's hair had to do with marrying, and he'd hardly classify her as clumsy. It was more exuberance, in his opinion.

Beacham appeared unmoved, but then again, he always did. "Beacham, what is your opinion?"

"I am honored that you have taken us into your confidence, sir. It is now clear why her ladyship did not want a footman with her in the garden. She feared his seeing her trip. Imagine the gossip below stairs that might begin. I shall notify all of them that they should not insist on accompanying her in the future." The butler sat straighter, though it was a feat, as the man was always straight, even if he was of an age with Mrs. Torbett.

Darius wasn't sure how he felt about his head staff pitying his wife, so until he did, he wouldn't argue the point. He just needed everyone to adjust smoothly so his own problems remained a secret from all but the two who sat before him. "I appreciate anything you two can do to help the staff accept their new mistress."

"I promise to do all in my power, my lord." Mrs. Torbett pressed her handkerchief to her chest. "I know in my heart that you wouldn't choose a lady of harsh temperament. I am grateful to have your trust."

"You can depend upon me, sir, as always." Beacham rose and gave a formal bow.

Relieved to have it all settled to a satisfactory conclusion, Darius gave them a nod. "Very good. Do not let me keep you from your duties any longer."

As Mrs. Torbett rose to follow the already-disappearing Beacham, Darius pulled out his chair.

But Mrs. Torbett did not follow his butler. "My lord—if I might have one more moment of your time?"

He forestalled his inclination to sit. "Of course." Surely it couldn't be more about his wife. He had hoped he'd settled that. Even as irritation flared, he recognized it for what it was. The beginnings of a black mood. Damn, he'd hoped to have more time.

"With the wedding and all the guests, I'm sure you haven't thought much about Christmas and the New Year, but I have prepared a list of foodstuffs for the festivities and wondered if you would like to see it. I can leave it on your desk before dinner-time."

Relief that it was nothing more than the holiday, he waved her off. "I believe Lady Ferncroft would prefer to be consulted on that. In fact, I leave the entire holiday in her capable hands."

Mrs. Torbett's brows rose for a moment. "Yes, of course." Her brows returned to their rightful position. "It will be a pleasure to help my lady create a wonderful holiday. Thank you, my lord." With that, the woman strode out of the study, closing the door quietly behind her.

He finally sank into his chair. Despite everything having been put to rights, his unease grew. After dinner. He'd wait to disappear until after dinner, for Lady Fer—for *Eleanor's* sake.

CHAPTER THREE

ELLIE SAT BEFORE her dressing table admiring how the peach dinner dress gave her complexion a soft glow. It also complemented her hair, or so Sophie had told her. She did hope Sophie and the other Curious Ladies were enjoying their studies before the term break. As for herself, she planned to continue hers when not teaching the children or making important decisions about the household.

She looked forward to her first dinner alone with her new husband. Secretly, she hoped to impress him with her knowledge. She had learned he was an Oxford graduate, so she had no doubt they could have a rousing conversation about any number of topics.

"Mary, bring me the red ribbon and the pretty purple butterfly for my hair. I do love that butterfly. It reminds me of my outing with Lissa at Talley on the Green."

Her lady's maid came up behind her. "I already had this white ribbon and snowflake comb."

"No, no. I want the red and purple." Though she valued Mary's opinion, Ellie wanted to make a very good impression on Darius.

Mary set the white ribbon and snowflake comb on the dressing table and disappeared back into the dressing room.

Ellie hoped to make her husband smile again, perhaps with an analogy of her new wedded status being much like the caterpillar's journey to becoming a butterfly. She certainly felt like one. She might even bring up the Greek goddess Psyche and the butterfly as the soul. There was so much to talk about regarding butterflies, if she needed a topic. Then again, there was also the cinnabar moth that flew at night, one of her favorites. She was far more familiar with night creatures because that was when the stars were most visible.

"I have them, my lady." Mary walked up behind her. "But I'm not sure about the red ribbon. It may give you a sad pallor in this dress."

Ellie waved off the comment. "Put it around my throat and I'll decide."

As Mary wrapped the ribbon around her neck, keeping the small red stone at the front, Ellie examined her reflection. It seemed to counteract all the dress did for her skin tone. As usual, Mary was correct. "Let's try the white ribbon."

Mary took the red off and hooked the white one, which had a tiny light-pink flower in the front.

"Yes, the white looks better. But then, will the purple comb look appropriate in my hair?"

Sophie had told Ellie that blue was actually the best to wear with her hair color. She watched in the mirror as Mary added the butterfly comb.

"Now try the snowflake." The white comb worked better, but she couldn't think of anything to discuss about snowflakes, except possibly one of the planets like Ceres, which would be incredibly cold.

"I will wear the butterfly." The butterfly had so much more potential for conversation.

As soon as Mary finished, Ellie rose. It was odd how nervous she was. She'd never been so around men before, but Darius was not just any man. In addition to being darkly handsome, he was her husband, until death do they part. Their first dinner alone would be the beginning of hundreds more, and she wanted it to go well. That must be why she felt unsure. Her expectations were too high. Her mother had always warned her about her high expectations that never materialized.

"My lady, I found a brown package in your chest. I think it might be from your classmates, as it wasn't there when I packed your clothes. I put it on the nightstand by the bed."

Her heart skipped a beat as she turned her attention to the paper-wrapped book at her bedside. Her cheeks heated at what was inside. At Lissa's insistence, after the proposal was made, Ellie had finally opened the book entitled *The Education of the Feminine Species*.

But that was the fake cover. Inside was *The Illustrated Pleasures of Seduction*. She'd only made it to page nine. With her knowledge of biology, which the duchesses insisted every woman know, and seeing the illustrations, the thought of how a man and woman created a child no longer made her ill. In fact, from what she'd learned so far, she'd been excited, since Lissa had told her that her betrothed was quite handsome and younger than her father. Unfortunately, she'd run out of time to read more, but had purposely left the book behind to prevent her new husband and staff from finding it. Sometimes Lissa was too forward.

She didn't have time to hide the book, so she left it there. "Thank you, Mary. I'll open it another time." With that announcement, she swept from the room feeling every bit the marchioness she now was.

The confident feeling lasted all the way down the stairs, then she walked through the parlor and bumped into a table with an empty vase. She caught the copper vase and set it aright before looking to see if her husband had seen the near miss.

He was there, but not seated, nor looking her way. Instead, he stood before the tall window looking out at the darkness.

Relieved he hadn't seen her, she slowed her walk and joined him at the window. "Good evening, Darius. What is it that has your attention in the dark?" She looked at the window but only saw their reflections in it. It was a sight she quite admired. His tall, dark frame next to her brighter one meant they complement-ed each other well, at least according to Isaac Newton, or so Lady Sommerset had instructed them.

"I merely ponder the dark itself."

At his answer, she looked up at him, as he was a bit taller than her, though not so much as to make it difficult to dance or walk and converse. "I quite enjoy the dark, particularly the nights with no moon, as then the stars are far easier to see. Even some of the planets can be seen, depending on the time of year."

He didn't look at her. "Of course. I had forgotten that you studied astronomy." He finally turned toward her and held his arm out toward the table. "Shall we sit?"

As she walked to the place setting at the end of a table that could easily sit twenty, she realized her predicament. When his parents had been their guests, they all ate at one end, something his mother arranged. Now the staff had obviously returned to the more formal setting. She would have to speak very loudly to hold a conversation with her husband. Luckily, she had a naturally loud voice.

After taking her seat, she studied the many dishes before her. She chose what appeared to be white soup to start. Curious as to what her husband would start with, she found him taking a piece of fish onto his plate. "Is bream your favorite fish?"

His hand froze in mid-transfer, as if he were surprised by her voice. He gave her a nod and finished putting the fish on his plate.

She'd be sure to confer with the cook on all his favorite dish-es. Taking a sip of her soup, she found it quite good, as had the other meals she'd had at Hawthorne Park. Again, a sense of confidence filled her. She had a good cook, which meant having guests and parties would be possible. She couldn't wait to meet everyone associated with her husband's land, from neighbors to tenants. "Will we be leaving soon to make our rounds about your estate? I do so look forward to learning all there is to know about Hawthorne Park."

Again, his hand stilled as he lifted his wine glass. "In the New

Year." He brought the glass to his mouth and took a sip.

The New Year? That was disappointing, but she supposed it made sense, since the year was ending in just over a month. He probably wished her to settle in first. She would make that her goal for bringing young Peter around. Perhaps a special gift at yuletide. "Do you have any special traditions I should be aware of concerning Christmastide?"

She wasn't sure, but something about the way he set his fork down had her thinking he was becoming irritated.

"Mrs. Torbett will be sharing all such information with you."

Though he used his usual polite tone, she sensed there had been a change in his mood since they spoke earlier in the afternoon. She'd always been able to sense people's changes in mood, but with a man who was so formal, she found it was more of a guess. "I'm looking forward to talking with Mrs. Torbett. She seems a very capable woman."

He gave a short nod before waving the footman over to remove the course.

She looked down at her half-filled bowl of soup and decided she didn't need any more either. While all was cleared, she watched her husband, wishing she were closer to better study him. What had happened between the afternoon and now? Was there a problem with the estate? If it was Peter or Maggie, surely he'd tell her. Then again, he wasn't used to having a wife yet. "Are the children well?"

That got his undivided attention. "I believe so. Why? Did the nursemaid say something to you?"

She waved off his concern. "No, not at all. I was just curious if you had seen them since this afternoon."

"No." The answer came out quick and flat.

The footman placed the next course before them and the scents of duck and nutmeg caught her attention. She piled her plate with the roasted duck, stewed mutton, and vegetable pie. She started by taking a bite of each to determine which was best, then began with her least favorite, which was the mutton. She had eaten that and was halfway through the vegetable pie when she remembered her manners. Her mother always said she ate too quickly and needed to converse with her companions.

But that was to attract a husband. Now she had one.

She smiled and looked down the table to find said husband staring at his food as he turned the barely touched wine glass in his hand. Concern immediately filled her. "Are you unwell?"

His head snapped up at her question. "No. I am…distracted."

That was obvious. "Is it anything I can help with?"

"No." Again the word came out far too quickly. Darius stood, his napkin in his hand. "I will not be about for a few days. I have business to attend to. I apologize that I cannot stay to help you settle in, but I know that you're very capable."

Not a little surprised by the sudden announcement, she set down her fork. "Would you like me to accompany you?"

"No. No, I want you to be here for the children. You will do that for me?" He squeezed his napkin, and there was a slight hint of desperation in his voice.

Truly worried now, she rose as well. "Of course. I will be with them every day. I promise." She started to walk toward him, to touch him and offer comfort. Whatever it was must be serious.

"Thank you." He looked at the napkin in his hand and threw it on the table before striding out of the room.

She halted, stymied by his behavior. Then she moved closer to his plate. Nothing had been touched. Truly worried now, she contemplated going to his rooms. She was his wife, after all. She would have, had it been anyone but Darius. It was his formality that stopped her. Perhaps if they'd been married for a month or even a fortnight, she would.

Whatever it was, he wouldn't solve it on an empty stomach. If he would be traveling on the morrow, he needed to eat. She waved over a footman. "Bring this up to his lordship's rooms."

"Yes, my lady." Immediately, the man took the plate and wine glass to the sideboard and placed them on a tray before walking out of the room with them.

Surprised the man hadn't argued with her, she turned back to her end of the table and sat. Though her own appetite had fled, she forced herself to eat. Worrying on an empty stomach was never a good occurrence. She'd done all she could...for now.

Slowly, she ate her meal. Though she wasn't as enthusiastic about it as she'd been before Darius left, she still appreciated the flavors the cook had brought out in the roasted duck. She looked forward to talking with her, in addition to Mrs. Torbett. With Darius gone for a few days, it gave her the chance to truly become the lady of the house.

There were a few changes she wished to make. The first was to either acquire a smaller table or have the places set next to each other. She would not have another conversation over dinner from so far away. Though to be fair, it hadn't been much of a conversation. Darius's worry had taken over. She should have noticed that right away, but she'd been too excited about talking about butterflies. How frivolous.

After taking a final sip of wine, she set her glass down and rose, ready to make her first change. She waved over the footman who had served her. "I will take my tea in the drawing room an hour from now."

Not waiting for his response, if he had one, she strode out of the dining room, through the drawing room, and to the front door where her cloak was hung.

The butler, a Mr. Beacham, appeared. "My lady. May I be of service?"

"Yes, you may, Beacham. Please assist me with my cloak."

"Your cloak, my lady?"

"Yes, I'm going for a walk in the garden...without a footman."

"Of course, my lady." He lifted the garment from the rack and held it out for her. "I will have the footmen light the lanterns on the terrace."

She fastened the top buttons. "No. No lanterns. The moon is at three-quarters and will be quite bright enough as it is."

"Are you certain? You might trip on a step or over a stone. I wouldn't want you to get hurt."

She turned around and faced the butler. "Beacham, I'm not a child. I can walk in the moonlight without hurting myself. And so it's not a surprise to you or the staff, I will walk outside every night, but not at the same time every night. However, I wish no lanterns to be lit when I do venture forth, is that understood?"

"Yes, my lady."

Pleased that she'd made her first official edict in her new home, she gave the butler a smile. "Not to worry, Beacham. I only go to gaze at the stars." With that, she turned back to the drawing room and strode across it, motioning for the footman to open the doors to the terrace.

The man jumped to do her bidding, and she walked onto the stone terrace and down the steps into the dormant garden. She stopped for a moment to determine her route, as three pathways led from the half-circle before her. Choosing the pathway to the right, as she'd already explored the one straight ahead, she started forward, anxious to get as far from the lights of the house as possible.

The air was crisp, and she pulled her cloak closer about her. The light from the moon was far brighter than she'd hoped. Though it made it easier to see the path, it would obscure the stars appearing closer to it. She focused on the ground and shrubs around her until she came upon a dry fountain. It looked to have a number of stone fish around it that would allow water to flow into the basin, while at the center was what appeared to be a cherub sitting on a dais. Now where did the water flow from him? It was impossible to tell in the moonlight.

She walked around the fountain before sitting on its stone edge next to a fish and looking up into the night sky. She'd chosen the eastern side of the fountain as that put the moon behind her. As she searched the stars, her gaze immediately landed on the Pleiades. The cluster of stars usually called the Seven Sisters made her think of the Curious Ladies who had already married. Had their transitions from being classmates to having a husband for company been similar?

But she knew it not to be true. Elsbeth, Dory, and Lissa had all married for love. She'd married to avoid another Season of men twice her age and possible spinsterhood. Still, it didn't mean that love couldn't come.

She moved her gaze from the Pleiades, which were particularly bright in winter. Aphrodite, the goddess of love, was in the Pisces constellation, along with her son Eros. She searched the sky for the elusive goddess of love, but it was too close to the moon and not visible.

She needed one of her telescopes. She had the very latest refraction lenses and multiple sizes. She'd love to have a spot away from the house where she could set up her largest one for stargazing…in the springtime.

The cold was starting to seep through her cloak and dress, causing her behind to get chilled. She rubbed her hands together to warm them up before rising. Maybe she could come out on the next sunny day and truly explore. If she found a good place, she could talk to Darius about having a small platform built, and maybe a wooden bench.

She kept her eyes on the sky and turned full circle. If she couldn't find Aphrodite, maybe she could find Venus. Squinting against the moon's light, she looked to the west. "Hah! Found you." She smiled, as the planet was quite bright, letting all the world, or rather the northern hemisphere, know that love was out tonight. That just proved that love was still possible in her marriage.

Happy with her discovery, she stepped forward and banged her knee against the fountain. "Ow." She rubbed the sore spot. Her mother, Lady Dulac, always complained she had her head in the clouds and needed to watch where she walked. But she didn't have her head in the clouds. She had it in the stars, which was far more impressive in her estimation.

Once the initial pain had lessened, she headed back the way

she came. Since Darius would be gone for a few days, she'd be sure to dress warmer, bring a telescope, and come out much longer, but right now, her after-dinner tea was calling her.

Even as she stepped back onto the terrace, she imagined a warm fire to stand before, as her fingers were turning quite numb. Quickly, she moved to the French doors and pulled one open. Warmth hit her cheeks, causing them to sting a little.

As the footman closed the door behind her, Beacham came into the room. "My lady, you look frozen. Allow me."

He took her cloak, and she moved to stand in front of the fire, holding her hands out to the heat.

Beacham returned within a moment. "My lady, I know you have just returned, but I received a request for your presence."

She turned around, silently wishing she could lift her skirts and warm her backside. "Mine?"

"Yes. Lady Margaret wished for you to say goodnight if you weren't otherwise occupied. I can tell her that you are just now having your tea."

Her heart filled with contentment. To be wanted by the child made any doubts about marrying float away. Besides, Darius had asked her to see to the children while he was gone, and though he wouldn't leave until the morrow, that Maggie had asked for her specifically had her anxious to fulfill her promise. "No, my tea can wait. I will go up and see her immediately."

Beacham stepped back. "I will have a new pot ready for you then."

"Thank you." She strode out of the room and up the stairs. Not only had she issued her first edict as lady of the house today, but now she would fulfill her first request as a mother. Marrying Darius had been the best decision of her life.

CHAPTER FOUR

Marrying Lady Eleanor had been the worst decision of his life. What had Darius been thinking to bring a new wife into his home when he couldn't be there?

He paced the confines of the converted bathhouse in the northern wood of his estate, far removed from the children he loved and the staff he employed. He'd hoped his black mood would stay away a little longer, but it had come swiftly and unexpectedly. What must she think of him?

It didn't matter what she thought. They were married for life, even if one day he was thrown into Bedlam, where he belonged. She would take care of his children and, eventually, Peter would get word that he'd died, probably by his own hand, like his uncle.

Dropping onto the settee near the fire, he untied his cravat and threw it onto the floor. He didn't want to die in Bedlam. He wanted to die at Hawthorne Park. How he would die was still a debate in his own mind. There were plenty of ways to kill oneself. His uncle had chosen drowning. Darius shivered at the thought. Poison, laudanum, or even a pistol were much better options. He just had to be smarter than his uncle.

He sat up to pull his boots off. They felt stifling, like his responsibilities. He cupped the back of his head in his hands as he leaned over his knees. He was supposed to take over his dukedom and all the responsibilities that entailed when his father passed away. But that would never come to pass.

He just had to hold on long enough for his parents to pass first. That and seeing his children settled were what kept him holding on. But he didn't know if he was strong enough. Dinah was supposed to have taken over for him, but she'd gone and died on him.

He pulled on his neck, beyond irritated. Everything he tried to do failed. What if his new wife discovered where he was and why?

He lifted his head. "Hell and damnation." He should have consummated the marriage on their wedding night. She was too clever and too curious not to become suspicious. Once she found out, she'd request an annulment, and then everything he'd been fighting for and fighting against would have been for naught.

Frustrated, he rose, running his hand through his hair as every worst possible future filled his mind. He returned to pacing, his stocking feet making little sound as he moved from one end of the building to the other, each step taking him deeper and deeper into his despair.

Images of being bound and brought to Bedlam filled his head, followed by his children crying, his parents arguing with some unknown adversary, and the new Lady Ferncroft pointing forward, demanding he be taken away. In his mind, he didn't resist, knowing he should have been gone years ago. He was a coward, hiding away. He was useless to his family and duties. He didn't deserve to be content, despite it being his fervent wish.

Why *couldn't* he be content? He didn't ask for happiness, just contentment. Was that so large a request that he must be plagued by—

The side door of the building opened, and he spun around, ready to fight.

"Saw the light in here. Back at it again, are you?"

"Archer." He scowled. "Go away."

The gray-haired gamekeeper closed the door before shrugging out of his heavy wool coat. "Not sure what I would think if you didn't greet me the same way every time."

"Damn it, old man."

"A drink? That's very kind of you." Archer moved to the sideboard and poured himself a scotch. He raised the glass. "Felicitations on your recent nuptials."

Darius snorted. "There's nothing to celebrate. You should have stopped me. Talked some sense into me."

Thomas Archer took a seat in the wingback chair by the fireplace. "Now, why would I do that? You have a second chance at happiness." He saluted with the glass. "If anyone deserves it, it's you."

The words infuriated Darius, and he swung his arm, knocking a candlestick from its holder on the wall. The force was so strong, the flame went out before it hit the floor—not that it mattered. "If I deserved damned happiness, I wouldn't be hiding out here right now, you fool."

"Actually, it's *because* you hide out here that you deserve happiness. You're not like your uncle was. You come out here to protect others. He came here to hurt them."

Darius ignored his glint of curiosity. "Maybe no one deserves to be happy." He found the thought comforting.

Archer took a sip as if contemplating his words. "That's an interesting theory. Perhaps we should dissect it."

Darius shouldn't give in, but the temptation was too much. Contemplating the idea that no one deserved to be happy was far too enticing. "Yes, let's."

Archer raised his gray brows before throwing back the rest of his drink. "Then I need more." He rose and poured himself another. When he had returned to his seat and made himself comfortable, he gestured with his glass. "Go ahead. Why is it that no one deserves to be happy?"

Darius moved closer and set his hand upon the fireplace mantel, the warmth of the fire heating his body even if it couldn't reach his heart. "Adam and Eve."

Archer waved his comment aside. "Surely you can do better

than religion and original sin. That's a belief. You can't argue a belief. What else?"

"Man is imperfect, and happiness demands perfection."

This time Archer spat out some whisky as he laughed, his weathered face crinkling like well-worn leather. "What does perfection have to do with happiness?"

Confused, Darius frowned. "Everything. If one conducts themselves perfectly then everything a man touches would be correct and therefore bring him happiness."

"So, you're saying that if your accounts all add up perfectly, that brings you happiness?"

His accounts always added up exactly as they should, but that wasn't happiness. "No, that brings satisfaction."

"Satisfaction. So that is not happiness? I must say, I find it so when tupping the missus."

He waved off the man's comment. "That's just physical release. It is not happiness."

Archer took another sip of whisky then contemplated his glass before speaking. "For you, it's physical release. For those who know what it is to love a woman and be loved in return, it is happiness. And you, my young lord, have no idea what that's like."

"Exactly. Because despite my best efforts, I chose wrong in my wife. If I had chosen correctly, life would have been perfect and I would have been happy, ergo, perfection equals happiness. Man is not perfect, and is therefore doomed to be unhappy." Feeling an odd sense of triumph in his dark reasoning, Darius pushed away from the fireplace and walked to the sideboard. He was halfway through his pour when his gamekeeper spoke.

"You have it all backward, Ferncroft."

He turned at the use of his title. "Do I? I think not."

Archer rose before walking over and setting his empty glass on the sideboard. "It is the imperfections that make us unique. They are what make us loveable, and it is love that brings true happiness. Think upon that." He poured himself yet another glass and lifted it up in salute. "It's damned cold out there tonight." He moved toward the fireplace as if just talking about the cold gave him a chill.

Darius poured a brandy. "Then maybe I should go for a walk. This room feels like a cave."

Archer turned at that. "You could always lock yourself in your rooms at the house."

Darius shivered at the thought. "That's worse, being locked in a space within a space. Here I can leave at night. Unless your son is about."

Archer shook his head. "No. I don't let anyone walk the north wood as a precaution, since I never know when you'll be here."

"Yes, and here I am. The monster in his cave needing to be released." Darius swirled his brandy in the glass, the reddish-brown liquor reminding him of a painting of hell by Hieronymus Bosch. He felt like one of the creatures in the painting.

"Then go. This is your estate. I just suggest you stay away from the lake. Young Peter is not ready to lose another parent."

At the mention of his son, some of the dark anger left him and he took a sip of his brandy before returning to the settee. "I would not do that to him."

"And glad I am to hear that. I know you don't believe it right now, but you're a good man, Ferncroft...for a swell."

Darius snorted, seeing no reason to reply to such idiocy.

Archer moved away from the fire and set his half-empty glass on the sideboard. "I'd best get back to my rounds or my lord will take issue with my work."

"Bugger it, Archer."

The gamekeeper ambled to the side door and shrugged into his coat. "Have as good as a night as you're able."

And with that, the man left to complete his travels around the estate, watching for poachers until the wee hours of dawn.

"Not perfect? If my imperfections made me loveable, I'd be surrounded by love." Darius snorted then held his glass high as he toasted to the closed door. "Have a safe night, my friend, and I will endeavor to do the same." He took a gulp of the brandy, reveling in the strong burn as it made its way down his throat and into his stomach.

He held the glass in both hands. Now that he was alone once more, as he should be, he could continue down the dark path of his thoughts, but once again Archer had piqued his interest when he least wished to be interested in anything.

Though the old man had missed the mark on what brought happiness, he had made some interesting points that could be investigated. Determined to prove his gamekeeper wrong, Darius searched for reasonable, logical reasons for happiness. Wealth, family, and success brought comfort. Because he was a marquess, he had no need to prowl the woods in search of poachers all night.

He took another sip of brandy. Yet here he was, hiding from his children and staff to avoid saying anything that would hurt them, keeping them in the dark, as it were, so as not to visit his pain and melancholy upon them. While Archer would return home to his wife in the cottage he was provided and enjoy her with laughter and body and be happy.

Swirling the liquid in his glass, Darius stared at it as if it could answer him before becoming frustrated with his inability to come to a satisfying conclusion. Downing the rest, he waited for the harsh burn before throwing the glass into the fireplace. Rising, he looked about, feeling trapped again.

He strode to the door, opened it, and walked outside into the trees of his own forest. He'd barely gone a few yards before the cold frost of the night seeped into his stockings, chilling his feet, but still he walked off the path and into the dense wood. The moon shone down between the leafless trees, making their shadows look like crooked arms reaching toward it.

He halted and looked up through the bare branches that grabbed for the shining partial orb. It had been full days ago. He only knew because he'd woken to its light, unable to sleep. Luna. The mother of the lunatics. He should feel a kinship with her, but he didn't.

A chill ran through him. It was too damn cold.

"Who, who." An owl sounded nearby.

He spun to search it out. "It's me."

The bird was eerily silent.

Determined to have one success this night, he let his gaze roam over every branch within his view. Not seeing the elusive bird, he moved a couple of yards and searched more trees. Finally, he found it, sitting on a branch as if the weather was of no import. Its head swiveled away from him before it turned its fathomless gaze back upon him.

"I'm far too big to be your prey and far too limited to be a threat. I am no more than a curiosity. You do not realize that you live here in this wood by my munificence. I envy you, envy your lack of self-awareness."

The owl blinked before turning its head to the side. Within seconds it took flight, swooping between the branches, soaring beyond sight.

"I envy you your flight, too." Darius shivered, the cold making itself known from his feet to his fingers. As he strode back through the wood to the small clearing where his hideaway sat, he crossed another way to die off his mental list. Dying from exposure would be a horrific way to go.

He quickly opened the door, stepped inside, and closed it against the cold. Walking directly to the fireplace, he stopped before it. Pulling his cold shirt from his body, he threw it on the chair previously vacated by Archer then stripped off his pantaloons before sitting on his clothes and removing his wet stockings. Naked, he rose and stood before the warmth of the fire, but it wasn't enough.

He stepped to the simple bed and wrapped the large quilt around him, intending to return to the fire. Sleep would be welcome, a relief from his dark thoughts for a short while. He looked to the clock. It was not yet midnight. Groaning, he sat on the bed. At least eight more hours of darkness to close in on him, swallow him up, and prove his worthlessness.

Archer knew not what was in his heart. Half of it must surely be dead already, putrefied by his disappointing past and hopeless future. He didn't deserve to live. What man resented his dead wife for pushing him away after discovering his secret? He even resented that she had died before him. It wasn't fair. She was meant to live, to ensure his son lived. Now he had to stay alive. Why could nothing go as he'd planned?

He lay down, still wrapped in the quilt like a caterpillar in a cocoon. If only he could awake and rise like a butterfly, or even as a moth, attracted to the light only to burn in the flames of its fire.

Either was acceptable to him.

CHAPTER FIVE

ELEANOR SEALED HER letter to Sophie and rang the bell for a footman. She hoped some of the Curious Ladies would accept her invitation before they went home on their break. After a sennight without them and no husband, she was feeling a little lonely. She hadn't realized how much she relied on the company of her friends.

"Yes, my lady?"

She snapped her head around, having not heard Beacham enter the parlor. "Oh, I just needed to send this letter to Sliver Meadows."

"I will have it done at once." Beacham held out his hand.

She lifted the letter, but didn't give it to him. "Have you heard when my husband expects to be home?"

"No, I haven't. But I'm sure it will be soon. He doesn't always let us know in advance."

"I see." Actually, she didn't. "Does he often leave so suddenly, or has something happened?"

"I cannot say, my lady. But it is not unusual for him to leave. He does have many responsibilities."

"Yes, of course. I will converse with him on the matter when he returns. It was just so unexpected, so soon after our marriage. I did expect we would meet his neighbors."

Beacham, who continued to hold his hand out, didn't blink.

"I'm sure he was planning for that, my lady. My lord is very attuned to the social requirements of his position."

Though it hadn't been a rebuke, she felt as if she'd cast doubt upon Darius's ability to fulfill his responsibilities. She should never have said anything, as usual. She placed the letter in the butler's hand. "Thank you, Beacham."

The man took the letter, gave her a nod, and turned on his heel.

"And Beacham?"

He halted then turned back to face her. "Yes, my lady?"

"Alert the nursemaid that I will be taking Maggie and Peter for a walk in the garden at noon. They need some fresh air."

The man's eyebrows twitched as if he'd been about to raise them but refrained. "There was frost on the ground this morning."

She waved away his concern. "So there was. But it has melted, and the sun is shining. The children need to walk outside today."

"Of course." Once again, the man gave a nod and turned, leaving the parlor as quietly as he'd come.

She greatly appreciated how helpful all the staff had been. At first there had been resistance, but they seemed to have come to appreciate having a new mistress of the house. Carefully, she pushed back her chair, not willing to cause another mess like she had not two days past, when she'd moved too quickly and knocked the small clock from her writing desk, sending glass across the floor.

She rose and wished for that very clock's presence, as she was sure Mrs. Torbett was to meet with her soon. Scanning the room, she noticed a clock on the mantel that hadn't been there before. She smiled softly. If she were to hazard a guess as to who'd set it there, it would be Beacham. Noticing it was almost eleven exactly, she walked to the chair with the cornflower-blue upholstery sprinkled with tiny peach flowers. It was her favorite.

When Darius returned, she would request to redo the colors

in her bedroom. The pale yellows and golds weren't very cheery, especially in winter with the heavy curtains closed to keep out the cold. He did say she could do any remodeling she wished, which was quite generous of him. She enjoyed spending time in the parlor, as it was a pretty peach color, which, next to imperial blue, was her favorite.

She heard the footsteps in the corridor before Mrs. Torbett strode in.

"My lady." The woman's face was quite flushed, as usual. She always seemed to be rushed.

"Mrs. Torbett, you are punctual as usual. Do take a seat." Ellie moved to her chair and sat.

"Thank you kindly, my lady. How may I be of help?"

She smiled. Mrs. Torbett was far different from her family's housekeeper. She was not nearly as bulky and tended toward smiles, not frowns, even with other staff. Also, Mrs. Torbett seemed genuinely pleased to help and often nodded in approval at Ellie's suggestions, not something that had ever happened back at home. In fact, her family's housekeeper looked down on her!

"You have already been such a wonderful help to me. You have made my first week here at Hawthorne Park so much easier than I expected. I admit to being a bit nervous at becoming the second Lady Ferncroft. I want you to know that your kindness has been appreciated."

Mrs. Torbett blushed, but didn't look away. "It has been an absolute pleasure. This house, this family, needs a lady to bring it all together."

Hearing that, Ellie felt more confident in her next request. "It's fortuitous that you bring up family, as I have always felt that Christmastide is the season for family." It was also the only time of the year that she heard praise from her mother for her efforts.

The housekeeper's eyes lit up. "Oh, my lady, do you mean to celebrate the season?"

At the excitement in the older woman's voice, Ellie's heart warmed. "I do. I wish to do everything, from the stir-up to a

Twelfth Night ball." She grinned, already envisioning the Christmas pudding, the gifts, the greenery, and the scents.

Mrs. Torbett's smile disappeared. "Is my lord willing to host a ball?"

"I have not discussed it with him. Surely he has in the past."

"My lady, there hasn't been a ball hosted here since I took over as housekeeper when Lord Ferncroft arrived over a dozen years ago."

"No balls? Did the former Lady Ferncroft not wish to host a ball?" Ellie found that difficult to believe.

Mrs. Torbett looked away. "I cannot be certain, but I believe it is my lord who does not wish to have one." The woman's gaze came back to Ellie as she smiled. "But I do think he would enjoy all the other festivities."

Obviously, Ellie would have to discuss the season when her husband returned. He would know why no balls were hosted at Hawthorne Park.

She was about to move forward with sharing her ideas when Mrs. Torbett's wording struck her. "You said you *think* the lord would enjoy the festivities. Has he not enjoyed them before?"

Again, the housekeeper looked away, clearly uncomfortable.

Now Ellie's pleasant mood had completely evaporated. "Truly, Mrs. Torbett, I don't wish you to divulge any secrets, but I do need such pertinent information if I am to move forward in an acceptable manner for all those under my care, be it the children or my lord. And you, my good woman, are the only one who can reveal all that I need to know. I promise you, I am no young debutante just out of the schoolroom, nor am I faint of heart. Now, do be blunt. I want to know everything necessary to ensure a pleasant and joyful Christmastide."

Mrs. Torbett's brown eyes rounded for a moment before she straightened in the chair and clasped her hands before her. "Right. You should know. The former lady chose not to celebrate the season and only allowed the nursemaid to decorate with greenery on Christmas Eve within the nursery. I was not privy to why this decision was made. I do know that the lady, who was at first content with her marriage to my lord, soon grew discontented. It was just before Christmastide began that she decided there would be no festivities."

Ellie's first thought was of Maggie and Peter. "Did Lord Ferncroft have nothing to say about such a decision?"

The housekeeper just shook her head.

It wasn't difficult to figure out that the two had had an argument of some kind, which led to such a drastic change. If it was a change. "Tell me, did the lord celebrate the season before being married?"

"I don't know. He did not spend the season at Hawthorne Park before he was betrothed."

Now Ellie had a decision to make—do as she planned or continue as it had always been. But the mere thought of no celebrations made her sad. "Thank you for telling me this. It is quite helpful."

"It is?"

"Yes, it is. Now, let us get back to planning this year's Christmastide at Hawthorne Park. First, we must be ready for Stir-up Sunday next week. We have little time to prepare. If you don't have the ingredients for the Christmas pudding, be sure to procure them. That is a priority."

"Right."

"We will also need the gardener to identify a few potential yule logs. The children and I will spend a few days identifying any holly, ivy, rosemary, evergreen, hawthorn, bay leaf, laurel, or hellebore on the property. I'm guessing there is hawthorn." She grinned at her deduction based on the name of the estate. "The outings will make for good science lessons and will help them appreciate it more when the greenery is brought inside."

"A wonderful idea, my lady." Mrs. Torbett's grin was as wide as Ellie's own. It was such a pleasure to find a fellow Christmastide enthusiast.

"I will need you to do some secret work for me and discover

what the children like, as we can't forget St. Nicholas Day, as it is less than a fortnight away. I want to be sure our gifts to the children on that day are something they are yearning for. I will also ask the nursemaid, but I want as many ideas as possible, since it will be difficult to find items here in the area, I'm sure. Maggie might tell me, but Peter is still not talking to me except for his lessons. Still, it should be a surprise to both."

"I will do my best."

"That is quite enough for now. Let us discuss this more in a few days. I've already invited a few friends, but I will wait for Lord Ferncroft to return home to discuss the possibility of a ball. Even if he feels it would be inconvenient, I believe all the other activities will be quite welcome."

"Oh, yes." Mrs. Torbett practically jumped from her chair. "We shall start preparing right away." The woman started for the open double doors then stopped and turned back. "Thank you, my lady. This is just what this old house needs." Then, not waiting to be dismissed, she scurried off at her usual pace.

That interview had gone much better than Ellie had hoped. It had also given her much to think upon…and to investigate.

But first it was time to bring the children outside. Rising, Ellie brushed out her maroon dress before heading for her room. As Beacham had mentioned, it was cold outside, and her red pelisse would keep her warmer than her blue wool cloak.

Once donning her preferred outerwear, she descended the staircase to find the children and nursemaid waiting for her, all dressed for outside. "Anna, thank you for preparing the children. You may take the time to tidy up the nursery and have tea."

The woman's brows lowered. "Are you sure, my lady? I wouldn't want Peter to run off and get lost."

What an odd thing to say. "I do not believe that Peter would misbehave in such a way. I'm sure he wants me to report only good behavior to Lord Ferncroft."

"Yes, my lady. But he's prone to colds and such."

"Not to worry. We will only be out half an hour and no

more. Now off you go."

Anna appeared to want to argue more but thought better of it. "Yes, my lady."

Ellie almost wished the young woman *had* argued. It had been a while since she'd had a good debate. Maybe Darius would humor her when he arrived home. "Come, children. Let us go exploring like Christopher Columbus or Ponce de León."

Maggie immediately took her hand, while Peter stalked off toward the now-open door in the parlor.

At the feel of the cold air brushing her face, Ellie started forward, anxious to share her knowledge with the two under her care. "Today, we are on the hunt for evergreen plants. Do you know what those are?"

"Are they plants that stay green all winter?" Maggie looked up at her.

"Indeed, they are. You are very bright."

"Daft plants," Peter grumbled as they reached the bottom of the terrace steps.

Ellie ignored him. "This way." She pointed to the far-right pathway. "This is my favorite path so far, as it gives the best view of the stars."

"You come out here at night?"

At Maggie's question, even Peter stopped to hear the answer.

"I do. Did you know the stars in the winter are different than the stars we see in the summer?"

Maggie looked up at the overcast sky. "Is that because the Earth turns?"

"That's a very good guess. Do you have a guess, Peter?"

The boy shook his head.

"It's actually because of the Earth's oblong orbit around the sun." At Maggie's confused look, Ellie remembered how Lissa had taught her about the ancient phalanx formation. "Let's go to the fish fountain and I'll show you what I mean."

"Fish fountain?" Maggie looked up at her. "I don't think there's any water in the fountains for fish at this time of year."

"We only have fish in the lake." Peter shook his head as if Ellie were daft.

"Well then, you'll just have to tell me what you call this particular fountain." Ellie led them along, surreptitiously checking every few minutes to be sure Peter followed.

"Oh, you mean Neptune's fountain." Maggie let go of her hand and ran to sit on the side of the dry fountain. She put her hand on one of the fishes. "I thought you meant there were fishes *in* the fountain."

Ellie laughed, pleased that the children were so invested in what she had to say. "That makes sense. I should have been more precise in my wording and said 'the fountain with five concrete fish on the edges and a baby on the top.'"

Peter pointed to the baby. "Neptune." His tone made it very clear he thought she was not very intelligent.

She studied the sculpture in the daylight. Now she could see where that the water would come out of three spires of a trident the baby leaned back against. "This must be when Neptune was just born. What a clever fountain."

"Mother said that he was born of the Earth and the stars."

Ellie glanced over Maggie's head to see Peter bending down and looking at something. "You're correct. He's supposed to be the son of Saturn, who represented the universe, and Terra, who was considered the Earth. No wonder I am able to see the stars so well from here. It's as if whoever placed it had stargazing in mind."

Maggie looked over her shoulder. "Peter, where are your mitts? Put them on right now, or you'll catch a cold."

"No."

Ellie walked around the fountain to see what had Peter so enthralled. "I'm sure not having his mitts on for a few minutes won't hurt."

Maggie jumped down from the fountain. "He was born too early. Nursemaid says he will get sick before anyone else."

"Will not." Peter rose, a black ground beetle in his hand.

"Will too."

Ellie bit down on a smile. "I'm not so sure, Maggie. Peter looks rather sturdy to me, and he's almost as tall as you already."

Peter stood straighter, and his little chest puffed out. "I'm *hardy*. That's what Mrs. Torbett said."

"Indeed, you are. What is it you have there, Peter?" Ellie lifted her brows as if she had no idea.

He thrust his hand out toward her and Maggie. "Beetle."

"Eek!" Maggie scrambled behind Ellie.

Peter's shoulders fell.

Ellie's heart squeezed at his disappointment. "That's quite a brave fellow to be out here in this cold. He's braver than Maggie."

That seemed to make Peter feel a little better, but the bond between the siblings was strong.

"Come, Maggie. Have a look. Beetles move slow in winter, so it won't jump on you or anything." Ellie looked behind her. "If this little beetle can brave the cold, surely you can be brave enough to look at it."

Maggie grabbed on to Ellie's arm and slowly stepped around her to peer at the beetle. "It's not very big, is it?"

Peter shook his head. "No. I think he's little. I'll put him back so he can go home to his family."

Ellie barely kept herself from sighing. The child was such a sweet boy who just needed some love and affection.

After depositing the beetle where he found him, Peter stood.

"Don't forget your mitts," Ellie pointed to the ground.

Peter's eyes widened—he had obviously forgotten them already—and he bent down to retrieve them.

"I'll help you." Maggie stepped forward.

"I can do it." Peter stepped back and managed to don one of his mitts, but getting the second one on while wearing the other was proving difficult.

Ellie gave Maggie a nudge, and the girl looked at her. Nodding toward Peter, Ellie turned her back and strolled slowly around the fountain again.

Within moments, the two children had joined her, both with their mitts on.

"I see there's quite a bit of laurel on this side of the garden, but with such a nicely laid-out plan, I doubt the gardener would appreciate having any of it cut."

"Why would we cut it?"

Maggie's question reminded Ellie of why they were there. She faced both the children. "We will need to cut some greenery to bring in on Christmas Eve, of course."

Both children's eyes lit up with excitement, but Maggie spoke first. "Mother and nursemaid always decorated the nursery. I'm so glad we get to do that again."

"Oh, I plan to decorate more than the nursery. I'm going to have the whole house decorated." Ellie threw her arms out wide, smacking her fingers on a stone fish. "Ouch!" She curled in her fingers and pressed her hand against her chest.

"Are you all right?"

Maggie's furrowed brow had Ellie fighting the pain. She swallowed hard. "I'll be fine." The sting in her fingers began to throb. "Let us return to the house now. I promised we wouldn't be outside more than half an hour, and surely it must have been that by now."

"Must we?" Peter was back to being petulant.

"I'm afraid we must. But if you like, we can come out again in a few days." He shrugged his shoulders as if it didn't matter to him, but she knew it did. Still, it was quite cold, and even if her fingers weren't throbbing, she wouldn't want the children to become ill. "I know I, for one, am ready for a cup of warm tea and some rout cakes."

As they started back, Maggie launched into a tale of one of the neighbors, who had a very bad cook and had gifted them with a failed trifle.

Despite the pain in her fingers, Ellie felt more at home in that moment than she had her whole life. She'd finally found her place, and she couldn't be happier.

CHAPTER SIX

DARIUS LEFT HIS study and headed down the corridor to break his fast. Surely his wife would be up by now. They had a lot to discuss after his ten-day absence, and he was anxious to move forward with securing his legacy.

It had been remiss of him to not consummate their marriage immediately, but he hadn't expected to fall into a black mood so soon. He'd risen to a state of panic more than once over the past days at the thought of his wife requesting an annulment. Then he'd been sure she thought him odd or not interested in women or even sex. Nothing could be farther from the truth, but he had to broach the subject delicately.

He just hoped she wasn't as timid as his last wife. Though some of his late wife's reluctance occurred after she'd discovered his reason for leaving suddenly. While she never learned whence he'd gone, she'd not been anxious to be bedded by a "madman," as she called him.

His step slowed at the thought. Memories of Dinah in bed, refusing to engage in any of the joy that could be experienced, had left him cold until he realized that was her intent. With him more determined than ever, every coupling had become a battle of wills, but he had much more to lose by not having an heir, and he made her feel the thrill of sex, whether she wished to or not. Sometimes he wondered if Peter was born too soon because

Dinah didn't wish him to live, but he resolutely dismissed that. After all, if Peter hadn't lived, then there would be even more coupling.

Stepping into the parlor, he scanned the area for signs Eleanor was up and about, but saw none. He strode into the dining room and took a seat at the head of the table as a footman served him coffee. The place setting to his left was a change that must have been made by his new wife. He would wait, albeit not patiently, for her to join him…unless she'd decided to eat in her rooms.

Taking a sip, he contemplated his options, quickly determining that he should discover if she'd already broken her fast. About to call over a footman, he opened his mouth only to close it again on the chance the rustling skirts he heard in the corridor belonged to his wife. He listened to the rapid tread, which was far from ladylike, but he had noticed she tended toward a more brisk form of movement, much to the detriment of items nearby.

Within moments, his wait was rewarded as his wife strode through the parlor door in a flurry of blue skirts—complete with green shawl. It was an unusual color combination. He stood as she entered the dining room. "My lady."

"Oh, Darius. It's so wonderful to see you. When I heard you'd arrived, I couldn't wait another moment to see if your trip was successful and you were in good health." She strode up to him and took his hands. "Let me gaze upon you for but a moment, relief in my heart."

A little surprised by the warm greeting, he held her hands just as tightly, not unaware of the unusual scent she exuded. He'd noticed it at the church, the last time they were so close, and it made him think of citrus, but it wasn't orange or lemon. "It is a pleasure to see you looking healthy. You do appear to be fairly glowing, Lady Ferncroft."

She shook her head as if to dismiss his compliment. "If I glow, it is because of your safe return. And we did agree to call each other by our given names, remember?" She squeezed his hands a bit harder, then rose up and kissed him on the cheek before letting go and stepping back.

He tensed, as it looked as if she'd bump into the chair held out by the footman, but luckily the kind fellow pulled it back another foot and no mishap occurred. "Please." Darius opened his hand toward the chair. "Do join me. I would like to hear all that has occurred in my absence."

As she took her seat, he gave the footman a grateful smile. The man reacted by standing even straighter now that Lady Ferncroft was safely seated.

"I'm happy to tell you all, but first you must relieve my mind. Did your business end successfully?" Ellie lifted her brows with her inquiry.

He resumed his own seat. "It did indeed. I appreciate your kind patience in starting our marital life together. Unfortunately, I am often called away suddenly, but I promise to always return so that I may enjoy my days here with you and my children." The lie did not sit well with him, but his experience with Dinah kept him from changing it.

"Truly? That is most wonderful to hear. Mayhap I can accompany you on occasion. I wouldn't be in the way, as I'm quite adept at keeping myself entertained." She paused as the footmen poured hot cocoa into a cup for her. "While my embroidery is not quite on par with my mother's, I do enjoy reading, shopping, and studying the night sky. Oh, I do hope it's acceptable that I promised the children a nighttime excursion into the garden tomorrow evening to give them their first lesson on the universe, beyond the mythological one that I covered a few days ago while we were out by the fish fountain. No, I mean the baby Neptune fountain."

He set down his coffee cup and relaxed as she moved away from the topic of accompanying him and addressed the latter part of her statements. "Peter and Maggie went outside? In this cold?"

"We all bundled up quite warmly and stayed out for a very short time. Just enough for a lesson, an encounter with a beetle, and to share that we will be having a lovely Christmastide this year." She patted his hand where it lay on the table near his cup as if to reassure him.

Normally, he would not enjoy such mothering, but if her instincts were so kind and visited upon his children, he would not discourage it. Not when she spoke about bringing back a tradition he had fully participated in as a youth. "Christmastide... It has been a long time since I took part in such festivities. Do you have great plans for Hawthorne Park, then?"

She clapped her hands together. "I have so many, and I'm pleased that you do not mind. Mrs. Torbett wanted to be sure that you approved. She's such a capable housekeeper and very loyal to you and the children. I simply adore her." She lifted her cup and was about to take a sip when her stomach made a noise.

Immediately, his wife's face turned a bright red, and she hid some of it from his gaze with her cup.

Realizing that she must be hungry, he rose. "I'm anxious to hear all your plans, but first I think it best if we have some sustenance. Allow me to get you a plate." Even as he strode toward the sideboard, he tried to remember what she'd eaten when his parents had been with them the morning after they married. Since he'd been curious about his wife since the moment he met her at the church, he'd observed her more than might be usual for a new husband. He filled a dish with items he was certain she liked, then added a couple that he liked to see where she stood on them.

After piling a dish with poached eggs, rashers, and honey cakes for himself, he returned to the table and set her dish down before her. "I hope most of this is to your taste."

"Darius, you are so thoughtful. All of this is exactly what I would have chosen."

He set his own plate down then resumed his seat. "Truly? All of it? Even the kippers and honey cakes?

She studied his plate for a moment before grinning. "Yes, especially the honey cakes. I see you enjoy them too. It is fortuitous that we have some things in common. And I know something else we have in common."

Pleased by her astuteness, he raised his right eyebrow. "And what is that?"

"Your children." She actually sighed and raised her hand to her chest. "I cannot truly express how grateful I am to you for bringing them into my care. I dearly love them both."

He couldn't quite believe his luck, even though it had been he who had requested a woman who would be a mother to his children when he sent Anthony in search of one. "They must be behaving very well for you to be enamored so soon. To be fair, I must be honest and admit they are not always so well behaved."

Eleanor laughed, a loud though not unpleasant sound that seemed to fill the room. "I wouldn't say they have been on their best behavior. No, they have been acting like children, and I absolutely adore it. I don't wish them to be formal with me any more than I wish you to be." Her smile left her and her mood seemed to shift even as she lifted a honey cake. "I know what it is to grow up in a formal household. It was not to my liking, and was one of the reasons I was anxious to attend the Belinda School for Curious Ladies. Everyone knows the Duchess of Northwick, who was a Mabry, grew up in a rather unusual home, and it was one I envied when I was younger. So when she opened the school, I begged my mother to allow me to attend. It was just as I had hoped." Her smile was back before she took a large bite.

Despite her improved disposition, he didn't like that she'd been uncomfortable in her youth and resolved to try to be less formal. He was grateful to her for not only marrying him, but for adoring his children. "Then I must confess to you that while my upbringing was less formal, as I studied and trained to take over my duties here, I have practiced formality in all areas. So I will ask you to help me be less formal when the situation allows for it."

Once again, she reached for his hand that held his fork, but instead of patting it, she grasped it, fork and all. "Darius, I would be honored to do so. Perhaps then you could start by calling me Ellie."

"Ellie." It felt strange to say it.

Her pretty blue eyes lit at his response. "Yes, exactly. Like an elephant. One of my brothers used to tease me and call me Ellie the elephant, but it was all in fun. Do you think you can do that?"

"Call you an elephant? I think not. But I will endeavor to remember you're Ellie." Her request made him feel as if they had a special relationship, beyond the obvious. Dinah had been called Dee by her sisters, but had never mentioned it to him. And, of course, after her discovery, they were nothing *but* formal.

Ellie, as he would attempt to think of her, let go of his hand, patting his forearm once again. "Excellent. Then let me tell you about our Christmastide for Hawthorne Park."

As his wife launched into her plans in between bites of her meal, she grew more animated. Her eyes almost sparkled with glee as she gestured here and there, sending one poor kipper off her fork and onto the floor. He tried not to watch the footman discreetly pick it up.

She was the complete opposite of Dinah, loud where his deceased wife was quiet, animated where Dinah had an economy of movement to the point of being able to sit for hours barely moving. Even Ellie's dress stood out for its brightness, while Dinah had worn very light pastels. Hope grew inside him that, perhaps, with his first marriage being such a failure, this one could be a success.

"—hope you will allow the children to participate in the stir-up. I want them to be able to participate in almost every part of the season."

The mention of the stir-up filled him with memories. "Of course the children must take part. I, myself, as the eldest, was the first child to stir the Christmas pudding. Lady Margaret should enjoy that honor."

"You mean Maggie, I'm sure." She gave him a knowing smile.

In turn, he nodded in acknowledgment of her request to be less formal. "Yes, Maggie and, though he is yet small, Peter. It seems like such a small affair with only two children to take part.

I do hope we can expand upon them with children of our own."

This time when her cheeks heated, it didn't cover her entire face, neck, and chest as it had earlier. Instead, it made her glow quite becomingly. "Darius, I would love nothing more than to be a mother to more children." Her gaze turned sly as one side of her mouth lifted. "I think at least a dozen, don't you?"

Startled, he pulled his head back and cocked it as he searched for an appropriate response.

Her laughter filled the room once again. "I'm only jesting. I would be grateful to be blessed with any children." She moved her hand to her chest once more, her strong feelings on the matter very clear.

Her happy demeanor called to him like a lost horse to his warm stall, and he found himself not simply curious about her, but attracted to her as well. "Then, my fine lady, I shall be sure to visit you tonight so that we may begin our expanding family."

For the first time since he'd met her, she didn't look at him directly. "I will be honored."

With her ready candor, he'd almost forgotten that she was a virgin and he needed to be careful. He also needed to make haste. Perhaps a day spent in her company would make the evening easier. Surprisingly, he found her company quite pleasant.

He set down his fork and used his fingers to turn her head toward him. "Ellie, I am very content to have you as my wife."

Her eyes grew wide and her lips lifted in a soft, tremulous smile.

It was the uncertainty in her face that must have had him leaning forward and brushing a soft kiss against her lips. Though the second kiss was because one touch was not enough. Her lips opened under his, and he forced himself not to deepen the kiss, despite a rising need to. Not wishing to frighten her, he pulled back, stroking her cheek with his thumb before releasing her.

Her eyes remained closed, her whole body leaning toward him though he sat back in his chair.

"Ellie?" He kept his voice low.

Her eyes fluttered open. "Yes?"

It was the quietest word he'd heard her speak yet. "Would you like to accompany me in visiting the tenants today? If you're planning Christmastide festivities, they will need to be involved."

She gave herself a quick shake then sat back in her chair. "I would enjoy that. I'm sure the children won't mind one day without me, especially since we will be going into the garden tonight."

"One day? You have spent part of every day with them?"

She nodded as she waved a footman over to pour her more cocoa. "Indeed I have, and many times I've spent the entire day. I do think I'm wearing down Peter. He was determined not to like me as his new mother, but I believe he's growing fond of me, despite his own wishes." She chuckled as she brushed back a stray piece of fiery red hair.

Suddenly, Mrs. Torbett's focus on Eleanor's—*Ellie's* hair color had his thoughts wandering. Would her passion be just as fiery once he'd taught her the joys of the marriage bed? Even at the thought, he found his gaze dipping to her neckline, where her over-bountiful breasts pushed hard against her dress. His own desire started in his groin, and he shifted his seat, trying to remember what they spoke of. "Peter should not make you feel unwanted."

She waved away his comment. "He doesn't. I'm pleased that he is reluctant to accept me as his new mother. It shows a depth of feeling and loyalty, both of which you can be proud of. In fact, I think a day away from me may help him realize that he actually likes me."

He stared at her as she took another sip of cocoa, both admiration and dread tumbling in his stomach. He'd expected her to be intelligent, as his brother's wife was, and they came from the same school, but he hadn't expected such depth of thought. He would need to be careful the next time he must leave. At least for his children, though, he could rest assured they would be looked after. No—rather, they would be loved.

"So tell me, Darius. Who will we visit first? Is there an order you plan on? We will need to visit your neighbors as well, but you are right that I should meet our tenants first. I think—"

"Excuse me, my lord."

Beacham strode in much faster than normal, which immediately had Darius tensing. "What is it, Beacham?"

"I have just been informed that Peter has taken ill."

"Oh dear." Ellie rose immediately. "I must see him."

Darius stood as well. "We will go to him at once."

Beacham stepped aside quickly to avoid being knocked over by Ellie, who was already in the parlor.

"Thank you, Beacham. Come with us, as we may need to send for a doctor." Darius followed after his wife, any doubts as to his children's welfare fully removed by her reaction. He sincerely hoped it was just something Peter had eaten. If he had taken a chill, it could greatly affect his constitution.

When he reached the nursery, the door was open and his wife sat upon Peter's bed, her hand moving from his head to his stomach.

"Is this where it hurts?"

His son's face, so pale, scrunched up as he nodded, and Darius halted as fear rifled through him.

The nursemaid ran over to him. "My lord, I'm so glad you're home. I believe Peter caught a chill when he went on the outing with Maggie and Lady Ferncroft. I don't know what to do."

He moved his gaze to the nursemaid, who clenched her hands together, clearly concerned. "We will be sure he gets better. Do not worry." He started past her, worrying enough for them all.

As he reached the bed, he stood behind Ellie, the nursemaid's words finally sinking in. He'd caught a chill under Ellie's care. Tamping down his anger, he addressed his wife. "Is it a chill?"

She shook her head. "No. If he'd taken a chill, he would have been ill days ago."

The nursemaid ran over, avoiding the vomit on the other side of the bed. "But I saw him shiver."

Ellie shook her head. "A shiver is not always due to the cold. If the body is heated or in a weakened state, a shiver can be caused by the trauma associated with it."

"How do you know this?" He couldn't help the doubt in his voice.

His wife looked up at him over her shoulder. "Because the Duchess of Northwick is learned in the medical arts and made sure we all knew the basics."

He studied his son. "This doesn't look basic to me."

She waved off his comment and returned her attention to Peter. "When did you start feeling sick?"

"My belly ached when I woke."

"And did you have more than two sugared plums before you fell asleep last night?"

Peter groaned and turned his head to the side, causing Darius's own stomach to feel uncomfortable.

Maggie spoke from behind them. "He had eight."

"Oh dear." Ellie brushed Peter's wet hair from his forehead. "Your poor belly." She looked to the nursemaid. "Did you give him ginger or peppermint?"

The nursemaid shook her head. "No, my lady. I gave him ipecac sherry. That's what my mother always gave us."

Darius wasn't touching his wife, but he sensed her tension. "And did you always vomit after taking that?"

"Yes, we did. It gets the bad humors out of our body." Anna nodded enthusiastically.

He found it odd that his wife didn't respond. Somehow, he knew she didn't approve. "We should send for a doctor."

"No!" Eleanor rose at that and faced him. "Do not send for a doctor. He will only bleed Peter and make him weaker. What he needs is to have a clean bed and some ginger tea to settle his belly." She stepped around him. "Maggie, would you allow Peter to rest in your bed while his is changed?"

"Yes. I just want him to get better."

For the first time since entering the room, his wife smiled. "Don't worry. Peter is going to be fine."

She sounded so sure that he found some of his own worry dissipating. "What do we need to do?"

She turned toward him. "If you don't mind, could you bring Peter over to Maggie's bed? Leave all his bedding behind. Beacham, please have a maid sent up to clean the floor and the bedding. Also, have Mrs. Torbett send up some ginger tea with a bit of ground cinnamon as well as sugar."

"At once, my lady." Beacham turned on his heel and strode out in haste.

Darius pulled down the quilt from Peter and lifted his son in his arms. His heart skipped a beat at how light Peter was, and how warm. Quickly, he walked to Maggie's bed, where Eleanor had pulled back the cover. He laid his son down carefully as if he could break, then stepped aside as his wife covered Peter to his neck.

She pushed Peter's hair away from his forehead. "We will have you feeling better in due course, but only if you do as I say. Will you do that?"

He nodded.

"Good." She straightened. "Now, Anna, show me where the ipecac sherry is kept."

The nursemaid gave a start before looking at Darius for permission.

He remained unmoving. The sooner the nursemaid understood that Eleanor was to be obeyed, the better.

"Anna?" Eleanor's hands had found her hips, and she looked none too pleased.

"It's over here, my lady." The nursemaid walked to a cabinet and opened it.

Eleanor's purposeful stride brought her across the room in a trice. Immediately, she took a bottle. Then she uncorked another bottle and sniffed. Recorking it, she took that one too. She read the writing on two others, leaving them where they were before taking another off the shelf. Turning, she scanned the room then strode to the chamber pot and proceeded to empty the contents of all three bottles.

"My lady!" Anna started forward then stopped. Wringing her hands, she looked to him, but once again, he didn't move.

When Eleanor had finished, she handed the empty bottles to the nursemaid. "Bring these down to Mrs. Torbett and have her dispose of them forthwith. These substances are to never to be kept in this house again. Understood?"

The nursemaid nodded, took the bottles, and left the room.

"Now, we shall concentrate on getting better." Eleanor went back to Peter and sat on the other side of the bed from where Darius stood. She laid her hand over Peter's forehead. "Your belly has had a rough time. But we are going to make it feel better so you can sleep. By tomorrow, you will be hungrier than an elephant."

His brow furrowed. "What's an elephant?" His voice was barely above a whisper.

Darius answered. "It's an animal as big as a coach. It walks on four legs, has gray, leathery skin, a very small tail, big, floppy ears, and a long trunk. They live in India."

Peter clearly didn't believe him. He would have to find a painting of one somewhere and gift it to him. Or maybe he could have a wooden elephant commissioned for St. Nicholas Day.

Eleanor waved away the explanation. "We will learn all about elephants soon, but know that it is a big animal and eats a lot."

"I'm not hungry," Peter whined.

"I know, dear. But you will have a little sweet ginger tea, which will soothe your belly, and then you can sleep. Sleep is very important for feeling better."

Maggie stepped up to the bed and laid a hand on her brother's shoulder. "I won't go outside and see the stars until you can too."

Peter attempted a small smile.

"And I won't got out to see them either, even though I usually do every night. I am going to wait until you feel better."

Eleanor gave an emphatic nod, sealing her promise. "In fact, I am not going to leave this room until you are feeling better."

Peter looked at Darius, as he clearly didn't believe Eleanor. That was of little surprise, since Dinah had never even entered the nursery when one of the children was ill. She'd left it to the servants to take care of the illness, cut, or bruise. Since he had no reason to believe Eleanor would lie, he nodded.

Yet, even as he did so, he found himself moving away from the bed, the realization that they may not consummate the marriage tonight frustrating him. He tried to ignore the panic beginning to swell. He hated that he felt this way, but it was common after his black moods.

Hearing footsteps approaching the nursery, he opened the door to hide his angst, and gave directions to the servants.

Beacham had also returned. "Is there anything else we can do, my lord?"

The man's concern for his son was appreciated. "Yes. Once I move Peter back to his bed, have the maid change Maggie's."

Eleanor turned around to address Beacham. "And tell Mrs. Torbett that I will want a full accounting of all medicinal powders, herbs, tinctures, and tonics that are currently at Hawthorne Park, as well as any herbs, dried or living."

"I will tell her." The butler nodded.

"Also, please have a settee or cot brought in. I will remain here with Peter, and if he is not well by evening, I will sleep here."

Beacham didn't react at all for a moment, clearly shocked. But he kept his face impassive nonetheless. "May I suggest a quilt and pillow as well?"

"Thank you for thinking of that. It would be most appreciated."

After the servants left to address their next tasks for his wife, Darius tapped her on the shoulder. "I would like to speak with you."

She gave a short nod. "I'll be right over there, Peter."

His son shrugged his shoulders, but it was clear he was nervous.

Darius walked to the far corner of the room, Eleanor by his side. When they reached it, he kept his voice low. "Do you know what ails him?"

"I am quite sure that he ate too many sugared plums, which made his belly ache. The nursemaid, misguided as she was, tried to help him by giving him ipecac, which caused vomiting, so it only made him feel worse." Her voice, which had begun quietly, grew a bit louder. "The ginger tea with cinnamon and sugar will not only settle his belly but taste good. After a few hours, if the vomiting has ceased completely, I will have him eat simple toast and more tea." Now she spoke in normal tones that even the children were sure to hear. "If he has quite recovered by nightfall, then he can eat normally on the morrow."

He glanced over at his children to see them both listening avidly. He pressed his finger to his lips before asking his next question. "And if it was not the ipecac sherry?"

Her gaze flitted toward the children before returning to him. "Then he will continue to vomit and I will send for the duchess." Though her voice had returned to a quieter level, her pronouncement shocked him.

"The duchess?"

"Yes. She is well learned in the way the body works and what is best when ill. She saved Lord Bellamore after he was shot and nursed Lady Georgina to health after she caught scarlet fever. She will know what to do." His wife took his hand. "Do not worry it will come to that. I am quite sure my guess is correct." She leaned in close, her unique scent filling his nostrils as she whispered in his ear. "I've had Mrs. Torbett and Cook keeping track of what Peter has been eating. I did not wish him to starve just to make the point that he wasn't happy I am here."

Many contradictory feelings assailed him at once. While her caring and kindness filled him with relief, her cleverness caused him concern. But it was her scent, her hand in his, and the air from her lips brushing against his ear that had him wanting to take her in his arms and kiss her. He reached around with his free arm just as she stepped back, and he used his position to pretend a concern for her balance.

"Oh."

"I didn't wish you to bump into the table. Thank you for your knowledge and informed hypothesis. If you would be so good as to update me throughout the day, I would be much relieved."

"Of course. Do not worry." She squeezed his hand in hers before letting go. "I will have Peter up and running about as soon as possible."

His hand felt cold, now that hers wasn't in it, and he took a step toward the door. "Thank you." With one last look at Peter, his sister sitting on the bed by his side, he left the room and strode downstairs to his study.

No sooner had he entered than he poured himself a scotch and took a gulp. It was not his drink of choice, but its particular burn helped distract his mind for a moment. He walked to the wingback chair before the fireplace, but did not sit, standing behind it to shield himself from the heat. Finding himself attracted to his new wife was enough heat for the moment, especially if they could not consummate the marriage this night.

He set the drink down on the small, round table next to the chair and strode toward the window, too anxious to stand still. He was torn by his need to see Peter well and the need to bind his wife to him so that his children would have someone caring for them. In the back of his mind, he was aware that he worried needlessly. If not tonight, there was always tomorrow night, since he never had two black moods in quick succession. He needed to be confident his son would heal. And he was quite sure she wouldn't welcome him to her bed until Peter was well once more.

Striding to the bookcases on the other side of the room, he didn't halt until he reached the bust of Plato. "Your words, dear philosopher, ring hollow before my quandary. For what did you know of marriage and children? Great thinker that you are, even you are limited. Which makes me far more limited, for I am merely a man, and a fatally flawed one at that."

He returned to the small table and took a sip of the whisky. He should be celebrating the easy attraction he had for his wife. But in his current state of mind, wanting to enjoy her and bring them both fulfillment immediately, it would just make it more difficult to be courteous and understanding of her naïveté on their first coupling.

Setting the glass down again, he examined the room. He needed a distraction. He strode to his desk and unlocked the second drawer, pulling out the ledger. He opened it to the last page that still needed to be totaled and forced himself to sit. After concentrating for a few minutes and coming up with three different totals, he set the quill back in the ink and rose.

It would be better to arrange the shelves so his wife couldn't knock anything else from them. He moved to the bookcase behind his desk and immediately removed a vase and set it on his desk. That raised the question about all other vases in the house. There was a very valuable vase in the parlor, an area she would use quite often. Immediately, he headed out of his office, anxious to make any changes necessary to ensure his wife's continued happiness in the house.

CHAPTER SEVEN

ELLIE, IN HER nightclothes and robe, hurried through the dark corridor toward her husband's bedroom, her small lamp lighting her way. It was well past midnight, but Peter was finally sleeping peacefully and had held down his last plate of toast and breakfast tea. She'd promised Darius an update, but didn't feel waking the servants at such an hour was necessary. Besides, she wanted to give him the news herself.

She counted the doors past his dressing room and parlor until she came to his bedroom. There was only her dressing room between their two beds, a fact that had made her nervous when she first arrived, but one she appreciated now. She'd not been immune to the excitement she'd felt at touching him in the nursery. The heady feeling had her wishing she'd read more of the book Lissa had given her, which sat in the chest at the end of her bed, still wrapped in its brown paper. She would rectify that oversight as soon as possible, but first she needed to talk to her husband.

Even as she thought the word, her step slowed. She was truly married, at least according to the law. She was quite sure that Darius wished to consummate the marriage this very night, which was part of her reasoning for telling him about Peter. Would he be fast asleep or barely resting, worried about his son? Should she wake him with a kiss on the cheek, or would that be too bold? While she knew what to expect—Lady Northwick had been adamant that they all know—she didn't know how it would feel. Both Dory and Lissa had been quite thrilled with their marriage beds.

She stopped before Darius's bedroom door. Her friends had married the men they loved. Her marriage was quite different, but she could easily see herself loving Darius. She already loved his children and it hadn't been a fortnight yet. But could he love her?

Doubt assailed her. Her mother had made her aware that she was not quite up to snuff as marriage material due to her hair color, lack of grace, and inability to be quiet and sit still. Would those characteristics still be important to a man who had already married? She thought back on her limited interactions with Darius. Not once had he remarked on her hair, nor had she had a mishap, as she liked to call them, while in his presence since the signing of their marriage register, and he'd only had to suggest she quiet her voice once.

There may very well be a chance that he could fall in love with her!

Unable to wait another moment, she opened the door and walked in, remembering to close the door softly. Quickly, she lowered the flame on her lamp and strode to the bed, which boasted four posts and a large canopy, much like her own. Limited moonlight shone through the windows, as the curtains hadn't been drawn. She stepped up to the bed and held the lamp aloft, but it was empty.

Empty? Where could he be at such an hour? Had he gone to her bedroom in the hope that she'd return? The thought warmed her heart, and she quickly made her way through the door that connected to her dressing room and then moved into her bedroom, only to find it empty as well.

Where was he? Did he stay awake in his study pacing, waiting for news? Was he in the dining room having a late-night meal to settle his worried belly? Had he been called away on business again so soon?

Even as questions filled her head, she strode to her door and out into the corridor once more. She would find her husband. She opened the door to his bedroom once again and walked into his dressing room before shining her lamp on his parlor. He was absent.

Not deterred, she left the room and headed downstairs. Walking into the parlor, she held her lamp aloft, shedding light on the quiet furniture, but no one was present. Proceeding into the dining room despite the lack of a fire, she bumped into a chair in the dark, bruising her elbow. She halted and set the lamp on the table to rub her arm. Clearly he wasn't in the room, or he would have remarked on the loud noise. Still, she lifted her lamp, just to be sure he hadn't fallen asleep at the table, but he wasn't there.

Now she worried that he might have been called away after all. Deep disappointment filled her, but she straightened her shoulders and carefully avoided the chair she'd bumped into as she made her way out of the dining room and parlor and into the corridor once again. There was a lamp lit on the wall, which made traversing the narrow space a bit easier. When she came to the double doors of Darius's study, she composed herself in case he was there. Then she slowly opened the door.

The room was dark except for limited light from what was left of a fire in the fireplace. That wasn't a good sign. She started forward and bumped into a stack of books, which toppled over onto the dark Persian rug. Barely keeping herself upright, she turned up her lamp and held it higher.

There were stacks of books all over the floor. Her first thought was that the Duke and Duchess of Northwick would be appalled, since they revered books so completely. She turned toward the fireplace and slowly walked between the books to see if Darius was there, as she could see a half-empty glass on a small round table. As she stepped around the large wingback chair, she halted. Darius wasn't in it, but Plato, Caesar, and—if she wasn't mistaken—Alexander the Great, or their busts, were. All quite notable men, but not her husband.

Turning back toward the rest of the room, she held her lamp high and navigated toward where she knew his desk to be. Was the room like this because the servants were reorganizing, since he had indeed left on business once again? As she drew closer to the desk, the light reflected off a number of vases placed haphazardly upon it. It must be the servants. Disappointed she hadn't found him, she'd started to turn back when she noticed his desk chair was not at the desk. It had probably been moved out of the way, but still she was bent upon finding it.

Staying closer to the half-empty shelves of the bookcases, where there seemed to be an easier path, she followed them around the room until she came upon the chair…and her husband. Her breath caught at the sight. He'd discarded his waistcoat and cravat, the opening of his shirt revealing very dark hair upon his chest. In sleep, his face was relaxed, even friendly. His hair was messy as if he'd run his hand through it more than once. His feet rested on the windowsill, of all places, crossed at the ankles.

If she didn't know better, she would say he was drunk, but no glass was nearby and a book lay open upon his lap. Curious, she crept closer. It was a poem by Samuel Taylor Coleridge, but she couldn't see which one, though a few lines were visible beneath Darius's hand. Sophie would know which one it was on sight, but Ellie's own knowledge was more earthbound. She stood in indecision. Should she wake him or should she allow him sleep?

By the state of his study, he'd been very busy, and most likely that was to while away the time until Peter was better. She took a step back. If he'd finally found rest, she wouldn't disturb it. Carefully, she made her way back to the doors. As she pulled the first one closed, she caught it just as it was about to slam, having already forgotten to be careful. Silently, she pulled it shut. Relieved that Darius was home and they could speak in the morning, she climbed the stairs once again to her bedroom.

Inside, she set the lamp down and dropped her robe on the

chair by her fireplace. After adding bits of coal to the fire, she waited until heat poured forth before moving to the chest at the end of her bed. She was far too excited about Peter getting well and finding her husband to go to sleep. She knelt before her chest and lifted the lid. Inside were various shifts, sheets, and a dozen or so unfinished embroidery squares.

She dug her hands underneath everything until she felt the brown paper. Pulling the large book from its hiding space, she immediately ripped open the paper. *The Education of the Feminine Species* revealed itself in all its leather-bound glory. She opened the cover and breathed in at the real title of the tome, *The Illustrated Pleasure of Seduction*. This was what she would read, as there was no better time to read such a scandalous book.

Quickly, she stuffed the brown paper back under the linens and closed her chest. She rose and brought the book to the chair before the fire. After lighting another lamp on the mantel, she sat and opened the book. She flipped through the inscription, the pages of illustrations of a naked man and a naked woman familiar. She may only have now to learn more before she became a wife in truth, and she wanted to know as much as possible about how it felt.

The next few pages she'd already viewed. Page five was a naked pair coupling, with the woman below the man, but the next few pages had the two people clothed as the man touched the woman in rather innocuous places. When Ellie had first seen these, she'd thought them silly. But at the remembered feeling of touching Darius, she could now see why a man's knuckles stroked gently across a woman's cheek, or the touch of his bare finger on her collarbone, would cause her belly to react like a meteorite fell inside her.

She passed by the next few pages and quickly focused on page ten. At this illustration, she felt herself heat. The man and woman, still completely dressed, kissed as he held her tight against him, his hand cupping her behind and her arms around his neck as he pressed her full length against him. To be wanted so much that a man would hold her in such a way had her heart melting. Would Darius do this?

She'd previously refused to read the book Lissa had found buried in the stacks at the school because she'd given up hope that she would ever feel what was shown. But now, the possibility loomed large and enticing. The idea of being wanted by Darius, not simply for an heir but for herself, was a heady thought, and one she'd never hoped for. After being told by her family and Society, both verbally and otherwise, that she wasn't worthy, not quite lady enough, to be wanted for any reason was tantalizing.

After turning the page, she studied it. The man now had half the woman's dress undone as he kissed her bare back. Despite the heat of the fireplace, Ellie shivered, but it wasn't due to cold so much as the thought of Darius doing the same to her. It was such a simple process, to undress, but the kiss…

She closed her eyes and imagined it happening to her. The image wouldn't come into focus, so she opened her eyes. The illustrations were well done and she could easily see them, so they'd do.

She couldn't wait for what came next, and turned the page. The woman's dress had fallen to the floor and puddled at her feet. She stood in her shift and stays, her head cocked to the side as the man kissed her neck. Ellie touched her neck in the same place, trying to imagine the feeling, but failing. Hopefully, she'd soon know.

As she turned the page, her breath caught. The man had lifted the woman's bare breast above her limited clothing, and his thumbs lay across the nipples. Ellie looked down at her own breasts, which were far more than a handful, and even now she could see her nipples pushing against her shift. Would Darius think them too big? She'd never had a man touch her breasts, but she was quite sure she would like it. She hadn't even had a man kiss her or take her hand, until Darius.

She sighed, hopeful but also afraid to hope that her life could continue on such a wonderful track. She'd never had such luck before. She read the single sentence below the illustration. *Always this...*

Always curious, as she'd seen the book do these back-to-back pages before. The next page would be a reprimand of some sort. She turned the page and stared at the drawing, at first not sure what she was seeing. The woman was completely dressed and against a brick wall of some kind, the skirts of her dress in the front bunched up to her waist, as the man, who looked completely dressed, stood against her. At the bottom it simply stated, *Not this...until later.*

Now *that* was a puzzle. She turned the page again to find the couple back to being half dressed. The man now had no tailcoat, waistcoat, or shirt as he held the woman, her torso bare against his as he kissed her. His other hand held up her shift as it grasped her behind. There was so much to the undressing part. It would be so much more practical to wait until nighttime, when each had little on their person.

Ellie turned the page. The illustration took an interesting viewpoint. It was from behind the woman, who lay on the bed looking at the naked man, but this was no ordinary naked image. His masculine member jutted out like a horse's did, and the woman was reaching for it with her hand. Ellie ran her finger over the man. It was most indecent of her, but she yearned to feel that piece of anatomy. As awkward as she'd known the copulating act to be, her friend's smiles when hinting at it told her it must be satisfying. She did long to be satisfied in that way.

She yawned and glanced at the clock, noticing the room was growing lighter. It was after six in the morning! Closing the book, she quickly rose and buried it back under the linens in her chest. Crawling into bed, she pulled the covers over her and closed her eyes, willing herself to sleep. After turning over a couple of times, she threw off the covers, finding them too heavy. She kept thinking about the illustrations. She needed to think of something else—the planets.

Yes, she would think about the eight planets and all that was known about them. From the sun, they were Mercury, Venus, Earth, Mars, Jupiter, Saturn, Uranus, and Ceres. First was Mercury…

—

Ellie rushed toward the stairs. It was past noon and she had yet to break her fast. What would Darius think? Did he know that Peter was better? Of course he would. No doubt Anna had sent word first thing in the morning.

She ran down the stairs, anxious to talk to Darius, but her foot missed the step. She grabbed for the banister, catching it just as her behind hit a step. "Oof." She sat down hard, the breath knocked from her.

Her heart raced at the scare, as she still had at least a dozen steps to descend. She set her hand against her chest, chiding herself for not holding the rail as she'd been taught. It wouldn't do her any good to fall and break her neck just because she was embarrassed that she'd slept so late. The time wasn't terrible if she'd attended a grand ball, but to be reading her secret book until dawn wasn't acceptable.

Impatiently, she waited for her heartbeat to slow a bit before getting to her feet, her legs shaking a bit.

"Beacham!" The yell came from down the corridor and echoed in the entryway.

The butler scurried past, disappearing in the direction of her husband's study. Thinking of the word *husband* calmed her nerves a bit, and she smiled. How wonderful that simply having a husband could make her feel so happy. Slowly, she continued down the stairs, her hand tight on the banister. When she reached the entryway, she increased her pace in time to hear Beacham address Darius.

"You yelled, my lord?"

She reached the study to see Darius raise his right eyebrow at his man. "I did indeed. Has Lady Ferncroft—"

She stepped around the butler. "I have. Or I believe I have. If not, I'm sure I will."

"Ah, here you are. I was about to inquire of Beacham if you had broken your fast." Darius looked at his butler. "You may go."

There was something about her husband that had changed since yesterday, but she wasn't sure what it was. However, the change in his study *was* significant. "Darius, you have changed this room about."

"Indeed I have. I do so on occasion. Each configuration caters to my current focus."

She studied the room, which looked far different than it had in the wee hours of the morning. First, there were absolutely no more piles of books on the floor. Second, his desk, which used to be across from the door and covered with vases, had been moved to the far wall, opposite the windows. Third, the wingback chair that previously sat by the fireplace was set by a window.

"Do you approve?"

She walked farther into the room. "I do not think it my place to approve or disapprove, as this is your study, and as such, should be arranged as befits your purposes." She scanned the bookcases, searching for the vases and busts she'd seen last night. On the top shelf of a bookcase near one of the windows, she found the vases.

"But I rearranged it because you are now my wife and may come in here to confer with me on any number of matters, so I would very much like your thoughts."

She pointed to the vases. "Do you not like vases? If so, why do you have so many?" The top shelf had at least fourteen that she could see.

Darius, who stood near the windows, now strode toward her. "I hope you will not think less of me, but I find them a rather feminine item." He raised his hand toward the shelf. "These are gifts from my mother or purchased by my late wife. Would you like me to put them elsewhere?"

She was rather pleased at their placement because there would be much less chance that she sent them to the floor as she walked by them. One in particular that had been in the parlor had two large handles that she'd steered clear of. "I have no particular love of vases, so in this we are in accord."

"Excellent."

"But what happened to your busts of Plato, Caesar, and Alexander the Great?"

He gave her a look of pure satisfaction. "You are very observant. They now grace the mantel above the fireplace." He gestured toward the area behind her.

She turned around to see Plato in the center and the other two men on either end, but not too close to the end. The mantel sat above her shoulder, and she couldn't get too close to the fire because of her dresses, something she'd learned accidentally before she came out. "I do believe they look very regal there." She turned back. "It is such a pleasure to learn that you value men of wisdom as much as I do."

He gave her a nod. "Something else we have in common. Perhaps we will find even more as we travel to visit my tenants."

She'd completely forgotten that they had planned to do so the day before, which reminded her of Peter. "Did Anna tell you about Peter?"

His features changed from polite to relaxed in an instant. It was that moment that clarified for her what was different. He was being very formal.

"Since I heard nothing, I visited him as soon as the sun had risen. He seems quite himself again."

Surprised that the nursemaid hadn't sent someone to tell Darius, Ellie felt guilty now for not waking earlier. "I did come down here to your study at about four in the morning to inform you of Peter's improved health, but I found you asleep in your desk chair over there." She pointed to the window where she'd found him.

"You were here?"

She wasn't sure, but it looked as if he'd lost some color in his face. "I was. I believe I walked in on your project of yesterday, as the room was full of book stacks. I'm guessing you were trying to keep your mind off Peter's illness."

He blinked then nodded. "So I was. I am heartily relieved that he is better."

She lifted her hand to touch his arm, but quickly brought it to her chest. She wore no gloves, and images from her reading the night before quickly crowded her mind. "As am I. So if you wish to travel today, I am at your disposal."

"Have you broken your fast?"

She looked away, embarrassed to admit the truth, but seeing no help for it. "I'm afraid I just rose, as I was up quite late."

"Of course, and I thank you for tending to Peter. I am very pleased at your caring."

Though the words were kind, no smile accompanied them. It was as if he hid himself behind his formality. He had said that it was required of him. "I'd best see what Cook has available. When would you like to depart?"

He glanced at the clock, which had been moved from the mantel to a bookcase. "Shall we say in an hour?"

She would have to change into a traveling dress, but if she had her food sent up, she could make that. "I shall be back downstairs in an hour."

He gave another short nod, then walked over to his desk.

Feeling a bit confused by the new Darius, she left the room, completely confident that once they were alone in the coach, he would relax once again.

CHAPTER EIGHT

STANDING IN THE front courtyard of the last tenant for the day, Darius watched in amazement as his new wife explained to Mrs. Gerey how to mix a lotion for her chapped hands. When Dinah had met his tenants, she'd smiled politely and nodded, adding little to the conversation. But Eleanor engaged them completely, even touching them upon the arm once and again, no matter their age or gender. And it appeared that every person genuinely liked his new wife.

He had tried to keep their conversations quite formal, but with her it was rather difficult. His formality was his shield, a way to stay in control and meet his responsibilities to his family, friends, and tenants. However, his new wife was anything but formal. Nothing about her was subtle, and she continually surprised him. In fact, in her deep-blue spencer and bonnet to match, with just a hint of her red hair wisping about her face, she was looking particularly pretty. So much so that, like his tenants, he found himself looking forward to the next time she turned her attention on him.

"Lord Ferncroft?"

Bringing his attention back to Mr. Gerey, he tried to remember what they'd been speaking about.

The man, not ten years older than him, gave him a sly smile. "Taken with the new missus, are ye?"

Darius would hardly say he was *taken* with her. "I am pleased to have a wife again."

The man looked over at his own wife. "They do lessen the burden of living, don't they?"

Studying the man who'd been married a good thirty years and had four grown sons and two daughters to prove it, Darius could see he was still fond of his wife. The woman was twice his size in girth, and while he remained fairly still, his wife's hands never stopped moving as she spoke earnestly to Lady Ferncroft. They appeared an unlikely pair, but perhaps when they had first met, they were more in accord.

However, Mr. Gerey was correct—having a wife did lessen the burden of living. Darius already felt a certain amount of relief over Eleanor's care of his children, and in particular Peter's illness. "They do, indeed, Mr. Gerey."

Eleanor and Mrs. Gerey approached, the older woman still talking.

The woman addressed her husband on seeing his attention on her. "Samuel, Hawthorne Park is going to celebrate St. Stephen's Day this year. Is that not wonderful news?"

The man looked to Darius for confirmation, and he nodded.

"Well, how about that? It is a welcome change after last year's troubles."

Though Mr. Gerey didn't elaborate, Darius knew the man thought more of the poor crops due to the Year Without a Summer the year before, and less about the lack of Christmastide celebrations at Hawthorne Park.

Eleanor clasped her hands together. "I'm so pleased you both are quite as excited as I am. I have always loved this time of the year, where everyone is appreciated for their part in the year's toils. After all, our labors deserve celebration and merriment." Her cheeks were rosy from the cold, which just made the sparkle in her eyes appear that much brighter.

At her pronouncement, Mrs. Gerey turned to Darius. "My lord, I am so happy for you. Thank you for gracing us with such a treasure as my lady."

"Mrs. Gerey, it is my pleasure."

"So it is," Mr. Gerey nudged his wife.

She batted her husband's shoulder. "Now you behave before his lordship, Samuel. We don't want him thinking poorly of us."

Eleanor, whose rosy cheeks were now full of red from a blush and not simply the cold, shook her head. "I could never think poorly of such wonderful tenants. Do let me know when your granddaughter is born, and what name your son decides upon."

"Oh, I will, my lady."

Darius held his arm out to his wife. "I believe we should return to the house, as the hour grows late."

She took his arm with poise. "Indeed it does."

With well wishes, they parted from the Gereys only to encounter a lone horseman riding up to the gate. Darius recognized him immediately, and wished they'd departed just a few minutes earlier.

"My lord."

"Archer." He tried to keep his voice neutral but, from the glance his wife sent him, hadn't succeeded.

His gamekeeper jumped down from his horse and bowed to Lady Ferncroft. "My lady. I am Thomas Archer, head gamekeeper. It is a pleasure to make your acquaintance."

"Oh, what a pleasant surprise. I met your wife on my first day here."

"Yes, my lady. And she's been singing your praises ever since. I must sleep during the day to best patrol the estate at night and keep it safe from poachers. That is why we did not meet that day. I do apologize."

She turned to Darius. "So that is why you said it was safe for me to walk about at night."

Archer's bushy gray brows rose. "My lady, do you walk in the dark?"

"Only a bit. I walk with my telescope so I can view the stars. Full-moon nights are my least favorite, but when there is no moon, the stars can be absolutely breathtaking. Have you ever noticed?"

"Indeed I have. I often get my bearings in the wood based upon Orion." Archer smiled kindly as if talking to his daughter.

"You don't use the North Star?"

The man shook his head. "Orion is the easiest to spot. He's a hunter, after all." Archer winked.

Not excited to have the one man who knew of his sanctuary becoming friendly with his wife, Darius interrupted any further conversation. "We were just heading back to the house. Did you have anything you wished to report?"

Archer shook his head. "My sole purpose for being out and about so early was to make the acquaintance of my lady. I shall wish you both a pleasant evening, then."

"It was wonderful to meet you, Mr. Archer. I am grateful to you for keeping our game safe."

Archer gave a short nod and a warm smile before mounting up and galloping back the way he'd come.

Eleanor watched him leave. "What a lovely man. To have a gamekeeper who knows about the stars is quite a surprise."

"Yes, well, Archer has been with Hawthorne Park since long before I arrived. I believe it is his years that have given him much wisdom. Shall we continue home?"

She turned back to him. "Yes, of course."

He helped her into the relative warmth of the coach.

Immediately, she pulled the blanket over her legs, holding up one end. "Would you like to share?"

He hesitated, about to refuse, since it was hardly something he did. However, he did wish to bed her in the evening, and they'd spent so much time with others, it could be to his advantage. "Thank you." He stepped into the coach and sat beside her, accepting the blanket she offered.

"I have to say, Darius, you have very pleasing tenants, and all of them were so welcoming. I truly was not sure what to expect."

"They are quite happy to have a lady of the house again."

"I also believe they are as excited as I am about the season. When I spoke to Mrs. Hurlock at our first stop, she said Hawthorne Park has never celebrated Christmastide. Perhaps I should limit my plans, so as not to cause too much change at once."

That she thought of those dependent on them was refreshing. "No. Do as you wish. It is best that everyone experiences how life will continue from now on."

Her face lit with undisguised joy. "Lovely." She placed her gloved hand on his arm as it lay on his lap. "I can assure you that organizing the Christmas traditions is the one skill my mother said I excelled at. She even allowed me to do it all. So you will not be disappointed."

Surprised by her statement, especially because Maggie loved her already and she'd made Peter feel better, he turned to view her face. "Only one skill?"

She didn't look at him. "Oh, I have many. I'm just not as proficient at them as others, or rather, than I am at celebrating the season." She finally faced him. "But I promise a Christmastide you will always remember." She cocked her head as she smirked. "At least until next year."

Her absolute joy was palpable, and it seeped into his chest, despite his defenses, lighting up the buried darkness inside for a moment. It was irresistible. He leaned in to kiss her cheek, but she turned her head and his lips brushed her bonnet instead. He straightened, a bit taken aback at how awkward he felt. He was never awkward.

"I have already written to my classmate Sophie and invited her to visit after St. Nicholas Day. I'm quite excited to have the Christmastide visiting season starting soon." She turned her head back toward him, her face now devoid of happiness, her brows lowered. "Why has there been no Christmastide celebrations at Hawthorne Park? Was your wife a Quaker?"

Her question was such a surprise that he snorted before recalling himself. "Hardly. She was a devout Anglican."

"Then why did she not—Oh, was it beyond her abilities? I can understand that, as it has been pointed out that many tasks are beyond mine. Perhaps she just needed encouragement?"

As much as he didn't wish to have this particular conversation, it would come out eventually, so it was best that he explain as much as he could. "No, she was quite skilled at everything and was the epitome of a woman with all the social graces. The perfect bride, so I had expected. Unfortunately, I failed to account for emotions, particularly anger and vengeance. A—"

"What? Your wife was angry at you and that's why there were no festivities?"

He gave a short nod. "It is a bit more complicated than that, but yes. When she learned more about what her life would be like with me, she was furious. She felt betrayed." He held up his hand, as Eleanor was about to interrupt again. "Allow me to finish my explanation?"

She closed her mouth tightly and nodded.

"I did not blame her. We married in January. She gave birth to Maggie in October, but shortly after that, her anger erupted and we lived civilly, though mostly apart, as she truly did not wish to be in my presence. Luckily, my business took me away often. However, she refused to find joy in anything, and so no Christmastide celebrations took place, nor any other festivity. I did insist on celebrating St. Nicolas Day for the children and made sure the nursery was decorated on Christmas Eve, as I wanted them to have a sample of what I'd had."

This time there was no stopping his new wife from speaking. The grip she had on his arm tightened. "She would have kept the children from celebrating?" Her voice rose so loud that he barely kept from physically cringing.

"I don't know. When I heard the orders she'd given Mrs. Torbett that nothing be done, I added my own to ensure the children would know what I had known. I'm sure Dinah cared very much for Maggie and Peter—when I was in residence, she spent most of her time in the nursery, and according to the nursemaid, that was usual. It may be that she simply didn't like the season." Though he had often wondered what Dinah had done up there beyond embroidering and spending time with Maggie and Peter. At least she cared about them, despite her fear of birthing another "mad Taylour."

Eleanor let go of him and crossed her arms. Her entire posture reminded him of an alley cat he'd once seen protecting her kittens from a small dog. That his new wife's first thought had been for his children solidified his growing confidence in her. Unfortunately, her state of high dudgeon on behalf of his offspring did little to set the mood for the seduction he had hoped to begin.

Oddly enough, he wasn't entirely disappointed. There would be time later, and the ride back to the house was quickly becoming productive and revealing. He was also quite sure he knew how he could change her mood. "I heard you tell Mrs. Gerey that we would be celebrating St. Stephen's Day. You may wish to confer with Mrs. Torbett, because she would know best what each tenant would benefit from."

She uncrossed her arms and waved off his suggestion. "No need for that. When we visited your tenant Mrs. Youell, she offered to compile a short list after profusely explaining that anything would be welcome. Besides, Mrs. Torbett will be busy preparing everything else. We may need to procure a few additional servants, especially for the ball."

Any contentment he'd begun to feel with the day immediately vanished as his body grew cold. "What ball?"

"The Twelfth Night masquerade ball. Surely you remember that's the final night of Christmastide. What would be the point of celebrating all the other days and not that one?"

"I *had* forgotten. After my parents' accident, they no longer hosted a ball, allowing another peer in the vicinity to do so. Nor did any of us attend. Yet we still celebrated the rest of the season. So it's actually quite possible."

"But—Oh, did they stop hosting because of your mother's scars?"

"Not just because of her scars, but my father's missing leg as well."

"But he's a duke!" She shook her head. "Surely his title helps garner him the respect he's due." She sighed. "But I do understand that those who pretend to be perfect are the first to be rude to others, no matter their status."

He liked that she defended his father. "Yes, and don't forget my mother wasn't exactly accepted either. She was a shopkeeper before she married."

"I had forgotten. She is so ladylike but without all the extra stuffiness. She's the opposite of you."

He jerked his head back. "Me?"

She grinned at him, obviously quite pleased with herself. "Yes, you. Darius, even *you* admitted to being too formal."

"I admitted no such thing. I simply agreed that I *need* to be formal."

"Very well, I will allow you the point, but it doesn't dissuade me from thinking you stuffy at times. For example, I have yet to hear you address me as Ellie."

"I address you by your name, Lady Ferncroft or Eleanor."

"Exactly. Yet you call Margaret Maggie."

Surprised by her observation, he quietly agreed. "I do." He had no idea why.

"Therefore, you can call me Ellie." Her grin softened and she took his hand once again. "Only when you feel comfortable doing so. I just meant to prove a point."

And she had. Her intellect was far superior to those he'd encountered years ago while looking for a bride. If she had been out then, would he have chosen her?

"I see we are almost home. Thank you for distracting me from my pique over your late wife's actions. I do appreciate your effort to keep our day pleasant." She squeezed his hand then let go as the coach pulled to a stop. "Now I can look forward to a pleasant night with the children as I give them their first astronomy lesson. Would you like to join us?"

The footman opened the coach door, but Eleanor didn't move, waiting for his answer.

How could he have forgotten that she had other plans besides consummating their marriage? Frustrated, he shook his head.

"I understand. I'm sure there is much you wish to do to-night." With that, she pulled the blanket from them and set it on the opposite seat as she stood. Before he recognized the disappointment in her voice, she'd stepped out of the coach, ascended the steps, and reached the front door.

The loss of her warmth both in body and humor had him rising to exit the coach himself. He started up the steps, berating himself for being so focused on avoiding what Dinah had threatened, an annulment, that he had lost sight of his current wife's feelings. He wouldn't be in such a hurry to bed her if they had already consummated their marriage…or would he?

He halted. Damn, he actually desired his wife!

The thought cleared away any disappointment he'd been feeling, and he continued up the steps. It also calmed his anxiousness over bedding her. He should have recognized the difference in the situation. He'd already bedded Dinah long before she demanded an annulment, and that was only because he'd revealed his secret to her.

Elleanor—Ellie—would never know his secret, so there was no rush. He reached the top step and stopped again. But there was a rush of a different kind. He wished to bed her, not out of duty but out of desire. He'd never desired Dinah, though he'd done his duty by her and made her happy in bed, or so she'd said. Instinct told him he'd never have to wonder if Ellie was pleased. He was quite sure she would let him know whether in bed or out.

His lips quirked at the thought, and he continued into the house. Maybe it was best that he had been delayed in his goal to have his robust wife. Now, he could seduce her properly.

He didn't doubt that she found him pleasant to look upon, but as she was a virgin, he didn't wish to scare her from what could be a mutually satisfying lifetime of sex. Now that his manic need to solidify their marriage had dissipated, he could perhaps accomplish a short courtship and win her heart as well as her hand.

"My lord?" Beacham stood waiting to take his coat.

Darius turned his back and shrugged out of it, allowing Beacham to hang it. "Follow me into my study." Without waiting, he strode out of the entry, down the corridor, and into his study. He started toward where his desk used to be before changing direction. After stepping behind it, he opened a cabinet and pulled out the wedding gift he had planned to give his wife last week. His black mood had foiled those plans, but now it would mean even more. "Please have this wrapped up and brought to Lady Ferncroft when we finish dinner tomorrow evening."

Beacham didn't actually smile, but his face did relax. "Would you not like it presented tonight?"

"No." Darius sat in his chair, still focused on his butler. "Tonight, she will be taking the children into the garden for an astronomy lesson. I want her to know this is specifically for her, not for them."

Beacham nodded. "You wish to make her happy. I understand. I will have all done as you asked."

"Thank you."

As Beacham carried the gift out of the room, Darius allowed himself a smile. Already he could imagine Elean—*Ellie's* joy as she opened the package to find the double-refracting telescope. For the first time in years, he looked forward to giving a wife pleasure.

CHAPTER NINE

"S ET IT RIGHT there." Ellie pointed to the far side of the baby Neptune fountain.

Beacham put down the new telescope. "Did you wish it facing this way?" He pointed toward the path that continued through the gardens.

"Yes." She couldn't wait to try it. Setting her lantern down on the edge of the dry fountain, she moved to where Beacham stood, locking in the legs of the stand. She still couldn't believe Darius was so thoughtful as to gift it to her. "I've never owned one so powerful." She sighed, still overcome with her husband's kindness.

At dinner that very evening, after a wonderful discussion over the subjects that should be taught to further the children's education, he'd had a footman bring it in. Though it had been wrapped in brown paper, she'd known immediately what it was and hopped up to press a kiss to her husband's cheek. But as she'd done so, his distinct musk scent filled her nostrils and her whole body flushed with a different type of excitement. It had to be because of the book she'd been reading. She was barely halfway through it and already her dreams had woken her more than once, her breathing rapid and her heart beating faster than butterfly wings.

"There you are, my lady."

She refocused her attention on Beacham and held back a smile, as he'd set the telescope pointing at the ground. "I thank you for your assistance. I know I could have had a footman carry it for me, but I would have worried."

"I understand. May I assist you with anything else?"

"No. Thank you. I'll just need it brought into the parlor when I'm done."

"I will await your summons, then." Beacham gave a short bow before heading back the way they'd come.

It was early yet, and she anticipated at least a couple of hours before the night air grew too cold. Luckily, winter was an excellent time for viewing stars, since it darkened so much earlier. The night before she'd only kept the children out a half an hour. It was just enough time to point out the easiest constellations to find.

But now, with such a strong telescope as Darius had purchased, she was quite sure she could even look upon Ceres! Moving to the instrument, she tilted it into the right position and locked it in place. She put her eye to it and looked. "Oh, my." The stars appeared twice as large, and she moved her eye away to get her bearings in the night sky before looking through it once more.

Her heartbeat raced as she gazed upon the very distinct Pleiades. With her new telescope, she could clearly see hundreds of other stars beyond the usual seven, as well as wisps of the space cloud that she'd read about around them. The blue she'd seen in other telescopes was much stronger and brighter, making it easy finding the main stars as well as their parents, Atlas and Pleione. She could even make out the white at the center of the largest stars, like Alcyone and Maia. "So beautiful."

In fact, the beauty of the stars quite overwhelmed her and she pulled back from the telescope to blink back her tears.

"May I offer you my handkerchief?"

Startled, she jumped, her hand hitting the telescope and sending it toppling.

Darius jumped forward and kept it from crashing to the ground. "I did not mean to startle you. I thought you heard me when I stepped on that dry stick."

She pressed her hand to her chest, her emotions swirling, as she tried to catch her breath. "Whenever I view the heavens, I am there, not here, so I didn't hear you." She paused to gulp in more air. "Thank you for saving the telescope. I would have been heartbroken had I damaged your thoughtful gift."

"I would simply have had it repaired. Here." He held out his handkerchief.

Grateful, she took it, and patted at her watery eyes.

Darius studied her. "Why were you crying? Is the telescope not working properly?" His frown was clear in the light from his own lantern.

"Oh, not at all. I mean, it works perfectly. I can see the stars better than I have ever seen them. While I have read about their beauty, this is my first glimpse of it. That is why I teared up. The Pleiades are so truly *celestial*." She swallowed to keep from tearing up again.

"The Pleiades? The Seven Sisters from Greek mythology, as I recall." He looked up at the sky. "Are they not visible in the Taurus constellation?"

Pleased that he was familiar with them, she pointed at the stars. "Yes. Just follow the line created by Orion's Belt and you can see the star cluster."

"I admit, that particular star grouping has always bothered me. It appears unorganized, almost like a smudge on the night sky."

She was not surprised by his thoughts, as some of her own classmates had made similar remarks, though not quite in that way. "I understand, but I think if you see them through this telescope, you may change your mind. Would you like to see?"

His brows rose. "I suppose I can be open to an alternative view on this."

She stepped back to allow him to look, anxious to see his reaction.

He bent and put one eye to the telescope. In less than a minute, his head snapped up. "That is truly the Pleiades?"

She nodded, excitedly. "Are they not beautiful?"

He looked up at the sky once more before putting his eye to the glass again. This time he remained there for many minutes.

She'd begun to wonder if he were trying to find the right words to disagree with her, when he lifted his head.

"I stand corrected. They are not a smudge. They are a stain."

"What?" For some reason, she took umbrage at his conclusion.

His lips quirked up a bit. "A breathtakingly beautiful white stain that spreads a brilliant blue across the cold, dark black of the universe."

As her mind comprehended his image, she returned his smile. "I do believe I agree."

He stepped away from the telescope and closer to her. "They are much like you."

"Me?" Her hand found her chest as she struggled with the idea of being any kind of stain, though she was quite sure her mother would enjoy such a metaphor about her.

"I do not pretend to be a poet, but I have noticed how your enthusiasm for life spreads to others, enveloping them in the warmth of your personality."

"Oh, Darius." No one had ever given her such an absolutely perfect and very personal compliment. Her heart swelled, not because it was a compliment, but because in their few days together, he'd paid her close attention and truly recognized who she was as a person.

With the back of his knuckles, he stroked her cheek, sending tingles to run along her skin. "I am grateful to you for marrying me. You have brought a warmth back to my home that it hasn't seen in over a generation. We all feel it."

Her eyes started to tear again because his appreciation was so sincere. "You don't know what it means to me, to be here. I feel as if I have finally come home. It is I who is grateful."

He stepped even closer, his hand on her face moving behind her head.

Her heartbeat turned sporadic, as she knew what that meant. She let her eyes drift closed and waited to feel his kiss on her lips, her whole body almost vibrating with anticipation.

"My wife." His words whispered over her lips before she felt his own on her forehead.

She opened her eyes to see his head moving away. Unable to help herself, she wrapped her hand around his neck, stopping his retreat, and lifted onto her toes to press her lips to his. It was just a touch, but it filled her with happiness. Letting ago, she could see his surprise in the dim light of her lantern and sought an apology for her bold actions, but couldn't bring herself to form one. She may be a maiden, but she was his wife. Surely women kissed their husbands.

He recovered quickly, and his hand once again came to her face, but this time he cupped her cheek. "Ellie."

Her name on his lips caused her to sigh silently just before he pressed his mouth to hers. Not expecting the kiss this time, she opened her mouth only to have his tongue slip between her lips. Her knees weakened at his invasion, and she grabbed a hold of his arms to steady herself. Then, before she could commit the feeling to memory, he pulled away.

"I did not mean to disturb your observations. I only wished to discover if you found my gift acceptable."

Still off balance from his kiss, she couldn't quite form the words, so she nodded.

"Very good. Then I will leave you to your stargazing." With a brief nod, he turned and started down the path that would take him back to the house.

She stood frozen in place, heating from the inside as her mind swirled like a galaxy and her belly tumbled like a meteor crashing into a planet. She could still smell him—and taste him. The hint of brandy on his tongue as he'd touched hers made her want to taste more.

She stumbled to the fountain and sat, her legs far too unsteady.

What the book had shown and described didn't begin to touch the feelings inside her. Now she understood why such actions were usually completed in bed. She couldn't imagine standing up while he kissed her unless he held her to him, which he hadn't. He seemed completely confident in his kiss, but then again, why would he not? He was her husband and would take her to bed very soon. Maybe even tonight!

The thought had her heart racing again, and she took in gulps of the cold night air. She wanted to race back and ready herself for bed. She rose on shaky legs, her gaze falling on the telescope, his gift to her. She sat back down. No. It was far too early, and to return so soon might make him think she didn't truly enjoy his gift.

But she was quite sure she would never look at the Pleiades in quite the same way again. Maybe she could find something else to tell him about in the stars. Perhaps she could use the stars to talk about how much she wished to be his wife in truth.

Moving her gaze to the sky, she identified four constellations before settling on the Draco, or Dragon. She'd read that the Cat's Eye Nebula could be seen in the constellation, but she'd never owned a telescope powerful enough to see the colors it was said to have. Adjusting the telescope to point farther north, toward the North Star, she put her eye to it and made smaller adjustments. Before she could lock it in place, she found the nebula and sucked in a breath.

She could clearly see the star's white center and blue gases surrounding it, but what had her attention was the pale orange, almost-peach glow that seemed to float outside either end, making it appear oblong. The colors began to meld, and she quickly moved her head away to wipe at her watering eyes. She was glad there was no one to see her so overset. It was just that the universe truly was heavenly and always made her feel honored to be able to glimpse even a small portion of it.

Determined to enjoy the view in her telescope, she straightened her shoulders. William Herschel surely didn't cry when he first discovered the Cat's Eye Nebula, so she could certainly look upon it without becoming a watering pot. Setting her eye to the instrument once again, she concentrated on all the details, so she could tell Darius about it. Though the Pleiades took her breath away, she felt more kinship with the nebula. After all, it wore her colors. She grinned as she straightened.

Glancing toward the sky once more, she decided to unlock the telescope and follow all of the Draco constellation. As it was one of the largest, she was sure there would be much to see that she hadn't seen before. Bending once more, she began her exploration.

It wasn't until she tried to lock the telescope and found her fingers had grown numb from the cold that she straightened. She blew on her hand. It started to tingle as she looked worriedly at the night sky. She had stayed outside far too long. Quickly, she locked the telescope with her thawing fingers before hurrying up the path.

As soon as she stepped into the parlor, her cheeks began to sting. She glanced at the clock. "Oh, no." Almost two hours had passed. Moving to the entryway, she found Beacham talking to a footman.

Upon seeing her, he turned from the man and hurried forward. "My lady, you look frozen. Let me take your coat." He turned to the footman he'd been speaking to. "Armand, add coal to the fire in the parlor immediately."

She wanted to tell him she needed to go to her room, that Darius may be expecting her, but her teeth started to chatter. That wasn't good at all.

"Come, my lady." Beacham ushered her into the parlor, where poor Armand was still adding coal to the fire. "That's fine, Armand. I'll add more. Go tell Cook we need hot cocoa immediately, and have a blanket brought to her ladyship."

She sank down into one of the wingback chairs before the fire as Beacham added even more coal before walking past her, to return with a quilt.

She gratefully accepted it and rubbed her hands together underneath it to dissipate the tingling. Finally, it went away and she clasped her hands together tightly, as she clamped her jaw to keep her chattering teeth from making so much noise.

Beacham's usually stoic face revealed his worry as his brows lowered. "Would you like me to fetch my lord?"

"No! I mean, I'd rather not disturb him." The last thing she wished Darius to know was that she'd lost track of time and frozen outside. "I'll be fine."

The butler didn't appear convinced, but moved away and returned with a cup of hot cocoa, which he set on the small table next to her.

She pulled her hands out from beneath the quilt and lifted the cup, sure that once she started warming from the inside, she'd feel much better. No sooner had she taken a sip and set down the cup, though, she sneezed.

Beacham, who was in the process of carrying over a small footstool, halted. "God bless you."

She gave him a weak smile, not a little embarrassed by her situation. "Thank you."

He continued forward and set the stool down for her.

She set her feet on it, and immediately the heat from the fire began warming her frozen toes. "Oh, that's quite pleasant. Thank you. As soon as I am properly warmed, I shall go to my rooms."

"I shall have a hot water bottle prepared for your bed."

Before she could once more extend her appreciation, Beacham vanished again. She lifted the cup of cocoa and took a gulp now that it was no longer too hot but still quite warm. She felt the heat move down her torso into her belly, thinking of one of the lessons at school where they all learned how their food was processed. They'd even learned why the body needed clothes to stay warm. She grimaced as she imagined her mother's reaction to her lack of sense in staying outside too long. Hopefully, no one but the servants would ever hear of her poor judgment.

She was the lady of her own house now, and she needed to account for everything. She would simply tell Beacham to send someone for her after an hour every night, so she wouldn't take a chill. Luckily, she was no frail miss, and her error should not cause any undue hardship upon her person. Still, it was best to be careful. She took another large swallow of cocoa, happy with her decision.

The telescope! In her hurry to get warm, she'd forgotten about it. Anxious that it may be damaged by what was sure to be a frost, she set her cup down and rose, dropping the quilt on the chair. She was pleased to discover her toes were tingling, which was a very good sign. She'd taken mere steps toward the door when another sneeze took her.

Luckily, no one heard it, and she quickly made her way into the entry to dig out the handkerchief Darius had lent her. She'd just wiped her nose when Beacham appeared.

"I'm going to bed now. Please bring in my telescope and set it in the parlor. It will need to be dried off, as the change in temperature may cause condensation and I don't wish it to be ruined."

"I will do it myself, my lady."

She gave him a full smile. "I know I can depend upon you."

He gave her a short nod before disappearing into the parlor.

Now to ready herself for bed. She ascended the grand staircase and was halfway to her rooms before she sneezed again. Quickly, she wiped her nose and ducked into her room, where her maid awaited her. Now that she had warmed considerably, she could look forward to her husband's visit with due excitement.

CHAPTER TEN

Darius put down the letter from his youngest brother. Anthony was enjoying married life, but it had not kept him from his usual wanderings. He'd written to say that he planned to visit Hawthorne as soon as he and his wife returned from Scotland. It appeared that Ellie had invited Anthony and Lisette for Christmastide. Darius should probably confer with his wife to discover what her plans were, exactly. The last thing he needed was a house filled with family if a black mood came upon him.

He set down the letter and sipped his coffee. Now that he felt normal again, which always took a couple of days after returning home, he looked forward to continuing his courtship of his wife, though after the kiss last night, he was ready to consummate their marriage sooner rather than later. Ellie's boldness had taken him aback because it was so unexpected, but he was quite pleased. If she enjoyed their bed together like she enjoyed everything else, he could see a relatively content life ahead for them. That was not something he'd ever envisioned for himself.

That she was pleased with his gift was quite obvious. It had been hard to walk away after having just a taste of her, but he didn't want to take her in the garden at night, in the cold, for their first time together. He'd gone to her room later in the evening, but she wasn't there. Assuming she was in the nursery, he'd left disappointed.

He glanced at the clock on the mantel in the dining room. It was getting rather late. Did she not sleep well? He waved the footman over to send for her, then thought better of it. "Never mind."

Rising, he dropped his napkin on the table before heading upstairs to her rooms. This was a perfect opportunity to further his pursuit. He smirked at himself. He was accomplishing everything backward. Usually, the wooing preceded the seduction, which preceded the marriage. It was rather more enjoyable his way, though not without its pitfalls.

As he approached the door to Ellie's room, he heard voices. It must be her maid. He was reaching for the doorknob when a loud sneeze had him halting. His whole body tensed. Surely fate would not be so unkind as to take another wife from him. He pulled his hand back.

Images of his late wife from before she'd passed crowded his mind. Her harsh coughing and gasps for breath still echoed in his head. Her last words were that she was glad she'd finally be free of him. The physician said her lungs had given out. Remembering what Ellie had said about bleeding, he now wondered if that had made Dinah too weak.

He shook himself. Ellie wasn't weak, and he doubted she'd allow a physician to bleed her, but he must find out how he could help. Grabbing the knob again, he turned it and stepped into the room, surprised to find not the maid but Mrs. Torbett.

"My lord." The woman rose from the chair next to Ellie's bed.

In a glance, he noticed the curtains were wide open, the sun streaming in the room, the fire burned warm in the fireplace, and his wife sat up in bed, her bright hair pulled back by a simple peach ribbon, complementing the smile on her face. "Darius. What a surprise."

He stepped into the cheery room, a little confused. "You are not well?"

A blush filled her face. "I'm fine. I stayed outside last night enjoying your gift so very much that I couldn't seem to stop gazing at the stars. Oh, and I viewed the Cat's Eye Nebula for the first time. Darius, it was wondrous. Did you know that the nebula—"

"Your health?" He didn't bloody care a damn about the nebula. He strode forward, anxious to look at her closely.

"I'm perfectly fine. But your housekeeper is insisting I stay abed. Could you please speak with her? I have much to do."

He looked to Mrs. Torbett. "My lord, my lady has been sniffling, and I simply don't want her to feel worse. You must agree with me. Staying abed for a day can only help."

Pushing away thoughts of Dinah's last days, he studied his wife. She appeared twice as healthy as anyone else under his roof, yet he was not one to take a risk. He trusted his housekeeper, as she'd proven herself worthy. "I must agree with Mrs. Torbett. It is best to err on the side of caution."

Ellie blew air out between her lips as she crossed her arms.

"I'll return later, my lady." Mrs. Torbett scurried out, obviously not willing to engender anymore of Ellie's displeasure.

"Truly, Darius, there is nothing to worry about. I just have a bit of a sniffle. I will say, your handkerchief was very helpful last night." She gave him a bright smile.

"Are you having trouble breathing? Any coughing? Do you have a fever?" He'd thought he'd convinced himself she would feel better soon, but her nose was red, so he stepped next to the bed to examine her more closely.

"My breathing is very good. I haven't coughed, and I don't have a fever. Here." She took his hand and set it to her head, her neck, and then her arm. "See?"

The softness of her skin distracted him, but he did recognize that she had no fever, which was a great relief. "Then you must rest and get well."

She released his hand and waved away his comment. "Not at all. I am willing to stay in bed, but there is too much to do. I'm so glad we made our wedding rounds and I've met the tenants and neighbors, or I'd have to insist on going out. As it is, taking a day from my duties will put me behind. Besides, if I sleep all the day then I'll be awake all night."

At her statement, he realized that being awake part of the night was what he'd hoped for. Obviously, he must wait for her to feel better before joining her in her bed. Despite his disappointment, he was relieved that she was not seriously ill and did plan to stay abed. "And what do you plan to do in your bed all day?" Even as he asked the question, his own mind filled with far too many inappropriate ideas.

"Plan for the upcoming festivities, of course. That's why I sent for Mrs. Torbett. Cook has everything for the Christmas pudding. You will be joining us tomorrow for the stir-up, will you not?"

He'd completely lost track of the days, though that wasn't at all surprising. "I would be honored to join you."

"And the children. Is it true they've never stirred the Christmas pudding?"

He barely held back a grimace. "I must admit, that is true."

Her hand was back on his arm. "Do not feel ashamed. I have to admit a certain satisfaction in being able to introduce many of the Christmastide events to Maggie and Peter. I'm hoping they will always carry fond memories of their childhood at this time of year and do the same for their children."

It took him a moment to follow her train of thought, but when he did, he counted himself very fortunate to have her as his wife. "I have fond memories of my time as a child and look forward to building similar memories with my children as well. You mentioned that you planned all the activities for your family. Surely there was a time when you were far too young to accomplish that. Was your enjoyment of the season why you took on that task?"

Ellie laughed, not in a flirtatious manner, but in a full-throated laugh that had his body taking notice. "Not at all. It was because my family's celebrations were chaotic and a complete ruin. As soon as I learned how all was to commence, I took over. I was nine, I believe."

He stared in shock. Maggie was seven. In two years, he couldn't imagine her telling the servants what to do and orchestrating the festivities. "And your family was happy with that?"

This time Ellie gave a short chuckle. "Not at first. My first year, all I did was make sure all was done on the proper day. But by my third year, I had the house running perfectly, even getting my eldest brother to participate in Stir-up Sunday, which was no easy feat." She gave him a sly smile. "To be honest, my mother was quite surprised. I've never been known for being successful." Her smile faltered as she shrugged. "But I feel a certain kinship with the holidays. I was born on the sixteenth of December, so right in the middle of all the festivities. I do believe it was fate."

It wasn't the first time she'd mentioned her lack of skill, which surprised him. "Your fate is our family's fortune. But I'm confused. Why do you say that you aren't successful? In the mere couple of weeks we've been married, you have made life here at Hawthorne so much better than it was."

A blush filled her cheeks, and she squeezed his arm where her hand lay before pulling it away. "That is kind of you to say. It may simply be that some of my strengths fit into your needs. But please do not have high expectations of me, except with the season. I promise I will disappoint you."

Her words were said with such absolute confidence that he didn't know how to respond. Luckily, there was a knock at the door.

"Oh, I'm quite sure that is Beacham. I asked him to bring my telescope in here. I don't think going outside for a few nights would be a wise decision, even if I can't see the whole sky from in here." She turned her face toward the door. "Please enter."

The door flew open and Maggie stood there, her eyes wide with fear. "Are you going to die?"

Darius's chest tightened at the sight of tears on his daughter's cheeks, but before he could go to her, Ellie laughed.

"Of course not, Maggie. In fact, I do believe I'm going to feel better faster with you nearby. Come and sit on the bed with me."

Maggie looked to him for confirmation, and he strode toward her to take her hand. "It's true. Lady Ferncroft will feel better in just a few days or so." He sincerely hoped that was the case as he led Maggie to the bed.

Anna spoke from the doorway. "I'm sorry, my lady. Maggie insisted on coming to see you."

"And I'm glad she did, Anna. And did Peter also insist?"

Darius looked down to see that his son was indeed hiding behind the skirts of the nursemaid.

Peter shook his head, even as he let go of the nursemaid's skirts and pointed at his sister. "No. She made me come."

"Did not."

"Did too."

"Did n—"

"Darius, would you be so good as to move that chair that Mrs. Torbett sat in just a bit closer to the bed, so Peter can sit? Maggie, you can hop up next to my legs if you can. Anna, please fetch a maid to bring us all hot cocoa."

Within a minute, Ellie had organized them like a queen and her court, and despite Peter's supposed dislike of his new mother, even he seemed caught up in her explanation of why they all needed to learn not to stay out in the cold too long.

Darius leaned against the bedpost, listening as Ellie described what she'd seen in her telescope, his children not even fidgeting, as Peter was wont to do. Even Darius found himself seeing the nebula in his mind's eye.

"May we see too?" Maggie's voice was almost breathless.

"I would very much like to show you, but I think on these cold nights, stargazing will have to be done from inside." Ellie looked toward the windows. "I'm not sure which way we are facing in this room."

"We could look from the nursery," Magie offered.

"I'm not sure which room would be best, but I promise that tonight, I'll figure out where in the house we must be, so tomorrow you can gaze upon the Cat's Eye."

"I want to see the dragon." Peter folded his arms, clearly determined to have his way.

"Well, we can see that too. It was Draco that led me astray and caused my sniffle. He's one of the largest constellations in the sky!" Ellie raised her arms and spread them wide.

Maggie cocked her head. "Does it really look like a dragon?"

Ellie crossed her arms. "That's an interesting question. Have you ever seen a dragon?"

Peter piped up. "There's no such animal."

Maggie immediately turned on him. "That's what you said about an elephant, and yet there is."

Peter immediately pouted, but Ellie laughed. "No, there is no living dragon, while there *is* a living elephant. We shall have a lesson on mammals tomorrow."

Darius pushed away from the post. "Do you think that wise? You may need more rest."

"Yes, I see what you mean." She looked at the children. "I promise it will be our first lesson once I'm up and about." She leaned forward and whispered, "Hopefully, tomorrow."

He frowned. Surely she knew he could hear her. "Now you've seen that Lady Ferncroft is under the weather, so let's allow her to rest and feel better."

"Yes, Father." Maggie turned and slid off the side of the bed to join him.

But Peter continued to look at Ellie.

"Come, Peter."

Finally, he scrambled off the chair and joined them, taking Darius's hand.

He led his children out of the room and down the corridor toward the nursery. They had almost arrived when Peter tugged on his hand. "Yes, Peter?"

"Is our new mama really going to feel good again?"

He crouched down to look Peter in the eye. "I believe she will. She knows a lot about such things. Look at how she helped you get better."

His son thought for a moment. "She said that thinking happy thoughts for me made me get better faster. If we do that for her, do you think it will work?"

"Happy thoughts?" Darius had never heard of such a thing.

Maggie, who had continued toward the nursery, came back. "Yes. When I told her I was worried about Peter, she said that thinking happy thoughts for him would help. So I thought about all the things he likes, even beetles." She squinched her nose.

Now he understood. Ellie had given Maggie something to do so she'd feel that she was helping. "Ah, yes. I do believe it would work to help her feel better."

His son's chin lifted. "Then we will do that. What makes her happy?"

Darius blinked, caught off guard by the question.

"She likes the stars," Maggie supplied.

"And elephants, I think."

At Peter's suggestion, Darius nodded. "Yes, she does. And do you know what else makes her happy?"

Peter shook his head.

"You and Maggie. She told me just yesterday how happy she was that she had you and Maggie to look after. She even thanked me for that."

"Me?" Peter pointed to his chest.

Darius smiled at his son. "Yes, you. She believes you have a healthy curiosity and are quite intelligent, and that Maggie is very caring and very accomplished."

Peter straightened his little shoulders, his face serious. "Then we must think of all the happy thoughts for our new mother, so she can feel better and take care of us."

Darius had never been so proud of his son as he was right then. "That is a capital idea." He rose and held his hand out. "Maybe you could even do some drawing that will make her happy."

Maggie's face split into a grin. "Yes! We can draw stars and planets and a tela—tela—"

"Telescope."

"Yes, that. Come on, Peter. We have much to do to make Mother better." She grabbed Peter's hand, and the two strode quickly to the open nursery door.

From the corridor, Darius could hear Maggie telling the nursemaid what their lesson was for the day. He listened as she explained all the supplies they would need.

Smiling, he turned back toward Ellie's room. She'd barely been with them two weeks and already she had his children curious again, his staff and tenants excited for Christmastide, and himself feeling… What *was* he feeling? Happy? He hadn't been happy since he was a child. He'd been content with Dinah until he'd told her his secret, but not *happy*.

At the door to his wife's bedroom, he paused. Something inside told him he didn't deserve to be happy, but he rejected it. He *did* deserve happiness, even if it was fleeting.

He opened the door and walked in only to find that Ellie had fallen asleep. He continued toward her bed until he stood beside it, next to the chair his son had sat in.

She slept propped up against the pillows, her head falling to the side, revealing the lengths of her fiery hair. Unable to resist, he lifted a few locks, allowing the soft tresses to fall through his fingers. Her nose was still red and the few freckles about the bridge were quite easy to see. Her light eyebrows framed her closed eyes, her even lighter lashes resting on her cheeks. Though her nose was still a bit red, her lips were redder, and the memory of their softness filled him.

As his gaze traveled down, it was arrested by her large bosom rising and falling beneath her shift and robe. But his attention was caught by the object she clutched in her hand—his handkerchief. She didn't simply hold it, she grasped it like a lifeline, even in sleep.

His chest tightened and something shifted in his heart. He

wanted to protect her like he protected his children.

He silently laughed at himself. It was juvenile when he looked at it objectively. She simply held his handkerchief because she needed it for her nose. But his mind had taken a flight of fancy and wouldn't let go that it meant much more. She must have her own handkerchiefs and could have used one of those. Maybe it meant she valued it because it was his.

Again, his practical side laughed at him, and rightly so.

Turning, he quietly left the room. He would be sure she wasn't disturbed. The cook would know what was best to have sent up for his wife's recovery, and no doubt Mrs. Torbett had already relayed the news of Ellie's illness.

Even so, he found himself descending the grand staircase and heading for the kitchens. Perhaps if he mentioned the issue, the cook would understand exactly how important it was to him that his new wife feel better.

He stepped into the kitchens and found four people rushing about as if the sky were falling. One of them, his cook, Mrs. Clark, was pouring liquid into a bowl and setting it on a tray. Then, with a word to a young man who stirred a pot above the fireplace, she picked up the tray herself and started toward Darius. So bent on her purpose was she that she almost ran into him, and he quickly stepped aside, which finally caught her attention. "My lord!"

Everyone in the kitchen stopped to look.

"Mrs. Clark, where are you headed with that tray?" His cook never delivered a tray, not in the entire time he'd been in residence at Hawthorne Park.

"I made a hearty soup for my lady. It will warm her from inside and give her the stamina to fight what it is she's got. We'll get her well sooner than the cock can crow on a clear morning after a rain. I prom—" The woman stopped, her round face breaking into a sweat.

They both knew what she'd been about to say. She was promising Ellie would get better even though there had been nothing she could do to help Dinah. Yet Mrs. Clark had never brought a tray up to his late wife.

"If you are bringing that up to her now, may I suggest you wait an hour? I just came from her room, and she is sleeping."

"Oh, of course. She needs to rest." The cook turned around much faster than he would have expected from someone of her girth and returned to the hearth, where she emptied the bowl into the pot the young man stirred. She then set the tray down on a table and came back to him. "Do you know if there is any particular food her ladyship enjoys? I'd very much like to make her a special meal when she's better. It's best to plan ahead for happy events such as this."

Not accustomed to discussing meals with his cook, he felt ill-equipped to answer, but he was very pleased that his staff cared so much. "I shall have to think on that. I will write down a few items and give the list to Mrs. Torbett."

"Thank you, my lord." Mrs. Clark nodded energetically and started to turn away, then stopped, turning back. "Did you need something, my lord?"

Feeling ill at ease now that it was clear his reason for coming to the kitchens was no longer valid, he straightened his shoulders. He was about to simply leave, when his wife's mention of Stir-up Sunday gave him an excuse. "I want to be sure that all is ready for tomorrow's stir."

Mrs. Clark beamed. "Oh, yes! We are quite excited. Mrs. Torbett said my lady and the children will be participating. Will you, my lord?"

He gave her his most formal nod. "Indeed, I will."

"I promise everything will be in place and we will be sure everything is quite tidy."

"Thank you, Mrs. Clark. Please go about your duties. I have detained you long enough." With that final pronouncement he strode out the door, pleased with his quick thinking though still worried about Ellie.

Would she be able to participate on the morrow?

CHAPTER ELEVEN

November 30, 1817
Stir-up Sunday

ELLIE COULDN'T STOP smiling even as she wiped her brow. "Very well executed, Maggie."

Maggie immediately stopped stirring in the chunks of apples Mrs. Clark had added to the pot. "Will we be able to taste the apples?"

"Of course. You'll be able to taste everything we've stirred in, from the raisins your father added, to the currants I stirred in, to the orange rinds that Peter will stir. Come on up, Peter."

Darius helped Peter stand on the chair and pulled the long wooden spoon toward his son. "Mrs. Clark, we are ready for the next ingredient."

The robust lady stepped up and poured in a small bowl of orange rinds. "There you go, Master Peter. Be sure to stir from east to west now."

At Peter's furrowed brow, Darius moved the spoon in the correct direction until his son took over, though he struggled to get the spoon through the thickening mixture.

Ellie kept her eye on the rinds, waiting for it all to slip beneath the surface. Finally, the last bit of orange disappeared. She clapped her hands together. "All done. Wonderful work, Peter."

The boy brought the spoon back to where he'd started and let go. "Will it taste good? It looks like mud." He squinched his nose up much like his sister often did.

Ellie laughed, not sure the children would appreciate the flavor after the pudding was cooked then soaked in brandy. She was both surprised and pleased that this would be their first ever Christmas pudding and that she could be a part of it. "I promise it won't taste like mud. Did you know before we eat it, we set it on fire?"

Peter's eyes rounded before he looked to his father for confirmation. At Darius's nod, Peter grinned. "I wish Christmas was tomorrow."

As Darius helped Peter clamber down from the chair, he explained, "That would be unfortunate, because it takes weeks for the Christmas pudding to be ready."

Peter frowned at that, not happy at all.

Maggie looked up at Darius. "Father, why did we never stir the pudding before?"

Ellie glanced at him in time to see the concern cross his face before he hid it well. "I did not know if you would enjoy working in the kitchen. Is this something you would like to do again next year?"

Maggie didn't say anything, but Peter nodded. "Yes! Unless the pudding tastes like mud."

Darius set his hand on Peter's shoulder. "Then I will ask you again after it's served."

"Mrs. Clark?" Ellie motioned the woman over. "Please continue with the ingredients and stirring. We leave the Christmas pudding to your expert ministrations."

The cook beamed. "Thank you, my lady."

"Come, children. It's time for you to return to the nursery. I will visit later, and we will play bilboquet."

Maggie took her brother's hand as they all left the kitchen. Anna waited for the children in the entryway and continued upstairs with them.

Darius stopped to watch them go before turning to Ellie. "Would you like to rest now?"

Her nose had stopped running, and after all the rest she had the day before, that was the last activity she was interested in. "No. I'm feeling very much better."

"Then may I suggest we adjourn to the parlor, where you can tell me who, beside my brother Anthony and his wife, you have invited to descend upon us between St. Nicholas Day and Twelfth Night?"

Not sure if he was pleased or not, she nodded. "Of course." She strode into the parlor, narrowly missing the doorframe, glad that the vase which used to sit on a table there was high on a shelf in his study. When she reached the fireplace, she turned to face him. "I do hope you don't mind that I invited your brother. Lissa is one of my dearest friends."

His right eyebrow rose. "Why would I take issue with my own brother coming?"

She shrugged, not sure if what Lissa had told her was true—that Darius had little patience for Lord Bellamore. "Not all families enjoy each other's company." At her statement, memories of her brother laughing at her came to the fore.

"You're frowning. What is it you think about? Do you not treasure your family's company?"

Surprised by Darius's question, she snapped her gaze to his before looking at the wingback chair he stood behind. "I feel no ill will toward them, if that's what you ask."

He stepped around the chair. "No, that's not what I ask. But now I must know. Did they not treat you well?"

She waved her hand, pretending a nonchalance she didn't feel. "I assure you, I was raised like many of my classmates. I was trained to lead a household, dance, play the pianoforte, and attract a husband, for I must be married off. Luckily, my parents focused on my brothers. It was only after they were married that Mother realized I had not been successful—not that she'd expected me to be, as she said often." Ellie crossed her arms over her chest, refusing to feel the hurt of her mother's words again. "But then I proved them all wrong, didn't I? I married a marquess."

Darius's gray eyes did nothing to give away his thoughts on her confession. "Indeed you did."

She uncrossed her arms. "Do be assured that I will do my very best for you and the children." Anxious to change the subject, she moved to the small desk in the corner of the room. "I believe you wished to know who was invited to visit us. I have my list here." She shuffled through the papers filled with notes that cluttered the little writing desk. One fell to the floor, but she ignored it, certain it wasn't what she sought.

Finally, she found what she searched for. "Here it is." She lifted the sheet of paper and waved it high in triumph. "Of course, I invited your dear parents and your three brothers. Only Lord Bellamore has responded as of yet, and Lissa stated they weren't sure when they would arrive. He's investigating something for Lord Sommerset. Lord Sommerset is married to the duchess's sister. I assume that once your brother finds what he's looking for, they will settle in here for the season. I also invited my classmates, Lady Sophie, Lady Georgina, and Lady Rose. I did receive a letter from Sophie. She will be visiting next week with Georgina and one of the new ladies. Rose, unfortunately, must attend her mother's events and already left for Sunnydale Manor."

Darius didn't say a word.

Was he wondering about his friends? Quickly, she turned back to the desk and rifled through the papers once more. She'd almost forgot. Not finding what she wanted, she spied the paper on the floor and bent down to retrieve it, but when she stood, she bumped her head on the side of the desk, just where a decorative metal knob protruded. "Ow." She dropped the letter and grabbed the back of her head, rubbing it.

"Here, let me see."

Startled, she jumped forward, stumbling toward the desk, but before she made contact, Darius grabbed her to him, spinning her around.

Immediately, her head was forgotten as she breathed in his deep musk scent and reveled in the feel of his strong arms around her.

"Are you quite all right? Are you dizzy?"

She could actually feel his chest vibrate as he spoke. It was a heady feeling. Reluctantly, she lifted her face from his shoulder and looked up at him. "I don't think so."

As he set her away from him, but still held her by her shoulders, she wished she'd lied. She liked it when he held her. Maybe she should ask him to hold her more often. They were married, after all.

He pulled out the chair at the desk and guided her to sit. "Where did you hit your head?"

She raised her hand and set her fingers on the spot. "Here. It was just the knob on the side that makes it look like there are drawers there, but there aren't."

He moved her fingers and gently pushed aside her hair. "It looks red. It may swell."

She bit down on a smile. Her hair was red, so seeing her skin red would be rather difficult, but she was quite aware of what could happen. It wasn't the first time she'd hit her head, but she didn't plan to think back and count how many times she had. "If it swells, I can use a cold cloth." She stopped herself from explaining how she knew that.

He moved to stand before her. "I've had a few knocks on my head in my time. The best thing for it is ice."

"Yes, that's true, but as it's so small, I doubt I'll need any. Did you get knocked in the head playing with your brothers or at school?"

He grimaced. "Both. I hadn't truly understood that I was the heir, though I was quite filled with hubris over being the eldest, so I insisted on trying everything first and on being better than all my brothers."

"And were you? Better than they?" She could see him outshining all of them.

"At some things, but we all had our unique skills and abilities."

She very much enjoyed learning about him. Imagining him as a young man was fun. "And what were you especially good at? Was it math? No, riding. No, you were a perfect shot." She grinned, quite certain she must be right with *one* of her guesses.

"According to my mother, my best skill was telling others what was best for them and what they should do."

She laughed, absolutely delighted with his answer. "See, I told you that you were stuffy."

He raised his right eyebrow. "Actually, I was far from stuffy. Commanding? Yes. Authoritative? Absolutely. Beyond confident? Always. Right?" He gave her a self-deprecating smile. "Sometimes. As I said, I was rather filled with pride that I was the eldest. It wasn't until I began to learn the responsibilities of an estate and how to shoulder the wellbeing of all who depended on that estate that I shed my pride and allowed myself to truly learn. It was a humbling experience."

Though she'd been teasing, his serious answer had her respecting him all the more. "And here I thought I was so very smart because I could find all the stars." She shook her head. "My mother always said I had my head in the clouds." She chuckled at how apropos that was, since it was said before she'd taken an interest in astronomy. "It sounds as if your role as eldest brother helped you in becoming a well-respected lord."

"It did?"

She nodded. "Oh, yes. Because once you learned what you needed to know, you were able to command with authority and confidence." She grinned as she used his very words.

"I see that I have a very intelligent wife."

"And you show your own intelligence in recognizing that." She chuckled, truly enjoying teasing him.

His eyes rounded before a slow smile curved his lips. "I do, indeed."

She gazed at him, barely holding back a sigh at how pleasant he was to look upon when he smiled. "I may be intelligent, but I really should organize my correspondence a bit better."

At the mention of her letters, he bent and retrieved the one on the floor and looked at it. "This appears to be notes on a how to find a comet."

He lowered the paper for her to look at. "That it is. My teacher at school worked with Monsieur Messier for a time. Ever since I started studying the skies, I have wished to see a comet. But that wasn't the paper I sought."

She rose, intending to go through her papers to find the list about the ball.

"It's of no matter. I trust your abilities in this. Come, I have something I wish to show you."

"Show me?"

"Yes." He held out his arm.

Curious, she took it, and he led her out of the room and up the grand staircase. "You said when you promised Peter that you would show him Draco that you may not be able to see it from your room."

"That's true, though I may be able to. Our rooms face west, and the best view from inside would be facing north."

They reached the next floor, and he led her past their rooms. "Hawthorne Park is designed in a square shape, though various additions have been made over the years. I thought perhaps one of the empty rooms on the north side would be a better place for you to teach the children about astronomy, with no one becoming ill."

Even as he said the words, she felt his arm tense beneath her own. "I agree that would be the best circumstances if the angle of the window will work. It can be rather complicated." She was tempted to squinch her nose like the children but refrained.

"As it has been told, one of the marquesses who lived here in the past put his wife's mother on the north side of the house, to keep her from meddling. When she complained about not being able to enjoy the summer air because it was such a long trek downstairs, instead of moving her, he built a terrace out of the rooms next to hers. Later, during my uncle's stay here, he had the terrace glassed in, much like a conservatory. I believe it would be the perfect place for your stargazing without having to worry about the weather. It has been years since I've been there, but if I'm not mistaken, it's the fourth door on the left."

As she tried to imagine a glass room on the second floor of an estate house, Darius stopped.

He opened what looked like a door to a bedroom and led her inside.

She gasped, unable to close her mouth. Even with the partly cloudy day, the sky seemed to surround them. On a clear night, it would be almost like having her own observatory!

She finally closed her mouth and examined the room. There were comfortable chairs set about with small tables between them, two settees, a fireplace on each end, and two writing desks.

Her gaze fell on Darius, who watched her, and her heart filled with emotion. "This is the most wonderful present I've ever received. Thank you." She strode back to him, took his head in her hands, and kissed him.

His arms wrapped around her as he spoke against her lips. "I'm pleased you like it."

She wanted to tell him how much, but her thoughts wouldn't stay still as he kissed her again, this time slipping his tongue between her lips. Again, her knees seemed to lose all strength, and she held on to him as he tasted her. She hesitantly touched his tongue with her own, not sure if she was doing it right.

His arms tightened around her, even as he drew back. He touched his forehead to hers. "I want to make you mine."

Her heart skipped a beat at his words. Ellie was well aware of what he meant. She ran her fingers through the hair at the back of his head. "I want to be yours."

His head jerked back, and his gray eyes turned a dark charcoal. "Ellie…"

Her name on his lips had her melting just before he lowered

his mouth to hers and devoured her. It was all she could do to hold on as new feelings of desire swept through her. She tangled her tongue with his as she gripped his hair, not wanting him to stop. She felt beautiful, wanted, perfect!

Then he broke the kiss, much to her chagrin. Before she could protest, he unhooked her arms from about his neck and turned her around.

The familiar feeling of rejection cooled her blood instantly and her eyes began to water. She couldn't even kiss properly.

Cool air touched her back and jerked her from her misery. Darius's fingers grazed over her shift as he undid her dress buttons. Immediately, tingles of fire skipped down her back and into areas only illustrated in her secret book. The realization that, far from rejecting her, he was accepting her—and more than that, wanted her in truth—had pure happiness bursting through her.

Her dress started to slip down, and from instinct, she caught it to her. His lips found a spot at the back of her neck that made her heart race. He ran his hands over her shoulders, down past her shift to the bunched sleeves of her yellow day dress.

His mouth moved up the side of her neck to her ear before he whispered, "Let it fall."

A shiver ran through her at his words, and, gathering her courage, she let go of her dress and straightened her arms, allowing the soft material to fall in a puddle out her feet. She held her breath, not sure what he would do next.

His hands continued down her arms, and finally linked with her own. His chin came to rest on her shoulder. "Beautiful."

No one had ever said that to her. Clumsy? Yes. Loud? Yes. Opinionated? Yes. But never had anyone used the word *beautiful*. She could feel her eyes tearing up, and squeezed his hands in response.

He brought her hands together in front of her and encouraged her to clasp them. Then he let go and went to work on her stays.

It was no easy task, since her breasts were quite large. They matched her hips, which were too wide to be fashionable, but they were very good for childbearing, or so her mother had said.

He didn't let the tightness of the lacing deter him, working diligently to loosen it. When it was fairly hanging from her shoulders, he lifted it, forcing her to raise her arms.

She had no idea what he did with her stays, nor did she care as his arms came about her waist and he hugged her to him. His lips found her neck again, and she tilted her head to one side, lifting her hand to hold the back of his head, the feel of his silky black hair far too tantalizing.

His hands moved upward then and cupped her breasts over her shift. She sucked in her breath, the touch so new and different. Then his thumbs started to rub back and forth across her nipples. Spikes of need seemed to flow down to her very core, and her body grew hot, her shift almost stifling.

His mouth traveled across her jaw, and she turned her head toward him. "Darius." The word was one of wonder and need. His lips descended on hers again, and she moaned around his tongue, wanting more of him, never wanting the feelings inside her to stop.

But then he broke the kiss and let go of her to walk in front of her.

She grabbed the back of the settee next to her to keep from falling, even as she watched him divest himself of his tailcoat and throw it over a table. Then, pulling his shirt from his pantaloons, he lifted it over his head and dropped it on the table as well.

His torso was well muscled, his broad shoulders tapering to a narrower waist, but what caught her attention was the thin line of short black hair that traveled down the center of his chest to his hard stomach. She wanted more than anything to trace her fingers over the soft hairs. Unable to resist, she removed her hand from the settee and stepped forward, but forgot about her dress, and her foot got caught in the material. She stumbled, trying to catch her balance as she fell forward.

Darius caught her. "Here, let me help." He stood her up then knelt to untangle her skirts from her foot. "Hold my shoulders."

She felt the heat rising in her cheeks. He must think her a fool. Still, she did as he asked. Not only did he clear her dress from her feet, but he took off her kid slippers.

He rose to stand completely still as his gaze ran from her face to her breasts, past her shift, then down her stockinged legs to her feet and back up again. His eyes seemed to have turned almost black, and his stare was so intense, she could feel her nipples getting hard as if he stroked them again. The pure want in his gaze erased her embarrassment and gave her the confidence to reach out and touch his chest.

She traced the trail of hair as she'd wanted to do, awed by how soft it was against such a hardened body. Then she spread her hand across the mounds of his smooth chest. He was well made, not like the illustrations in her secret book and more like the great statues of Greece, which were far more to her liking. Touching him, though, made her feel even more confident, especially as she moved her hand down to his abdomen and he drew in breath.

He caught her hand and brought it to his lips before letting go and cupping her face. He gave her a gentle kiss before his hands ran down her sides to the bottom of her shift. Without a word, he slowly lifted it.

No one except her maid had ever seen her naked before. A small part of her wished to resist, but a larger part wanted more than anything to belong and be treasured, and this man offered her that. Slowly, she lifted her arms, and in a trice, her shift was gone.

As she stood naked before her husband in only her stockings, she blushed, not from embarrassment but from the heat in his gaze. He made her feel desired, a feeling so new to her that she found herself reveling in it.

But then he was there, holding her against his bare chest, kissing her, making her feel as if he couldn't live without her, and she grasped him to her, needing to let him know she wanted him just as much.

His hands roamed over her back and down to cup her behind and pull her even closer. She felt the hard ridge in his pantaloons pressing against her mons, and her muscles tensed deep inside her. He walked her backward until the settee hit the back of her knees and they buckled. But she didn't fall, and he gently sat her down then leaned her to the side so that she lay half on the furniture.

She thought to suggest that she move up as he knelt on the floor, but his mouth left hers to lick at her nipple, and her thoughts completely disappeared in the exquisite sensations flowing through her. As he laved one nipple and then the other, the feelings intensified, and she grabbed at his head to keep him focused on one.

It must have been the right thing to do, because he started to suck, causing her toes to curl as she felt moisture at the juncture of her thighs. She pressed her chest closer to his mouth, not wanting him to stop. That was when he scraped his teeth over her nipple, and she let out a low moan. He then sucked hard before releasing her.

She forced herself to loosen her hold on his head, anxious for him to do the same to her other breast.

Instead, he moved one of her legs over to the other side of the settee, spreading them.

Before she could demand that he get back to her breast, he kissed her. It was a long, luxurious, probing kiss that had her grasping his shoulders. Then she felt his fingers slipping through the red curls of her mons. She didn't have a chance to react before his hand continued its descent to the folds between her legs and his fingers began to explore her.

It was then that he ended the kiss and began his ministrations on her other breast.

There were so many sensations running through her that she could barely catch her breath. She found her hip pressing toward his fingers as she panted through the sharp trills of excitement running from her nipple to the very core of her. Then his fingers circled the nub at the apex of her sheath, and she almost forgot to breathe.

It was as if a comet shot through her, lighting her on fire everywhere. She hissed as she pressed her pelvis higher, anxious for more. He gave her more, making her spiral around like a galaxy, and her very inside grew hotter like a sun, threatening to explode.

And then she did!

Pure joy burst through her, sending her into a million pieces, touching upon the reason for being, continuing, never-ending, forever. This immense pleasure swept her away before slightly cooling as she drifted back together, every piece falling back into place, back into Darius's arms. She let her eyes drift open to find him looking down on her with some unspoken question. "Oh, Darius." The words came out in barely a whisper.

His gaze grew intense. "I must have you now."

His words, so guttural and strained, sent excitement lighting her up everywhere. She'd forgotten there would be more. "Yes." At her single word, his nostrils flared.

In one moment, he lay on her, and the next he stood, unbuttoning his pantaloons and stripping them off.

She had but a glance of his maleness before he covered her, kneeling between her legs. Then she felt him at the very entrance to her core. A primitive craving bubbled up inside her, and she lifted her legs to rest her feet on his behind, silently telling him to fill her.

And then he did, slowly, every inch of him filling every inch of her until she thought he could go no farther, and still she wanted more of him. Instinctually, she titled her hips, inching her feet up to his waist until his pelvis lay against hers. Despite the awkward position, she sighed with satisfaction.

"I will try to be gentle." The words barely made it out of his mouth, as if he held himself back.

She didn't *want* gentle. She wanted to feel how much he needed her. "I am no timid miss."

"Yes, but it is your first time."

That he struggled to make her happy had her heart opening completely. "And I'm loving it."

His eyes rounded just before he started to pull back.

She pulled his head down with her hand. "Take me to the stars, husband."

CHAPTER TWELVE

DARIUS OPENED HIS mouth only to have his vibrant wife thrust her tongue into it. Her boldness sent his hips down faster than he'd planned.

Letting go of him, she dropped her head back down on the cushion. "Yesss."

It was all he needed, and he thrust into her tight sheath, enjoying his long, slower strokes but unable to keep from increasing the pace. Her energetic reactions to his lovemaking had destroyed his control sooner than he'd thought. But her enjoyment was his primary focus for her first time, and he was grateful that she was so responsive.

In fact, her legs grasped him, and as he plunged into her faster, she tipped her hips, rubbing herself along his entire shaft. He tried to hold back, just one more, just one—her sheath squeezed around him, and a yell of sheer pleasure burst from her throat, sending his own release deep inside of her.

He continued to thrust, her body receptive, urging him on until he was completely spent. He let his head hang down as he held himself above her on the settee. He hadn't planned to take her in the middle of the afternoon in a room he hadn't seen in years, so neither of them was in the most comfortable position. Guilt started to build that he'd let his desire take precedence over her comfort.

"That far surpassed what I expected. Do you think we could do it again?"

At her words, all guilt vanished, and he chuckled. "Of course, but mayhap somewhere a bit more comfortable." He pulled out, thinking only of her comfort, and immediately wished he was back inside her.

She pulled herself into a sitting position against the high back on one side, looking like the finest of courtesans, her hair messed terribly, with a few long red locks trailing down toward her large breasts and nothing on except her stockings. He wanted to take her all over again but dared not. If she became too sore, she'd become hesitant about the marriage bed.

Looking down as he donned his pantaloons, he noticed the telltale sign of her virginity. Moving to his waistcoat, he pulled out his handkerchief and cleaned himself off before setting himself to rights. Then he picked up his cravat and brought it to her. "You may need this. I'm sorry there is no basin in here." He gave her a half-smile. "I hadn't planned for this to happen."

Her eyes rounded before she looked down at herself and the redness started in her chest before it climbed up into her face.

He didn't want her embarrassed. He promptly kneeled and took her face in his hands. "I am very pleased that I am your only lover."

She gave him an understanding nod.

He rose again and turned his back on her to give her some privacy, busying himself with putting on his shoes and shirt. He was reaching for his greatcoat when voices in the hall stopped him. He spun around to find Ellie only in her shift.

Bloody hell. Who was about this side of the house? Even as he strode toward the door closest to the voices, he worried about the other door. He glanced toward it, for the first time wondering where all the dust covers were, as the room wasn't used at all. He put his finger to his lips at Ellie's worried look then gestured for her to stand behind him. If the door opened, he could keep her from being seen.

He listened carefully to those in the corridor just outside.

"I swear, Mr. Beacham. I heared a low, terrible moan, I did. And a howl as long as any wolf's. It's haunted, I say. The former lord has come back to take another soul."

Darius bit down on a grin even as he contemplated whether to allow the staff to believe his uncle haunted the room, but he quickly dismissed it. Such a belief would be bound to get back to Ellie, and then she'd start asking questions.

Beacham's voice sounded right outside the door. "I promise you, there are no ghosts about Hawthorne Park, and I'll prove it."

As the doorknob turned, Darius grabbed it and opened it just enough so that he blocked the entrance with his body. "Beacham, just the man I wanted to see. Please have tea sent up here. Lady Ferncroft and I are enjoying the old solar."

"Of course, my lord." Beacham hid his surprise well. "By happenstance, did you hear noises up here?"

Darius raised his eyebrow. "Noises? I did move a chair to better suit Lady Ferncroft as we viewed the estate, but other than that, I did not. Why?"

Beacham turned his head to frown at the maid nearby before looking back at Darius. "I will have the tea sent up posthaste, my lord."

As Beacham turned, the poor maid following meekly behind him, Darius closed the door, only to find his wife smiling at him.

He wasn't quite sure why almost being caught making love by the servants thanks to her own noises would please her. "You are happy?"

She gave a nod before holding her arms wide and spinning around, almost hitting him as he barely stepped out of the way in time. "I'm more than happy. I am filled with bliss."

Not a little confused and certain they wouldn't have much time to get her clothed before tea arrived, he strode to where her dress and stays lay on a table and chair. "We'd best get you dressed."

She padded up behind him and wrapped her arms around his

waist. "Darius, do you not see the humor in this?"

"Humor?"

She felt hot against his back before she stepped in front of him, crossing her arms beneath her bountiful chest, which had his mind traveling in a completely different direction.

"Darius."

He moved his gaze to her face. "Yes?"

"You and I are married. This is our home. They are your servants. We don't need to hide what we were doing."

They didn't? "But it's the middle of the day and this is not the most proper place to take one's wife. You do understand that."

She stepped up to him and wrapped her arms around his neck, her familiar scent filling his nostrils, teasing him with what it could be. "My dear formal, stuffy husband… Do you not see that because you couldn't wait to have me that our encounter means that much more?" She brushed his hair back from his forehead. "For the first time in my life, I feel wanted, needed, and cared for. You have made me the happiest of women and the most contented of wives."

Now he understood. "I am very pleased that you feel so, because it's true. I do want you, need you in my life, and care for you." Even as he said the words, he was surprised by how true they were.

"Thank you." She rose up and brushed his lips with her own. "Now, please help me dress. Though it is quite warm in here with the sun pushing away the clouds right now, we may have company at any moment." She picked up her stays and handed them to him.

He blinked at the realization that though she'd been a virgin, she was completely comfortable with him though she was half dressed. Dinah would have—

He stopped his thought. Comparing Ellie to his late wife was unfair to both, especially to Ellie. She was a unique woman that he was just beginning to truly appreciate.

He dropped the stays over her head and quickly laced them

up, though a couple of the bottom holes remained empty, as the ties had come out and he didn't have time to thread them through. Next, he lifted the gown over her head, and when she had it settled where she liked it, he started to button her up, but footsteps in the corridor alerted them to an approaching servant. Immediately, he tied the top tie so it wouldn't fall from her shoulders.

Ellie stepped away from him and turned to face whoever arrived.

Too late he noticed her shoes and his cravat still lay on the floor before the settee. He pointed to a table and chairs set closer to the door, and they both headed for it. She had just sat down, facing the door, when it opened and a footman brought in the tea service.

After the man left, Darius stood listening to the footsteps fading away until a giggle from his wife had him turning. At her devious smile, he chuckled. "I admit I never expected to be hiding my activities from my own servants." He took a seat opposite her.

She patted his hand before lifting the teapot. "I didn't know how exciting it would be. I do hope we can do it again."

He raised his brows at that surprising statement. He had a feeling she would continue to surprise him for many days to come. After accepting the cup of tea, he took a sip, pleased that she'd remembered how much sugar he liked and that there was no cream in it. "Perfect."

"Of course. I may not be excellent at many tasks, but I do have a very good memory."

The phrasing of her response jarred him. Not because it was odd, but that he'd noticed it to be a common pattern. Setting down his teacup, he watched her for a moment. Her movements were typical, if a bit faster than most ladies were wont to do. She poured her own tea in an instant and stirred her sugar vigorously before dropping in a quick plop of cream and stirring loudly again.

"You often say that you are not good at many tasks. Why is that?"

At his question, she stilled, her teacup halfway to her mouth. After a moment, she continued to bring it to her lips and sipped. When she set it down in her saucer, it clinked hard and she stared at it as if it were the source of all her woes. "It is no secret that I am not quite gentle enough as a lady, nor accomplished as one. All my friends know it and my family is quite vocal about it. I do apologize if you had been hoping for someone more refined to better fit your formal bearing."

Anger flashed from his gut to his head in an instant, catching him by surprise. That anyone would be so cruel as to make her think she was unworthy to be a lady caused a strong protective instinct to rise hard up his back. "I reject your apology. You have no reason whatsoever to be apologetic. If anyone deserves an apology, it is you, from your family." He bit down on his next words, about to utter a curse that was not for a lady's ears.

Her gaze snapped to his in shock. "My family? But they are the ones that pointed out my shortcomings so that I may improve. It is entirely my fault that I have not been able to make progress." She gave him a self-deprecating smile. "Though I do admit that since my classmates are telling me I'm perfect the way I am, I did not work too hard on improving over the last two years."

"Then you must classify me with your classmates. I see no area that needs improvement."

Her brows lowered. "But you're so—"

He held up his hand. "I know. I'm so formal and stuffy. But that's why I need you to stay the way you are. It would be remiss of me to allow my children to become just like me. Please, do not make any improvements."

Her bright-blue gaze softened. "Truly?"

His anger almost boiled over at seeing tears in her eyes, but he kept it in check—barely. "Yes."

Ellie jumped up, knocking her chair over as she grasped his

face and gave him a resounding kiss. "Thank you. You don't know how happy you've made me." She let go and stood, clasping her hands to her chest. "Today has been the most marvelous day of my life."

He sat enthralled by the pure joy that seemed to emanate from her. It was, no doubt, simply the sun's rays coming from behind her, but he felt it inside him, as if she shed her warmth *through* him.

She reached out to him. "Come, stand with me while I view your beautiful estate."

He rose without thinking, taking her hand as she led him to the end of the glassed-in terrace to look at the gardens, forests, and fields. Only then did her words register. "It is our estate now."

She squeezed his hand without looking at him.

But he looked at her, trying to decide how he could be most worthy of her. Did she have a refined, aquiline nose? No, it actually turned up a bit at the end. Were her ears quite small? No, actually, they seemed larger than his own. Was she beautiful? Yes. Uniquely beautiful to look at and warmly beautiful to be with. If it hadn't been for his brother, Anthony, he would never have met her.

That was a sobering thought. Though Anthony had arranged the marriage because he owed Darius a favor, it appeared to have been overpaid.

Ellie's fascination with the view didn't last long. She let go of his hand and faced the rest of the room. "I must have my friends here. They will love this place. I'm so glad I asked Mrs. Torbett to have all the rooms on this floor prepared."

So that was why the furniture covers had been removed, and the staff had been about. "I thought you were only having three friends visit, plus my brother and his wife."

She strode into the center of the room, her partially open dress reminding him he still had a number of buttons to close. "Well, yes, after St. Nicholas Day, but I'm sure many people will wish to stay the night of the masquerade ball, maybe even the weekend."

His brief glimpse at contentment vanished in an instant. "I do not believe a Twelfth Night Ball necessary."

She turned at that. "Of course it is. It is the culmination of the season and will set the New Year off on the right foot."

And what if it started on the wrong foot, with him unable to attend? It was far too much of a risk. "No. I am opposed to it."

Her brow furrowed. "But why? Oh, will it be too much expense for our coffers? I do admit I did not—"

"No. You need never worry about that."

"Then why, Darius?"

Because if a black mood comes upon me, I won't be here—or worse, it may come upon me that night. Long ago he'd given up trying to figure out why they came. But he couldn't admit that. "This staff has never prepared for a ball. It will be too much." The excuse sounded weak even to his ears.

Ellie, though, gave his words consideration. "You're right, of course, that it would be new for the staff and there would be more needed. I will consult with Mrs. Torbett and tell her to be honest. It might be that a much smaller scale would be more appropriate."

He opened his mouth, but she held up her hand.

"I shall gather all the information necessary and then discuss my findings with you."

Confident that he could help Mrs. Torbett come up with a sufficient excuse, he nodded. After all, his housekeeper knew exactly where he went on his "trips." "That is acceptable."

She started toward him then halted. A blush filled her cheeks, and she changed her direction, stopping before the settee and bending over. Though she was discreet, it was obvious she'd picked up the stained cravat and hid it in the folds of her dress. "I think I will return to my room and rest before I prepare for tonight's activity with the children." She glanced at the sky, which had become more clouds than sun. "I just hope it's a clear night.

Peter is so looking forward to seeing Draco." With that, she strode toward the door and quickly left.

She seemed to take all the light from the room as she exited, for the sky turned completely gray and portended rain. He felt as if the universe was mimicking his actions, to dampen Ellie's excitement over the ball like he had. It was as if he was the very monster he called himself in his darkest of moods.

Now his simple gift seemed highly inadequate for showing how grateful he was that she had married him. He should allow the ball…for her. But how could he?

CHAPTER THIRTEEN

"WHAT'S THAT?" MAGGIE pointed to Peter's drawing. "A planet."

"A planet can't be square."

"Yes, it can."

"No, it can't."

Peter stood, holding his paper aloft. "Yes, it can!"

"No, it can't!" Maggie rose. "Mother!"

Ellie strode toward the table where the children stood. "There's no need to raise your voices."

Peter pointed to his sister. "She said I can't have a square planet. But you said there is a lot of the universe we don't know about. So just because she doesn't know about a square planet, doesn't mean there isn't one."

For a five-year-old, Peter's logic was impeccable. Rather than explain why that was highly unlikely, Ellie decided they needed a distraction. It had been raining for five days straight, and the children seemed to be on edge. Probably because St. Nicholas Day, which they couldn't wait for, was only two days away.

When she was young, she'd walk in the garden when she was upset by something her brothers had said to her, but there was no walking in the garden today. However...

"Let's go for a walk."

Maggie frowned. "We'll get wet."

"Yes!" Peter dropped his drawing on the table. "I'll go."

Ellie chuckled. "No, we're not going outside."

Peter crossed his arms. "Then I don't want to go."

"Where are we going to walk, then?" Maggie looked at her curiously.

Ellie put her hand on her hip. "I propose a race."

Peter dropped his arms, but didn't say anything.

Ellie continued, "And I know the perfect spot. Of course, Peter, if you don't come, then you lose."

"Where?" He looked at her skeptically.

In that moment, she could see Darius in him. His little eyebrow actually lifted a bit. "Well, if you want to find out, you'll need to follow me." She turned her back. "And do keep up." She headed for the door, but didn't look to see if they followed.

Once outside the nursery, she turned down the corridor and headed for the stairs. She distinctly heard two sets of footsteps behind her and grinned. When she reached the grand staircase, she descended the five steps to the center landing, then went up the five steps to the other side of the house. Once she was in that corridor, she picked up her pace. When she reached the end, she turned to face the long corridor that ran south to north and ended at the back of the house. In her opinion, Hawthrone Park's square layout was perfect for rainy days.

"Are we going to run down there?" Peter stepped up next to her and pointed.

"Yes, we are."

Maggie came to stand next to them. "I don't think Father would approve."

Ellie laughed. "Oh, I don't know. I think we could convince him that it would be fun."

Both children stared at her as if she'd grown antlers out of her head. She just smiled at them. "Are you ready to run?"

Peter's face split into a big grin before he turned his head and ran down the corridor.

"Hey, that's not fair." Maggie ran after him.

Ellie held up her skirts so she wouldn't trip and set out after them. About halfway down the corridor, she came up behind Peter. "I'm going to pass you."

He didn't even look at her. "No, you're not!" He increased his pace, almost catching up to his sister.

Ellie wasn't about to let the boy lose, so she slowed down a bit until he reached the end after Maggie. When Ellie reached them, they were both smiling.

"Can we do it again? Please?" Peter waved his arms in front of her as if she couldn't see him.

"Well, I will need to rest. So why don't you two run down and back to me?"

"Yes!" Peter jumped up before heading back down the corridor, his sister catching up.

Ellie leaned against the wall, pleased to note that even as an adult, she felt happier after a little run. She was also pleased that she hadn't tripped or bumped into anything, one reason she'd chosen the east wing. It was rarely used and so had no statues or obstacles that could get in her way. She had to admit that she'd been a bit short in patience herself. She couldn't wait for her classmates to arrive in just ten days. If it hadn't been for the nightly attentions of Darius, she was sure she'd be willing to run even in the rain.

She felt her cheeks heat, thankful the children hadn't reached the other end yet. Darius was teaching her so many ways to enjoy their time together in her bedroom. He insisted on leaving after making love, as he didn't wish to impose upon her, since she was new to the experience. He said if he stayed with her, he wouldn't be able to resist her, which was so sweet.

He wasn't home, having gone with his steward to review an issue with a tenant, so it wasn't as if he'd sought her out due to being cooped up in the house for days. In fact, the last three days, he'd been out and about quite a bit, insisting she stay inside for fear she'd fall ill. He obviously didn't realize she had a very sturdy constitution. If the sun came out tomorrow, she would make sure they all went for a walk, even Darius, no matter how cold it might be.

Maggie came running toward her and yelled, "I win!" She jumped up and down a moment then looked at Ellie.

Before Ellie knew what she was about, Maggie had thrown her arms around her hips and hugged her. "Thank you for being our mother."

Ellie wrapped her arms around the girl, swallowing a lump in her throat the size of Mars. "Thank you for being my daughter."

At the sound of Peter's footsteps, Ellie looked up. The little boy ran full tilt into both of them, wrapping his arms around Maggie and a bit of Ellie. She grabbed on to him, even as her behind hit the wall. She should say something, but her heart was bursting with joy, completely closing her throat.

Peter stepped back, and she let him go. "I heard someone coming. We better behave."

She stifled a chuckle as Maggie let go to peer down the corridor. "I hope it's not Father."

Ellie looked into the somewhat darkened space. "No, it's not your father." She watched the stride and the way the person moved. "I do believe it's Beacham."

Peter waved his hand. "Then we can run again."

Before she could suggest they not, he was off.

"I'll get him." Maggie ran after him.

Ellie shook her head as she strode forward to discover why Beacham searched for them, if he had. Peter sped past the man, Maggie after him, before Ellie reached the butler. "I hope we aren't disturbing anyone."

"No, my lady. I only sought you out because you have a caller."

She blinked. "Me?"

Beacham nodded confidently. "Indeed. The Baroness Watkins specifically asked for Lady Ferncroft."

She'd been so focused on her husband, children, and Christmastide, she'd forgotten her neighbors may call. "Then I'd best go to the parlor immediately. Please have tea brought for my guest. Thank you, Beacham. Oh, and would you be so kind as to ensure the children are returned to the nursery?"

"Of course, my lady."

"Thank you, Beacham." She strode toward the end of the corridor at a quicker pace than normal. When she reached the children, she stopped. "I have to attend to a guest, but I will check the sky again after dinner to determine if we can see anything tonight."

The two children nodded, smiles still on their faces from their races.

Quickly, she descended the staircase, holding on to the balustrade. When she reached the bottom, she paused and took a deep breath, patting at her hair, hoping it hadn't come too loose. Holding her head up and her shoulders straight, she breezed into the room. "Baroness, what a lovely surprise."

Prudence, the Baroness Watkins, sat on one of the pale-blue chairs, her sage-green day dress making it appear as if the chair were the flower and she the leaf. Her hair, liberally sprinkled with white, was pulled back in a tight bun as if she sought to erase the wrinkles in her face. Her brown eyes missed nothing, and she had a rather large nose, which she managed to look down, despite the fact she sat and Ellie still stood.

"I thought you might enjoy some company on such a dreary day. I believe the chill in the air could go right to one's bones."

Ellie sat in the chair adjacent to the older woman. "I haven't been out today, more's the pity. I do enjoy the fresh air."

"You would not enjoy it out there today. There is a mist hanging in the air that is sure to bring sickness to those out in it." The woman waved her hand and smiled. "But I am not here to discuss such a sad subject. Here you are, newly wedded and a dear neighbor. Do you find Hawthorne Park overwhelming? I'm not far if you need any advice."

Ellie smiled, ignoring the subtle hint that she wasn't quite able to handle the house. The woman was just being neighborly.

"I admit to quite enjoying my new home. The servants are so good at what they do, the children are a joy, and my husband is a wonderful companion." She felt a blush starting in her cheeks, but luckily a footman entered with tea service at just that moment.

Lady Watkins didn't reply while the footman was in the room, but as soon as he left, she spoke. "I do hope the children are not too much trouble. Lady Ferncroft—I mean the late Lady Ferncroft, Dinah—said they could be rather *untamed*. Yes, I believe that was the word she used."

Surprised, Ellie dropped the spoon she'd picked up. "Untamed? That is a rather odd description to use about one's own children. I find them absolutely delightful. Sugar?"

"No, just black."

She handed the woman her cup then proceeded to make her own. "Do you have children, Lady Watkins?"

"Indeed, I do. My eldest son is currently studying at Cambridge, my other two sons are at Eton, and my daughter is at a finishing school. They'll all descend on me in a fortnight." The baroness seemed to be proud and yet put upon at the same time.

"I'm sure you're anticipating their arrival." Ellie took a sip of her tea.

"The boys will go about hunting and visiting their friends, I'm sure. I will be sure to get my daughter to help with all the Christmastide preparations. I must say that I was surprised that you would be celebrating here."

Ellie set down her cup. "Many people have been surprised. I can understand, since it's not been celebrated here in generations, but I—" Voices in the entry had her pausing. She looked at Lady Watkins. "I do believe I have more guests." Though Ellie found herself quite excited, Lady Watkins appeared much less so.

Ellie rose to greet her new guests.

Two ladies strolled through the doorway arm and arm, but they couldn't have looked more different. Lady Saunders, a woman in her mid-thirties with very dark brown hair, wore a lovely blue day dress that complemented her blue eyes. Her companion, Lady Chelton, who was ten years younger and had golden-blonde hair and green eyes, wore a yellow day dress that complemented her hair.

"Lady Saunders. Lady Chelton. How wonderful to see you again."

Both ladies smiled, and Lady Saunders held out her hands. "We couldn't wait to see you. Lady Chelton wanted to come a fortnight ago, but I insisted that we wait to allow you to settle in. Last we saw you, you had yet to meet your tenants."

Ellie smiled warmly at Lady Saunders, took her proffered hands, and squeezed. "I'm so pleased you have come." She turned toward Lady Watkins. "As you can see, Lady Watkins thought as you did."

The two younger ladies sat on the settee together, and once everyone had tea, Lady Chelton spoke. "Are you pleased with Hawthorne Park and all who reside on the estate?"

Ellie nodded. "I am. Our tenants are lovely people, and I was just telling Lady Watkins how much I'm enjoying the children. The staff have been almost as excited as I am about celebrating the season. Mr. Beacham and Mrs. Torbett are truly expert and have the best dispositions."

Though the younger ladies smiled, Lady Watkins's brows drew together. "And what of your husband, Lord Ferncroft?"

Since she'd already told the woman she was quite pleased with Darius, Ellie had to assume the question was asked for the other ladies' benefit. "I couldn't be happier. I count myself very fortunate, for I did not meet my husband until I entered the church. He has been everything I had dreamed of and more." She lifted her cup to take a sip, trying not to blush.

"I'm so relieved to hear that." Lady Chelton smiled kindly. "Lord Ferncroft has always been so formal, and you seem very friendly, so I am pleased to hear that you two rub along nicely."

"Humph."

Ellie turned to Lady Watkins, who seemed to take issue with

Lady Chelton's words. "Do you not agree?"

"My dear, it is not for me to judge your happiness. I simply worry that you do not know all there is to know about him yet, since there was no courtship."

Lady Saunders set her teacup on the plate rather loudly. "Even with a long courtship, you cannot know everything. I was quite surprised to discover that Lord Saunders has absolutely no affinity for hot cocoa!"

Lady Chelton nodded. "I can attest to that. I promised never to tell." The sly smile on her face made it very clear that she'd told everyone as if it was the greatest secret in the kingdom.

"That hardly qualifies. The former Lady Ferncroft appeared happy until after the heir was born. The poor woman practically hid away here."

Since Ellie was aware of the discord between Darius and his late wife, the observation did not surprise her as much as the fact Lady Watkins would make it a topic of conversation. "Yes, my lord did explain that he and his late wife did not suit as well as they had both hoped."

Lady Watkins picked up her teacup. "It must have been him, because Dinah was an absolute angel."

A slight gasp came from the settee, but as Ellie faced Lady Watkins, she didn't know which woman had made the sound. "I do not pretend to know the former lady. However, I do know my husband, and I can see no reason why the former lady would complain of her lot."

Having defended Darius after Lady Watkins's rather bold statement, Ellie returned her attention to the other ladies, who were obviously aghast at the turn in the conversation.

"Has no one told you that he can be a monster? Or so Dinah named him. She said he was mad, and I'm very sure she was the target of his tirades. She told me she hid in the nursery, where it was safest. I do hope that you will find him more reasonable."

Ellie felt her face heat at such disparaging remarks about her husband. Boxing the ears of the baroness, as she'd done to Lord

Ferriday when he'd been rude at the Stocktons' final ball last Season, would not be looked at kindly by her neighbors, but she refused to put up with such behavior.

She turned her head back to look at the woman who tried to appear sympathetic but couldn't hide the glee in her gaze. "Lady Watkins, I find my husband very reasonable. In fact, I do believe he may find me to be the one who is less than reasonable. For example, by the fact that I must ask you to leave after being so rude as to blacken my husband's reputation only to satisfy your own need to gossip about those who are better."

The woman opened her mouth, but didn't say anything, as if no one had ever set her down for such behavior.

Ellie rose. "Plutarch was quite clear that while hate may be directed at any man or beast, envy's sole focus is on those of superior status. But it was Socrates who said, 'Envy is the ulcer of the soul.' I would suggest that you meet with the vicar to work on saving your soul. Thank you for calling, baroness." She held her arm out toward the open doorway.

The woman snapped her mouth shut and stood. She started toward the doorway then halted, looking at Lady Saunders and Lady Chelton. "This is the kindness I receive for trying to help. Forewarned is forearmed." With that, she breezed out the door into the entry.

Ellie stood frozen, trying to let go of her anger, but she couldn't seem to. It was one thing to attack *her*, as her family had often done, but to attack someone she cared so strongly for had her hands curling into fists.

The sound of the front door closing jarred her from her focus. She looked toward the ladies on the settee, trying to form an apology for such harsh behavior but finding herself unable to.

Lady Saunders clapped her hands together. "That was wonderful! I can't tell you how often I've wanted to throw her out. I'm beyond pleased that you are our new marchioness."

Ellie blinked. "Truly?"

Lady Chelton waved her hand as if to dismiss the entire ugly scene. "Do not worry. We will be sure to tell everyone how rude she was to you. I don't think there's a person within twenty miles from here who hasn't borne the brunt of her jealousy."

Relief swept through Ellie, and she sat again still a bit shaken, even if she hid it. "Do you truly think Dinah said those awful things about Lord Ferncroft?"

The two ladies exchanged a glance before Lady Saunders spoke. "I don't know if she confided in the baroness. She didn't confide in us, but she did let it be known that she wasn't happy."

"Every time we spoke." Lady Chelton rolled her eyes. "We all have our crosses to bear. No one's marriage is perfect. There's bound to be squabbles, misunderstandings, different opinions. It's just like living with our families. Everyone has their own unique personality. But Dinah seemed to *thrive* on being melancholy."

"I think she enjoyed people feeling sympathetic toward her, though why she'd want that kind of attention, I don't know." Lady Saunders paused. "To be honest, we stopped calling on her the last year, and she didn't visit either of us. So, unless she called on the other two ladies in the area, the baroness may have been the only one she could talk to."

"That wasn't very good of us." Lady Chelton shook her head.

Lady Saunders lifted her chin. "We didn't simply stop calling. We first asked her to converse about other topics and let her know that we felt sad instead of gladdened after visiting her, but she continued."

Ellie's sympathy for the late Lady Ferncoft had lessened after the baroness's revelations. "It would appear that the former lady made a poor match and wanted everyone to suffer with her. I do understand her being unhappy, but to say such horrid things about her husband is unconscionable."

Lady Chelton reached out and squeezed her hand. "No need to think about it anymore. We are both delighted that you and Lord Felton are pleased with each other."

"I am grateful to you both. I am happier than I have ever been, and I know that we will be great friends."

Lady Chelton sat back. "So tell us about your plans for the season. There is usually a small festival in the village that we all like to attend. I do hope you and the lord will be there."

Ellie smiled, finally relaxing. "Can children attend as well?"

"Yes, they can. We bring our three every year." Lady Saunders laughed. "They enjoy themselves immensely, as there is usually a puppet show and bobbing for apples."

"And do mention the widows." Lady Chelton set her hand on her friend's shoulder.

"I do believe you just did. But I shall elaborate."

Ellie listened intently, quick to add a tidbit here and there of what she had always done for the season.

It wasn't until Lady Saunders glanced at the clock and jumped up that they all realized they'd conversed for far longer than appropriate.

"I do hope you'll come again," Ellie smiled at the ladies.

Lady Chelton smiled, which really made her very pretty. "We most definitely will."

After they left, Ellie's mood was much lighter than it had started. Still, she was determined to get to the truth of the matter regarding Dinah's life at Hawthorne Park. As soon as she spoke to Mrs. Torbett, she planned to return to the nursery to see what more she could learn.

❦

Chapter Fourteen

DARIUS OPENED THE letter from his brother, anxious to read the response from Anthony. Skimming past the salutation and updates, he found what he sought. He sat down and read, relief filling him. As much as he hated to request a favor from his youngest brother, knowing he'd have to do something in return, he'd done so for Ellie. Now, he could tell her she could host her Twelfth Night ball.

He sat back, pleased that his brother would disguise himself as him for the masquerade. He'd criticized Anthony's penchant for disguises for years and felt more than a little guilt for his personal judgments. Now, he was grateful that Anthony had ignored his censure.

Sitting forward again, he lifted the letter, intending to read it in its entirety, but his mind went to what costume to wear. He couldn't dress as a Roman emperor or a Persian, as that would show too much of him. He could simply wear a domino, but the mask would need to cover his entire face. Anthony was a bit shorter and broader than him, so an animal costume like a bear would work best, but the idea of spending the entire night in such a costume if he was able to attend made him shudder. The domino with a full mask would work best, as the cape would hide Anthony's frame and face, and if Darius was actually able to host with his wife, he wouldn't be too uncomfortable.

Having made his decision, he moved his gaze back to the letter and read the full two pages. Anthony always did have much to say. He and Lissa were down in Kent and would be leaving soon, but had stops to make along the way. No exact date was given.

That did make him uncomfortable. He would have to write a letter explaining his costume in the event he could not be present. He would then bring Ellie into his confidence about the ruse so she could help Anthony pretend to be her husband and greet guests. He would simply tell her he had affairs that needed urgent attention, but didn't want to ruin her ball.

He didn't like the idea of Anthony posing as him, but it would make Ellie happy to host the ball, and so he would accept the consequences. Even as he thought of her as he'd last seen her, in her bed riding him hard and screaming out her ecstasy, he grinned. He'd never known such an enthusiastic lover. She was anxious to learn all there was to know about the art of lovemaking, and he was very pleased to show her.

Footsteps just outside his study had him slipping his brother's letter into the top desk drawer. He'd just closed it when the door opened and Ellie breezed in, Mrs. Torbett hurrying behind her as usual.

"Oh, Darius. I didn't know you were in here. I just wanted to write a quick note, and your study was closest. We can go to the parlor." She gave him a warm smile.

"Actually, you are just the person I wished to speak to. Then I would be pleased if you used my desk for your note." He rose and held his hand out to his chair.

Ellie turned to Mrs. Torbett. "I shall write it up and have a footman deliver it to you."

"Very good, my lady." Mrs. Torbett gave a quick nod before scurrying out of the room.

He hadn't realized until just that moment how perfect his housekeeper was for his wife, who also moved about the house quickly.

Ellie strode forward and stood just a bit closer than was normal for a conversation, laying her hand on his chest. "What is it you'd like to discuss?"

That she often touched him, and others, reminded him of his mother, as she did so as well. He had to admit it was a trait he enjoyed, and he wished he could be as comfortable doing so, especially with his children.

"I have decided that a Twelfth Night ball is exactly what we need to truly begin the New Year properly."

"Oh, Darius!" She flung her arms around his neck and pulled him down for a kiss. It wasn't a simple kiss of appreciation, either, as nothing was simple about Ellie. She thrust her tongue into his mouth and pressed her body against him.

He wrapped his arms around her, very pleased that his decision had made her so happy.

When her pelvis began to rock against his own, he felt himself grow hard. They had yet to make love in his study, or specifically on his desk. Even at the thought of her lying on her back, her skirts thrown up, her bountiful bosom unsecured, his body turned them in that direction.

"Mother! Mother! Peter needs you!"

He broke the kiss at the sound of Maggie's voice. "It's Maggie. She's downstairs." His daughter had never come downstairs alone.

Ellie pulled away from his arms and spun toward the door. "Maggie! We're in the study!"

He almost covered his ears at her yell before he followed her out the door. They'd just reached the parlor when Maggie burst out, "There you are! You must come upstairs. Peter fell."

As Maggie ran past them to ascend the stairs, he glanced at Ellie, whose face had paled.

"What do you mean he fell?" He strode for the stairs, Ellie next to him, his chest tightening with dread.

Maggie spoke over her shoulder but continued upward. "He was standing on his chair, explaining how birds take flight, when he lost his balance and fell. I think he hurt his ankle."

Though his daughter wasn't a physician, the fact that Peter hadn't fallen onto something, or hit his head, helped Darius to think more clearly.

"What did Anna say?"

"He won't let her near him. He just keeps wailing, 'Mama.'"

That his son wanted his mother had Darius feeling like a failure. Would Peter ever stop missing Dinah and embrace Ellie?

Ellie glanced at him, her gaze sympathetic. "The poor dear. I know he wants his mother, but I promise I will do all I can for him."

Maggie had reached the main landing, and they were about to step onto it with her when she spun around, halting their progress.

From the corner of his eye, Darius saw Ellie teeter at the sudden stop in her forward progression.

His heart stopped for a moment at the thought of her falling down the full staircase, and he grabbed her about the waist.

She grabbed his arm as she steadied herself, her hand securely on the balustrade. She looked at him, her face filling with her blush. "Thank you."

That she was embarrassed for almost falling down the stairs had irritation striking through him. He turned toward his daughter to reprimand her, but Ellie spoke first.

"Maggie, why did you stop?"

Maggie shook her head as if they were daft. "Peter doesn't want our dead mother. He wants *you*. Now hurry." And off she went up the last five steps.

He felt Ellie suck in her breath at Maggie's words, no doubt as surprised as he was. But he was very pleased. Still, he didn't release her until they'd made the top of the stairs, where Maggie waited impatiently.

As they all started down the hall, Ellie spoke, though her voice was a bit shaky. "Why would you think he calls out for me? I'm sure, being hurt, it makes him want your mother more."

He didn't understand why Ellie would question what he felt was a Christmastide miracle. His children had spent so much time with Dinah, every day, that it had to have been a significant emotional adjustment to have her no longer in the nursery.

Maggie spoke over her shoulder, "No, he doesn't, and neither do I. She never wanted us. She just sat near the window reading or sewing on the settee. Or she would write letters at her desk in the corner. Sometimes she'd yell for us to be quiet when we disturbed her."

His step faltered at his daughter's revelation, his surprise complete.

"That doesn't mean she didn't want you, Maggie." Ellie's voice was soothing.

"No. But she told us she didn't want us. She said we were 'Father's little problems.' I like you much better, and so does Peter."

Darius felt his wife looking at him, but he couldn't meet her gaze. Dinah had lied to him. She'd deliberately kept him from his children, having told him he needed to leave her alone with them, but her sole purpose was to take her anger at him out on them. Didn't she care that they were the innocent ones?

Fury burned inside him, and he curled his fingers into his palms to keep from showing it. "Maggie, you are not my problems. You are my joy."

Maggie shrugged. "We know. She was just unhappy and wanted everyone else to be, too."

He had a sinking feeling that Maggie had heard that from a servant, because as smart as she was, he doubted she'd come to that observation on her own.

The sound of his son crying came to his ears, and he strode forward faster. As he entered the nursery, he found Peter on the floor, his foot on a pillow, his cheeks wet from his tears. The nursemaid paced nearby.

After hearing what Maggie told them, Darius rushed forward. "Peter." He knelt beside his son, whose bottom lip trembled.

"I fell. I want Mama."

"She's here, Peter." Maggie ran forward and sat on the floor next to him.

Darius looked to his wife as she entered, a soft smile on her lips even though Peter started wailing again.

In that second, it struck him. He loved her.

Or did he? He'd never been in love. But as she knelt at Peter's feet, Darius felt it in his heart. He loved his wife.

"Now, Peter, you must stop crying and tell me what has happened, so I know what to do."

Peter's wailing stopped immediately, and he sniffed as he pointed to a chair that was tipped over. "I was showing Maggie how a falcon flies and the chair tipped. I tried to jump, but something happened."

The nursemaid, who'd been cowering not far away, stepped up. "My lady, his foot caught on the leg, and he screamed when he fell. I didn't know what to do, so I brought him a soft pillow. He wouldn't let me do anything else. He just cried for you."

Ellie set her hand on the nursemaid's shoulder. "You did well, Anna. That's what I would have done. Now, if you could please have some chips of ice sent up, that will be a great help."

The nursemaid nodded and quickly ran to do Ellie's bidding. What was it about his wife that made everyone feel better, even him?

"Now, Peter, I'm going to have to take off your shoe, so I can have a good look and treat your foot. I want you to think about being that great falcon and soaring high above the trees, looking for a rodent to eat."

As Ellie continued painting a picture for Peter with her words, she gently untied the shoe and slipped it off, never stopping in her narration. She had Peter's stocking off before he even noticed.

"Darius, could you hold Peter's hand while I examine his foot? Peter, I want you to squeeze your father's finger when it hurts. It will make it less painful."

Darius had never heard of such a thing, but didn't argue the point, and gave his little son his index finger.

"Now, Peter, you tell me when it hurts."

Darius watched as Ellie pressed her fingers in different places. His son squeezed his hand multiple times, making him wish he could take all the pain for him. Finally, she'd completed her examination.

"Well, Peter, you have sprained your ankle."

The boy's eyes widened. "Will it get better?"

The fear in Peter's expression was too much for Darius. "Yes, son. It will get better, but you have to listen to…your mother. Will you do that?"

Peter nodded. "Will I be able to walk again, or will I have to use a crutch like the boy in the village?"

Ellie answered before Darius could. "If you do everything I say, you will be able to walk and run with no crutch. But you *have* to do as I say. At first it will be easy, as it hurts, but as you feel better you will want to walk on it, and you can't or it will twist again and weaken. You don't want a weak ankle."

Peter shook his head.

Ellie took his other hand. "I knew you were a smart boy. Now, as soon as Anna comes back with the ice, we will set it on the swelling to bring it down. Then we will wrap your ankle and put you in bed with a bigger pillow under your foot. But no walking for at least a fortnight."

Peter's eyes rounded before he nodded, understanding the importance of the requirements.

The nursery door opened and Anna strode in. "I've got it, my lady." The nursemaid was out of breath but continued forward. "It took some time for Cook to chop it off." She handed over the bowl of ice.

"This is just the right amount, Anna. Very well done." Ellie smiled at the nursemaid, receiving a relieved smile in return.

Darius watched as his wife tended to his son, her actions sure and efficient. He found it odd that she moved so assuredly now, yet knocked items over or bumped into objects at other times. She was definitely a complex person, and one he planned to learn about for the rest of his life.

His breath hitched at the thought. *The rest of his life.* He wanted that to be a very long time, but what about when his next black mood took him? Or the one after that? Or the one next year? Or the final one? A cold chill swept through him, and he purposefully returned his attention to Ellie.

"There you go. Now, I need to leave the ice on for twenty minutes. That should be just the right amount of time, but if it starts to sting, call for me."

"You're leaving?" Peter grabbed her arm.

"Of course not. But I wish to talk to your father in private." She turned to Maggie. "Can you bring over some of Peter's toys and play with him?"

Maggie nodded and immediately went to the cabinet to get the toys.

"Darius, can you move that chest over behind Peter so he can sit up to play?"

Darius nodded before sliding the chest across the floor. Ellie took Peter's hands and pulled him into a sitting position, and Darius set the chest behind his back.

"That's capital."

Peter's unusual expression had Ellie shaking her head. Now where had he heard *that* from?

Ellie rose. "Twenty minutes." She nodded toward the corner.

Darius turned and walked with her until she stopped before the writing desk where Dinah had sat. Understanding dawned as he looked at it, and then the settee arranged next to the window to get the best light. Fury started in his gut and rose into his jaw as he gritted his teeth to keep from releasing his anger, his breathing turning shallow.

For over seven years, Dinah had made him believe she loved their children so much that she wished to be with them daily, when she'd simply used them as an excuse to avoid him. Or did she do it to make him suffer as she thought she'd suffered by being married to a madman? Whatever her motivation, she had kept him from showing his children how much he loved them, and had denied them her love as well. He curled his fingers into his palms as he tried to stem the hurt and rage at her perfidy.

Ellie's hands enveloped one of his fists. "I believe this writing desk would look lovely in my solar. It would be the perfect place to take notes on the heavens. The telescope you gave me allows me to see so much more than I've seen before. I want to be sure I can record it all."

Her voice, usually loud and clear, was soft, breaking through the pain. He uncurled his hand and grasped hers.

"And this settee would be perfect in the music recital room. Unfortunately, that room won't get much attention until, and if, Maggie takes up an instrument or singing. I can assure you, I will be doing neither, as I'm rather poorly skilled at both and wish to keep my family, friends, and staff." She chuckled.

He understood her purpose. She wanted the furniture out of the room to take away the memories Dinah had left behind. Her kindness and understanding soothed the edges of his anger just enough to allow him to speak. "You are the lady of the house, and I concur with your wishes on this matter."

"Oh, how stuffy you do sound." Her voice was back to normal levels. "Then you wouldn't mind if I had some footman bring up a couple of the sideboards from the gallery and set them there and there? I do believe they would make wonderful anchors for an Indian market tent."

"Please, Father!" Peter yelled from behind them, and Darius looked over his shoulder. Though Peter faced away from them, Maggie was nodding her head.

He looked back at Ellie, truly understanding how important she was to all of them. By asking him, she was making him the benefactor, even though it was her idea. "As Peter would say, I think that's a capital idea."

Ellie laughed. "It's settled, then. We shall have an Indian

marketplace for Peter to spend time in while not in bed." She turned back to the children, her hand still holding his, forcing him to walk with her. "We will need sheets for the roof and many blankets and pillows to lie upon."

"And they must be brightly colored. You did say they were so, right?" Maggie looked to Peter for confirmation.

Peter nodded. "She did."

Darius looked at his wife. "And why did we all learn about Indian marketplaces?"

Ellie opened her mouth, but Maggie spoke first. "Father, it's all a part of geography. Certainly you know *that*."

He raised his brows at his daughter's condescending tone.

Ellie nudged him with her shoulder. "She does so take after you in mannerisms."

"Me?"

"Well, she certainly doesn't have mine." She let go of his hand and knelt down at Peter's feet. "Let's see how the ankle is. Ah, perfect. I believe we can move Peter now. Darius, if you would, please carry Peter to his bed."

Darius crouched down. "Put your arms around my neck, son."

Ellie cradled the hurt foot as he lifted his son and brought him to his bed. The simple act had strong emotions clogging his throat. Gently, he laid his son down.

"Hold his back up. Maggie, fetch those pillows from the settee so he can sit. No need to sleep away the afternoon. Anna, have Cook send up a tray. This way Peter can still do his lessons."

"Lessons?" Peter whined.

"Yes, lessons. You hurt your foot, not your brain or your hands. You can draw a picture of an Indian marketplace."

Maggie brought the cushions and Ellie set them up. Darius let his son rest back against them.

Ellie gave a single clap of her hands. "Perfect. Now, as soon as Anna is back with the tray, Peter can draw, and Maggie, you can work on your numbers." She stepped up to Maggie and hugged her. "I'm very proud of you. You did everything right."

As Ellie let go, she looked to Darius.

Quickly, he stepped over to Maggie and set his hand on her shoulder. "You're a good sister."

Maggie threw her arms around his waist, and he held her close, his heart filling. He now had the family that he'd always wanted, and all because of Ellie…his wife…the woman he loved.

CHAPTER FIFTEEN

Ellie fairly floated down the stairs, though she still held the balustrade. Darius had not only made love to her twice in the night, but he'd stayed the night in her room. Waking up in his arms had her feeling as if she could do everything perfectly.

Their St. Nicolas Day, the week before, had been better than she'd hoped. With Peter's sprained ankle, she'd insisted that they have their breakfast together in the nursery. Seeing Darius relax, not even wearing his tailcoat or cravat and enjoying the children's joy over their small gifts, had been so fulfilling. That he had found a carved elephant that could fit in the palm of his hand for Peter was so thoughtful. Maggie had been very excited by the small telescope Ellie had given her. While she hoped Maggie found her own interests, the young girl had been excited to see the Pleiades when the skies had finally cleared.

And today, finally, Ellie's former classmates were due to arrive. She stepped into the entry and headed into the parlor to await the arrival of Sophie, Georgina, and Felicity. Truly, the day couldn't be better. While she waited for her friends, she would make out the invitation list for their Twelfth Night ball. She wanted to get the invitations out very soon, since people wouldn't be expecting them. She feared there would be very few people attending, as many made plans far in advance.

She pulled out the chair to the writing desk then opened the drawer to retrieve a piece of paper. Picking up the quill, she set to writing. After adding forty-seven family names to her list, she dropped the quill into the ink pot and counted the number of people there would be if they all came. Accounting for sons, daughters, and elder relatives, it didn't even reach two hundred. And unfortunately, a hostess could not expect all invitees to respond positively.

She lifted the paper and waved it to help it dry. Maybe her friends would have some ideas. Maybe she should write to Lady Saunders and Lady Chelton and see if they knew of anyone she should invite. Yes, they would know who lived nearby, even if not in the immediate area. The paper slipped from her fingers and floated toward the floor. She grabbed at it, catching it against her peach skirts just before it hit the ground. Triumphantly, she lifted it back onto the table and reviewed it. A couple of places were slightly smeared, but she still understood the names.

She could start writing out the invitations immediately. Happy with her plan, she pulled five more sheets of paper from the drawer and set four of them to the side of the desk. Picking up the quill again, she set it to the paper. Just then, she heard the main door open. Immediately, she dropped the quill on the paper and rose, almost toppling her chair in the process. After righting it, she strode out of the parlor and into the entry, where Georgina was just stepping inside to stand next to Sophie.

Ellie smiled widely, so happy she felt as if she were a star exploding. "Sophie! Georgie! I have missed you both so much." She embraced Sophie and then Georgie. As she stepped back, another woman stepped inside in a cloak with a hood. Not wanting Felicity to feel any less welcome, she turned to the woman.

The figure threw back her hood. "Surprise!"

"Rose! What are you doing here? Sophie said you could not come." Ellie didn't wait for an answer before giving the laughing Rose a hug as well. She stepped back and eyed her friend. "Whatever did you do to poor Felicity?"

Rose chuckled. "Do not worry, Mother Hen. Felicity never intended to come, as her brother was arriving home from his grand tour, and she missed him desperately. I made Sophie write a falsehood, which I will admit was no easy task." She waggled her brows.

"That is hardly true, Ellie," Sophie added. "I didn't mind at all, since it was to surprise you."

Ellie's heart filled with joy to have her classmates with her once again. Eventually, Lissa would arrive and then only Dory and Elsbeth would be missing...and the new ladies like Felicity, whom she'd just started to take under her wing. "I know you have just arrived, but would you like tea or cocoa before settling in?"

"Cocoa, please," Georgie answered immediately. "Can you have your staff add a bit of cinnamon?"

Ellie smiled warmly. Georgie loved anything sweet, yet remained thin, though she appeared even thinner because of her height. "I can. And I believe we have some marzipan to serve with the cocoa."

Georgie's eyes rounded, as marzipan was her favorite. "Oh, Ellie. We have sorely missed you."

"Then come into the parlor so I can learn all that has been going on at Silver Meadows since I left. I've missed you all." Ellie hooked her arm through Sophie's and led the way.

Sophie, who was petite, with caramel-colored hair, wore a white traveling dress and took the chair closest to the fireplace. She naturally gravitated toward like colors in the room, and as the fireplace was white, it didn't surprise Ellie in the least. Knowing her good friend hadn't changed her ways made things more comfortable.

Georgie took an enthusiastic seat upon the settee and patted the space next to her for Rose, who gracefully sat as requested. The two ladies complemented each other. Rose wore a pale-pink traveling dress that gave her a rosy hue, the two chestnut-colored ringlets she allowed loose on each side of her face giving her a sophisticated appearance. Georgie's pale spring-green dress complemented her amber eyes and dark brown hair.

Ellie took the chair next to Sophie, before speaking to Beacham, who, having hung their outerwear, had followed them in. "Beacham, we shall have hot cocoa and marzipan before my friends retire to their rooms to rest. Have their trunks sent up in the meantime."

"Yes, my lady." He turned and exited.

Rose waited until Beacham was out of the room. "So tell us, Ellie. How do you get along with the mysterious Lord Ferncroft?"

"Yes, tell us." Georgie leaned forward. "It was so brave of you to marry him without meeting him."

Ellie chuckled. "I wasn't brave at all. I was desperate to avoid another season. That, and I trusted Lissa's judgment, especially since she's so happy with Lord Bellamore."

Sophie set her hand on Ellie's arm. "But are you content?"

Ellie grasped dear Sophie's hand and squeezed. "I am more than content. I'm happier than a newly born star gathering its planets into orbit."

Rose waved her hand about and sat back. "If she's waxing about the universe, you know it's true."

"Oh, it's quite true. Not only am I very happy with him, but his daughter and son are delightful. I'm tutoring them, and of course, I get to show them the stars. In fact, Lord Ferncroft gifted me a double-refracting telescope that shows me so much more than I've ever seen before."

Sophie smiled. "I'm very pleased for you." Her voice was far too quiet for the footman, who entered the room with their refreshments, to hear.

After serving everyone, Ellie took a sip. She couldn't be happier to have her friends in her new home. All her favorite people under one roof made her almost giddy.

"And he doesn't mind the occasional mishap?" Georgie gave a little grimace before taking a bite of marzipan, closing her eyes as she did so.

Ellie leaned forward, so she could keep her voice lower than usual. "I don't believe he knows. I've only almost knocked something over once, and he caught it—and then two days ago, I almost fell back on the stairs."

Sophie gasped.

Ellie patted her friend's arm. "No need to worry. Not only did I have my hand on the balustrade, but my husband grasped me about the waist to keep me from falling. And to be fair, it was only because Maggie suddenly stopped in front of us that I lost my balance. So, I'm hoping I can keep him ignorant of that one foible. I've already told him I'm not as accomplished as most ladies."

All three of her friends started talking at once.

"You're perfect."

"You are as good as any other lady."

"He's lucky to have such an accomplished wife."

Her heart filled to hear them defend her to herself. "I thank you all, but I do not want his expectations too high. I am content with myself, even if I may not be as aware of my space as others."

Rose pointed toward the floor. "Is that what happened to your dress?"

Ellie looked down at her dress, lifting one foot in the air. "Oh dear. That's the ink from the list I was making before you arrived." She frowned, not happy to see the black smudges that made it look as if she'd splattered mud on her dress.

Georgie shook her head. "Don't worry a bit about it. No one looks at your feet when you are standing, and at a table no one can see them. A short hem and a bit of lace and no one will ever know."

"Thank you, Georgie. You've eased my mind mightily."

Sophie turned toward her. "Why not tell Lord Ferncroft of your…unintended tendencies? Wouldn't it be easier to have that known and not worry about the next potential unfortunate event?"

"Sophie, you are too honest by half and make me rethink my

ideas. I may very well tell him eventually, but I'm hoping, at least through the season, that he can focus on my ability to bring Christmastide to Hawthorne Park. Did you know they have never had a Twelfth Night ball?"

Georgie put her cup down hard. "Do tell me you are hosting one and we're invited." The hope in her voice was clear to them all. Georgie did so like to dance.

"I am, and yes, you are all invited."

Georgie actually jumped up to stand. "This will be wonderful! Mother will be so pleased that I've been invited, and you are bound to have many unmarried men."

Rose pulled on Georgie's hand, forcing her to sit down. "Whoa, there. Don't get ahead of yourself. Your parents may have other plans, as I know mine do. So I won't be able to attend. Unless…"

Ellie loved how Rose's mind worked, even if her pranks were so unexpected. "Unless what?"

"If I could get my brother to insist that I come with him and Dory because there will be many more available men here, I might be able to avoid the gathering at Thornwood Park, the duchess's parents' estate. It tends to be a small, subdued affair, no dancing, and we all know how much the duke and duchess enjoy dancing the waltz together."

Everyone nodded, as the pair were known to ignore the fashion of married couples standing on the sidelines, specifically when it came to a waltz.

Rose gave them all a sly grin. "And maybe, if you invite the duchess, then she'll want to come and convince her parents there's no reason to have a gathering at all."

To have Dory at the ball was more than Ellie could have hoped, but to have the Duke and Duchess of Northwick in attendance would ensure many would accept the invitations. "Then I suggest we think of all the men I can invite and reconvene at dinner to discuss the options. Rose, you determine the best way to convince Joanna. Georgie, I know you have posed for

Lady Sommerset, so perhaps you could convince her and the earl to attend. He has a younger brother as yet unwed. And if there is someone in particular any of you would like to have here, I'll be happy to invite them. I'll even ask Lord Ferncroft to make the introductions."

"Did I hear my name?"

Ellie snapped her head up to find Darius leaning against the open doorway of the parlor. Her heart fluttered at the sight. He looked particularly handsome in his gray pantaloons and black tailcoat. His hair was slightly messy, probably due to the wind, as he'd been visiting a tenant who had a problem.

She smiled softly and held out her hand. "Indeed you did. Do come and reacquaint yourself with my friends."

Darius strode forward and took her hand before standing next to her. "If I remember correctly, I have the honor of being in the presence Lady Sophie, Lady Georgina, and Lady Rose."

Rose gave a regal nod. "Your memory, my lord, is quite impressive."

Ellie couldn't quite take her eyes off her husband, so when he looked at her and squeezed her hand, a meteor seemed to speed through her chest.

"I couldn't forget anything about the day I married the woman who has brightened my life."

"Oh, my lord. Do you have a brother?"

Georgie's smitten voice forced Ellie to look at her. "He does. He has three. Why do you ask?"

Darius addressed her friend before Georgie could speak. "They are all happily wedded. My youngest brother married your classmate."

"Yes, of course." Georgie rearranged her skirts, avoiding eye contact.

Ellie didn't like seeing Georgie uncomfortable, so she spoke to Darius. "We were discussing the Twelfth Night ball. I do hope you can add some unmarried gentlemen to my invitation list."

"I will be happy to be of service in that regard. Now, however, I have a meeting with my steward, but I shall look forward to seeing you all at dinner."

Darius squeezed her hand once again before letting go and striding from the room.

Sophie spoke first, her voice quiet as always. "He seems a different man than the one we met at the church."

"I agree." Rose, who'd watched Darius leave, turned back toward them. "He's still formal, but less stiff."

Georgie finally looked up. "He's very intelligent."

"He is all of those." Ellie looked at each friend in turn. "I have learned much about him and discovered his first marriage was not all he had hoped it would be. I believe I am quite different from the late Lady Ferncroft, and for that he is grateful."

Rose nodded as if that explained everything. "I speak for all of us, Ellie—we are very pleased for you."

"Should we, perhaps, settle in and begin our visit in earnest?"

Sophie's gentle suggestion reminded Ellie of her hosting duties. "Yes. You must be tired from your journey. We have many days to enjoy each other's company." She picked up the small bell and rang it before rising.

Rose gracefully stood. "I'm looking forward to our holiday together."

Beacham stepped into the room. "My lady?"

"Please have Lady Rose, Lady Georgina, and Lady Sophie shown to their rooms." Ellie nodded to each in turn.

"Of course. This way, my ladies."

Georgie jumped up and followed Rose out, but Sophie simply rose.

Ellie turned toward her. "Thank you for the reminder. I have missed having you near."

"Thank you for inviting me. I admit to being a bit lost without you, but I'm learning."

She took Sophie's hands. "And I want to hear about everything you're learning and the literature I know you've read since I left...after you rest."

Sophie gave her a grateful smile before releasing her hands and following the others out.

Ellie sighed, her pure happiness almost too much to keep inside. She wanted to run and laugh and throw her hands up in joy, which would probably spook the servants. Instead, she would kiss her husband and tell him exactly how pleased she was to be his wife.

Her decision made, she strode out of the room and across the entry to seek out Darius in his study. When she reached the door she turned the knob, but the door didn't open. How odd. Could he still be meeting with his steward?

Turning about, she returned to the entry, where Beacham was overseeing a footman retrieving the cocoa cups and plates. "Beacham, is Lord Ferncroft still meeting with his steward?"

"No, my lady. The steward has left. He was only here for six minutes."

She frowned. "Do you know why the door to the study is locked?"

"My guess would be that my lord locked it."

"Yes, I surmised that as well, but do you know why he would?"

Beacham pulled himself even straighter, if that were possible. "I would not presume to understand my lord's thoughts."

Of course he wouldn't. She tried a different tack. "Has he locked it before, or is this the first time?"

"Since I have served here, that room, as well as the parlor, ballrooms, a few bedrooms, the billiard room, and the larder have been locked on occasion. But I cannot say why, except for the larder, which the cook often locks."

Beacham's answer made her feel that perhaps it wasn't such an unusual occurrence. "Do you know if my husband is in his study, then?"

This time Beacham blinked. "I do not know for certain. Last he called me he was in there."

Something told her Beacham was hiding something and knew

a bit more about the locked door. "I suppose I could knock and find out myself."

She'd started to turn to do just that when Beacham spoke. "Usually, a locked door means that one should not enter."

She studied the butler. He definitely knew something. Maybe she wasn't supposed to go in the study for some reason. But why wouldn't Darius want her in—

Oh. Could it be he had a gift just delivered for her and didn't wish her to see it?

She grinned. That must be it. Why else would Beacham not want her to see if Darius was in there? After all, it was the season for surprises. "You're right, Beacham. I promised Peter to check on him as soon as I was able, so I will head to the nursery. Did Mrs. Clark make the baked apples for him?"

"She did."

"Very good. He shall have them with his dinner. Thank you, Beacham." With that, she headed up the stairs smiling.

CHAPTER SIXTEEN

DARIUS STOOD OUTSIDE in the cold and mist, the bright moon of just a few nights ago obscured thoroughly. Instead of the darkest black, the evening was charcoal, the clouds and moisture droplets reflecting the slightest light.

He stood well beyond the light shining from the dining room windows, where he could clearly see his wife talking animatedly with her friends. Was she upset with him? No, not Ellie. She would support his need to take care of his people and estate. Did she miss him? He fervently hoped so. Even now he missed being in her warm presence, so much so that he'd debated leaving—but as usual, his logical side had won. For that he was thankful, even as he yearned to return to the house.

He'd known even as he rode up from meeting with the Gereys that his black mood was taking over. He'd barely held himself in check while discussing Mr. Gerey's concerns, and as he rode for home, his irritation worsened. He had nothing to be irritated about, which was so bloody frustrating. When he'd entered the house and heard the female chatter, he'd started toward his study, but even before Beacham raised his brows, he knew he must greet Ellie's friends…for her sake.

He'd barely made it through without revealing his unreasonable anger. Luckily, Beacham reminded him his steward was waiting before he entered his study, and he'd kept the meeting very brief, locking the door after the man. When the doorknob had been tried, he'd frozen in fear as if the lock wouldn't hold. But it did, keeping the warmth of Ellie from reaching him, or rather the coldness of his mood from touching her.

His heart skipped a beat as he watched Ellie through the window while she threw back her head and laughed at something one of her friends said. Her bright-red hair caught the light and her vibrancy mesmerized him. He could stand in the cold all night and watch her from a safe distance. He'd never expected to fall in love with his wife. He hadn't loved Dinah, but felt they rubbed along fairly well. That had been his gravest misjudgment. To discover she'd treated their children like she treated him made him want to hurt her, but she was far from his grasp now.

He'd thought having Dinah at Hawthorne Park, instead of letting her live elsewhere, as she'd asked, would be better for Maggie and Peter. How wrong he'd been. He'd failed his children, first by telling Dinah about his black moods and then by forcing her to stay. Why hadn't he asked his children? If he'd been a worthy father, he would have asked and not taken Dinah's assurances that she and the children enjoyed spending time together. She'd obviously done it to punish him.

He didn't deserve a second chance, and yet he'd found one in Ellie. His children deserved her, even if he didn't. But falling in love was the worst possible scenario. Hopefully, she didn't feel so about him. He was hardly worthy of her. He couldn't even tell her the truth. He was a coward, afraid he'd lose her.

Ellie rose from the table, and he watched as she herded her friends from the dining room into the parlor. Her smiles were constant as she hooked her arm with one lady and spoke to another. He couldn't tear his gaze from her as she played hostess to the others, instructing the footman, talking with her friends, and, if he didn't miss his guess, setting up a game of charades. It looked as if Lady Georgina was to go first.

Movement in the dining room caught his attention, and he glanced that way to see the servants closing the curtains against the cold night. He yanked his gaze back to Ellie. He didn't want to stop watching her. She half stood as she made a guess, only to fall back into her seat laughing. He could hear her inside his head, his angst dulling as he listened.

The servants came into the parlor and began to close the curtains. "No." He stood helpless as his view of Ellie was impeded by the thick peach curtains. He remained absolutely still, staring at the window, willing her to get up and open them. He waited, wanting to see her more than he wanted to live. He was her husband. He could simply walk into the parlor and take her in his arms. All he had to do was—

"Didn't your mother teach you that standing out in the cold isn't good for your wellbeing?"

Darius stiffened before growling, "Archer."

"Who else would be such a fool as to be out here when it's colder than the top of Ben Nevis?"

He spun, his frustration mounting. "What do you know about a mountain in the wilds of Scotland?"

"Been there when I was a lad. What are we watching?" Archer peered around him.

"Nothing," Darius ground out between his clenched teeth.

Archer stepped around him and studied the barren gardens. "Obviously. I'm guessing you were on your way to the bathhouse?"

Was he? Yes, that was why he was out in the cold. He'd started for his cave when he made the mistake of looking back and saw Ellie. "Yes."

"I'll walk with you."

He ignored Archer and started north. "I know the way."

"As it happens, so do I."

He didn't want to talk to his gamekeeper. He didn't want to talk to *anyone*.

Except Ellie.

His step slowed. He shook his head and forced himself to keep walking.

He entered the north wood and took the path toward the former bathhouse. If he didn't know the building was there, he would have walked right into it, because no light shone from the windows and no fire crackled inside. It fit his mood perfectly.

"Here, you better let me go inside first."

He started, having forgotten Archer was with him. The man walked on silent feet. "I'm not an invalid," he snapped at him before opening the door and stepping inside. It was just as cold inside as out, but not as damp. He walked forward toward the fireplace where the tinder was kept and bumped into the settee. "Damn!"

"I told you to let me enter before you. I can see in the dark."

He wasn't sure if Archer meant his words, but also didn't care. Feeling his way around the settee, he felt for the mantel and found it. Running his fingers along it, he found the tinder box, but he couldn't seem to get it opened. "Worthless box." He slammed it back on the mantel.

A chuckle came from in front of him as he scowled into the darkness.

The flint was struck and a tiny flame moved to a lantern, where it caught, and light shone on Archer's face and onto the sitting area. "I would have had the place prepared if you had sent me word you were leaving."

"Just light the fire, since you're here." Darius covered his cold ears with his hands. He could have started the fire himself, and had many times, but watching Ellie through her entire dinner had not helped his body heat.

Archer was not only expert but efficient, and by the time Darius's ears had warmed, the fire was going tolerably well.

"Here." Archer held out a glass. "It'll warm you from the inside."

Knowing Archer, it was probably whisky, but Darius didn't care. He took the glass and threw it back. The burn did indeed warm his chest, but he grimaced as he handed the glass back. "That'll burn your insides to ash."

Archer lifted his glass high in salute. "That's the whole idea." The gamekeeper threw back his own glass before returning to the sideboard.

Darius took off his greatcoat and hung it on a hook by the door next to Archer's. Then he sat down on the settee and managed to take off his boots.

"Here's your brandy." Archer held the glass out to him. "You might want to sip that."

Darius scowled at what the man thought was humorous. "I know how to drink good brandy." He took a sip and set it on the small table nearby.

Archer settled into the wingback chair with a larger glass of whisky. "The new Lady Ferncroft appears very different from the late Lady Ferncroft."

Darius ignored Archer as he untied his cravat.

"She has the whole village abuzz with talk of St. Thomas Day. The word is she has issued an invitation to all the widows to come to the house."

Darius had suggested she give the coin to the church to distribute, but she insisted on doing it herself and involving her friends. "She wants the many widows of our men who fought Napoleon to know they are not forgotten." He dropped his cravat over the side of the settee, before picking up his glass and taking another sip. It was so much better than the whisky.

"My missus is all aglow over her. She's made an impression on all the women. They say she's friendly and kind. It sounds like you found the perfect woman for your children."

Darius stopped in the process of unbuttoning his waistcoat at Archer's comment. "She is. Not only is she well versed in healing, but she's also most learned. I may not need to hire a tutor for Peter." Even as he said the words, he knew he held back what was the best of Ellie. It was almost as if he talked about it, he'd lose it.

"Don't know anything about that, but I can tell you are pleased. Congratulations on picking the right woman this time. I imagine it's easier to find a mother than a wife, since you focused only on your children."

Archer was right. That had been his motivation, but he'd found so much more, which meant he had to protect her even more, especially from himself.

"Of course, you'll probably need a few more children. You nabobs always like to have a good half-dozen. Hope she's not a cold fish like your last wife."

Even at the mention of Dinah, Darius felt his anger returning. "Ellie is nothing like Dinah." He rose, his agitation building. "Dinah was colder than the temperatures outside. I discovered this week that she hid in the nursery but ignored the children." He started to pace. "More than that, she called them 'my little problems,' and said it in front of them! And she called *me* a monster!" He fisted his hands as he paced the short distance from the bed, past the settee to the wall and back. "I should have asked the children what she did, what she said. It's my fault."

"I suppose it's your fault it's cold outside too, or that a year ago we had no summer."

Darius stopped, confused. "What?"

"All I'm saying is you can't know everything. You did what you thought best based upon the information you had. It's not your fault Dinah was selfish and spiteful. That lies firmly at her feet. You have always done what you thought best for everyone. Isn't that why you remarried?"

"Yes. I remarried someone nothing like Dinah. Ellie is kind and caring. She has a happy disposition, enjoys gazing at the stars, and loves my children."

"You sound like you have a lot of respect for her. That is a strong basis for a good marriage."

"Respect? Yes, I have much respect for her. I also admire her and worry about her and love—" Too late, he snapped his mouth closed, but a cold wave of fear raced up his back.

"You love her. Darius, this is wonderful. Does she feel the same way toward you?"

He sat on the settee, dread filling him. "I don't know. I hope not."

Archer stilled, his glass halfway to his lips. "You hope not? Why?"

"I don't want her to. She can't love a monster."

"If you love her, you should tell her about your problem. Tell her about your uncle and that you don't want to follow in his footsteps. Man, this is your chance."

Darius set his elbows on his knees and held his head in his hands. "I can't let her know about my black moods. She will turn away from me. I cannot lose her. My children cannot lose her. She's brought light and love to Hawthorne Park." He lifted his head and looked at his gamekeeper. "I cannot tell her."

Archer set his empty glass down. "If she's done so much for you, she deserves to know. Do you really think you can keep it from her forever?"

He shook his head. "Just a little while longer, until the children are older."

"And what about your future children?"

Darius felt his heart race at the thought that even now Ellie could carry a little girl or boy. He wanted that almost as much as he wanted her. "Then I'll have to wait even longer."

Archer rose. "If you respect her and love her, you need to tell her."

Why wouldn't he leave it alone? Darius sat up. "And have her hate me, maybe even hate my children? How can I risk it?"

Archer moved to the door, donned his coat, then looked at him. "And if she cares for you and discovers your secret on her own, then how do you think she'll feel? Think about it." The gamekeeper opened the door, looked at Darius once more, then strode out into the cold night, closing the door behind him.

Darius took another sip of brandy. Ellie wouldn't find out. He'd be extra careful. Yet even as he tried to reassure himself, his fear grew. She was very intelligent. Maybe he could take her on a trip where he had "business" to take care of, so she'd see it wasn't all that interesting. Of course, if she were with child, she couldn't go, but then she'd be focused on that. There was always another ball. If she kept busy with the house, children, and entertaining, maybe she wouldn't notice his absence that much.

He rose, his brandy still in hand. Even if she didn't discover his secret, he was still lying to her. He'd told Dinah because he didn't like lying to her even though he hadn't loved her. And that was the crux of his problem. He *did* love Ellie, and the thought of her leaving him because he should be in Bedlam, not trying to manage an estate and raise a family like others did, made it hard to breathe. Before her, he'd counted the months he managed to stay sane, knowing that eventually he'd either be committed or follow his uncle's path. Not to the pond, though. A pistol would be quicker, with no second thoughts.

He walked to the bed and set his brandy on the night table before lying down on his back. With the single lantern on the fireplace casting minimal light, he stared up at the barely visible ceiling. Maybe that was the best answer. Ellie and the children were better off without him. Peter would inherit and…he still needed another son. The thought of having to live long enough for that felt like a never-ending tunnel with no hope of escape, the dark walls closing in, cutting off his air, suffocating him as they crushed him.

A screech outside jarred him from his nightmare, and he took a deep breath, his heartbeat pounding inside his chest. It was just the resident owl, but a welcome one at that. For the first time since his moods had started, he didn't want to simply wait until his legacy was secure. He wanted to live every moment he could with Ellie.

"Ellie." Even as he whispered her name in the dimly lit room, the darkness inside him seemed to open up a bit.

He closed his eyes and pictured her as he'd last seen her, holding court among her friends. If he could just hold on to her, maybe there was a chance at life.

CHAPTER SEVENTEEN

December 22, Winter Solstice and St. Thomas Day

"ELLIE, IS THERE more food?" Georgie breezed into the entryway. "There's at least another dozen coming up the drive."

Ellie's chest tightened with compassion for all the widows in the area. She'd always been pleased to give to the widows on St. Thomas Day back at home, but around Hawthorne Park, there were so many more. The war had taken a toll. "Yes, there is." She looked at her butler. "Beacham?"

"I'll have it brought out at once, my lady."

As he strode off, Georgie smiled at her. "If you like, I can spell you for a while."

Though she knew Georgie was perfectly capable of directing the staff, Ellie simply preferred to do it herself. But she also liked meeting the women who had lost their husbands and still managed to carry on. "No need. I will join you." She moved to the wall by the door and lifted her pelisse from its hook.

Beacham reappeared with a footman in tow carrying twelve bags of food and cooked wheat. Immediately, he stepped up and helped Ellie on with her pelisse.

"Thank you, Beacham. Tell Mrs. Torbett if any more widows arrive after we give these bags away, she can hand them out. I will entrust you with the coins to be sure each widow receives some."

"Do you not wish to rest now, my lady? I'm quite sure Mrs. Torbett is capable of taking care of everyone."

Ellie smiled, pleased that her butler was concerned. "Not yet. I do so enjoy the smiles on their faces. While my mother enjoys planning charitable events, I've always preferred to help directly and meet those I can benefit."

Without another word about it, she headed back outside with Georgie, the footman carrying the sustenance.

"Ah, here she is now, the Lady Ferncroft with more food." Rose gestured toward Ellie as she descended the five steps to where Rose and Sophie stood.

It was lovely to see how easily Sophie interacted with the women. Was it that they were women or that they were in unfortunate circumstances? She had a feeling it was the latter. "Ladies, please, we have a bag for each of you. Do come over and take one."

The three women who had been speaking to Rose and Sophie came toward her. Each took a bag then thanked her warmly. No sooner had they left than two more approached Rose and Sophie, who gave out the coins. When the last bag of food was given, Ellie looked toward the end of the long drive and could see more ladies entering. "Let us repair to the house. My servants will take our places."

Sophie and Rose joined her and Georgie as they climbed the steps.

Rose looked toward the sky. "I wonder if you would have had so many women arrive if it hadn't dawned such a bright, sunny day."

"I'm sure that helped, and it's not too cold today either. I'm just thrilled that the vicar and Mrs. Gerey let as many people know as possible."

Georgie raced up the steps to the top. "Is she a neighbor?"

Ellie shook her head. "No, she's one of our tenants. She would know more widows than my neighbors, I'm sure."

Sophie spoke from behind her. "Do you have nice ladies

nearby that can be your friends now?"

Ellie stopped on the landing and faced Sophie. "You are such a dear to think of me. Yes. There are two ladies I've met that I think could be very good friends. And then there is the dragon."

Rose's blue eyes lit with curiosity. "Is she old and wrinkled, with a long, sharp nose and bad breath?"

Ellie laughed.

"No, you goose. She must have three heads, claws for hands, and scales for skin." Georgie punctuated her comment by curling her fingers into claws.

Sophie shook her head. "She must be a very unhappy woman."

"I believe you're right, Sophie." Ellie could always count on Sophie's observations. "I fear she is only happy when the unfortunate tidings of others reaches her ears." They'd all met ladies like the Baroness Watkins. "Now, let us repair to my glass terrace upstairs and enjoy the sun from there."

"And marzipan," Georgie grinned while taking off her coat as she walked through the door.

"Yes, I will have marzipan sent up." Georgie opened her mouth to speak, but Ellie held her hand up. "I've already informed Cook that you will need a couple dozen to take with you on your way home tomorrow."

Sophie grinned. "You are always thinking of us."

"Yes, I am. Now, upstairs you go. I'll be there in a moment."

Ellie watched her three friends climb the grand staircase. She'd thoroughly enjoyed her sennight with them, though it was too bad that Lissa had been delayed. Ellie was going to miss having her former classmates about, especially because Darius had not returned from his trip. It was already a day longer than his last one. She couldn't help but worry.

Beacham turned from hanging up the final cloak. "My lady, I have told Mrs. Torbett to expect more women."

"Thank you. Has there been any word from Lord Ferncroft?"

"I'm afraid not, but I promise I will tell you immediately."

"I do hope he comes home before Christmas."

Beacham gave her a sympathetic look. "I'm most sure that he is as anxious to be here with you as you are to have him home."

She nodded, in complete agreement with Beacham. Darius had seemed very happy with her and the children before he left. No doubt he was anxiously traveling homeward even now. "Please have tea and marzipan sent up to my terrace."

"No cocoa, my lady?"

She grinned. "No. I don't wish to spoil Lady Georgina too much. After all, she and Lady Rose must leave on the morrow and won't be able to have cocoa every day."

Beacham raised his brows. "Then would it not be kinder to allow them their final day of bliss?"

She laughed. "You make a good point. Send up the cocoa along with the tea."

—

Ellie moved the telescope toward the Cassiopeia constellation. It was well past midnight, and she couldn't sleep. She missed Darius, and her friends were to leave in the morning. She was so thankful that Sophie said she could stay a couple of more days, since she lived less than a day's journey away. Or maybe it was the moon keeping her awake. It had been full not three nights past, and was said to affect people. She probably should have dressed in more than her shift and robe, but she didn't expect to see anyone at this hour.

Though it had been sunny all day, the clouds had moved in during dinner, making it impossible to show Rose the constellation of Hercules that she wanted to see. But now there were parts of the sky visible, and with the moon behind a bank of clouds, Ellie could definitely do some stargazing. It always distracted her from her worries.

And she *was* worried. She worried about her husband.

Looking southward from the top point of Cassiopeia, she found what she sought. Not simply the Andromeda constellation but the Andromeda Nebula. She moved the telescope slightly and locked it into place. The nebula came into focus. Instead of the soft white oblong smear she usually saw, it now looked like a tilted plate. In the center appeared a very bright star that rose above and below the disk. She could even see a smaller nebula nearby. How different the universe looked with a better telescope. It made her want to share all her discoveries with Darius.

She lifted her head from the eyepiece. Marrying Darius had made her life very different, too. Like the telescope showed her so much more, Darius showed her how wonderful life could be. He granted her most fervent wish, to be a mother the very day they wed. Then he'd believed in her and her abilities, and he made all her dreams come true in their bed. As much as her friends insisted she deserved it, the voice of her mother still echoed in her mind, criticizing her, her brothers' laughter ringing in her ears.

Shaking her head, she chastised herself. Nothing was perfect. Soon Darius would notice her penchant for knocking things over and her shortcomings in running a household when it wasn't Christmastide. But in the meantime, she would enjoy every moment. So as soon as he came home, she would insist on showing him what she'd found in the stars. Not that he would resist. He was far too kind. So what else did she want to find to show him?

She walked to the cabinet and pulled out her notes, then set them on the small table nearby and gazed out into the darkness of the estate. Maybe she should research if there were any other nebula that had been discovered that she was unaware of.

With her decision made, she brought her gaze back to the sky, gauging if the clouds were dissipating or filling in. The moon's light remained blocked, except what shone down on the earth directly below it. The rest of the gardens and field were dark and, in the wood—

She frowned. It looked like there was light in the north wood. It was just a sprinkling through the trees, like a new star cluster.

She watched the light to see if it moved, as it could perhaps be the gamekeeper and his men, but the light remained steady. Did someone live there? The gamekeeper lived in the village, but maybe another out-of-doors servant, like the gardener? Curious, she continued to stare at it, wishing she knew what it was. Beacham would know, but he was abed, as was everyone else.

Turning back to her telescope, she grinned. She could make a new discovery, albeit not an astronomical one.

Without a second thought, she unlocked the telescope and turned it toward the light. Once she had it in place, she relocked it and put her eye to the eyepiece. As she focused, she could clearly see a little building. Someone definitely lived there, as light shone from the windows and smoke rose from the chimney. It looked very small, no bigger than her glass terrace. Whoever lived there was up quite late, especially for a laborer. A shadow moved across the light, proving someone was awake and about the small place.

She smiled, excited to see who it was. It could even be an old woman who was granted the small building by the former owner. Or maybe it was a man who'd been hurt saving the former owner and was given the little place to live out his days. Oh, the stories she could make up about the little place.

The shadows moved again, and then a man strode past the window. Her breath caught in her chest. She pulled her head back from the telescope. She knew that stride, but it couldn't be.

She shook her head. Her flights of fancy were playing tricks on her. Lowering her head to look through the telescope again, she waited. Long moments passed and still there was no movement. Then a man came into view. He looked like the gamekeeper. He stood still, talking to someone. Yes, it was Mr. Archer. Maybe it was a place where he could warm himself on his nightly rounds. That made sense, but that couldn't have been the original purpose. And whom was he talking to?

Oh, did the man have a mistress that he kept from his wife? She didn't like that idea at all. If that was the case, then Darius must know. She would have to speak to him about it.

As she watched, the gamekeeper moved out of view and

exited the building. Now she would see who was the woman the man dallied with. It was but a minute more before a figure moved to stand before the window.

Her heart stopped. She knew that silhouette. "Darius."

Confusion, concern, and anger twirled inside her like a galaxy. She lifted her head and looked out the window. What was her husband doing on the property when he was supposed to be traveling? Her chest tightened. Was it *he* that had a mistress? Tears sprang to her eyes. She knew it was the norm, but it hurt nonetheless, and to have the woman on the estate was too much to bear.

And she wouldn't.

She strode out of the room and headed down the hall. Quickly, she ducked into her bedroom and exchanged her light robe for a warmer one before continuing to the grand staircase. Descending quickly, she stopped long enough to wrap her cloak about her before striding through the parlor and outside. She stopped after coming to the half-circle at the bottom of the steps of the parlor terrace. She and the children always took the path to the right, toward the north wood, but only to the baby Neptune fountain. It hadn't occurred to her to explore further, to discover more.

Now, she would remedy that oversight. She continued through the gardens, past two more fountains, and out across a large field. Though she could see no lights, she knew the building to be in the north wood. Her pace quickened as her fury festered. But deep down, where she dared not look, was an immense hurt that made her belly ache far worse than Peter taking ipecac sherry.

When she reached the wood, she turned back to look at the house. Her glass terrace gave a faint glow from the two lanterns within it. She gauged her position and where she remembered seeing the lights.

She walked along the tree line, peering into the trees. The moonlight didn't shine where she was, as the bank of clouds remained in place. The one time she wished for moonlight, it hid as if in fear of a black hole.

Continuing on, she kept her gaze sharp, so when a distinct opening in the trees revealed a path, she silently shouted in triumph. It had to be a path to the little house. She didn't hesitate in starting forward. The ground sloped slightly upward at first before going into a gradual decline, no doubt what kept her from seeing any light in the field. The path also wound its way about as if purposely making it difficult to travel, but she wouldn't stop.

Finally, light revealed itself between the trees, and she quickened her pace. As the building came into view, she understood now what it was. It looked to be an old bathhouse—there was probably a pond nearby. She didn't care anymore what it was. All she cared about was confronting her husband and his mistress.

She'd thought Darius was happy with her. She was wrong. She hadn't been good enough, just as her mother always warned, but she'd let herself believe that she was.

She didn't slow her pace as she reached the door, turned the knob, and burst in.

—

Darius spun away from the fireplace at the sound of the door banging against the wall. "Ellie!" He stared in horror at his wife. Her finding him was far worse than any nightmare he'd ever had.

She slammed the door behind her and scanned the room as if looking for someone. Then she snapped her angry blue gaze back to him. "Why are you here?"

And there it was, the question he'd dreaded. The question he knew better than to answer. "You shouldn't be here."

"*I* shouldn't be here?" Her voice rose. "*I* shouldn't be here?" She took a step forward. "*You* shouldn't be here. You had business to attend to. You would be gone for days, or so you said."

She scanned the room again, this time her gaze stopping on the unmade bed, then continuing to the dirty glasses on the sideboard and his plate with the remnants of his meal still upon it—all of it making it clear he'd been hiding. *Damn.*

"You've been here." Her shock was clear in her whispered

words.

How could he deny it? Why did fate offer him a glimpse of what his life could be like only to take it away like this? But he couldn't let it go. He'd fight for what he'd seen could be.

"Yes. I will be home soon. I promise. You need to go back to the house." He snapped his mouth shut over the words that almost came out. He *wanted* to tell her she'd been duped into marrying a madman.

She cocked her head and lowered her brows. "I don't understand. Why are you here?"

He took a step toward her then halted. Her vibrancy and warmth called to him, but it would do no good. He would taint it, turn her cold if he said too much. "I promise, I will tell you when I return. But you must leave now." He curled his hands into fists, trying to stay in control of his tongue, and not let the doomed monster inside get out.

"Why? Are you expecting someone? A woman, perhaps?" Her tone was harsh.

"A woman?" He snorted. The idea was laughable. He couldn't even keep *one* woman happy. He certainly didn't need another. "It's not so simple as that. I can't explain it to you now. You must leave." His voice had turned cold, but he wasn't capable of changing it. He was losing ground.

She crossed her arms. "Why not now? I'm here. Why does where we are make a difference?"

"Damn it, it's not where, it's when! Just go." He pointed toward the door, praying she'd leave. *Please.*

He'd never raised his voice or cursed in front of her before, and it obviously startled her, but she wasn't Dinah, a faint miss, who perpetuated her revenge by stealth. Ellie was fire and brimstone personified, wanting him to confess his sins before her...*now.*

"I'm your wife. I deserve to know why you have lied to me."

Her only worry was that he'd lied? It was laughable compared to what she *should* be worried about. Yet guilt raised its ugly head, showing him the truth—that he didn't deserve her. But now he wasn't sure he could live without her. It wasn't fair! "I did it to protect you. Now leave!"

"You want me to leave? Why? Am I not your wife? Or is it because I'm not good enough to be your wife? I cannot be trusted to—" She dropped her arms and looked back at the sideboard.

He recognized the moment understanding dawned, as she sucked in a breath before facing him. "Who else knows you're here?"

He closed his eyes as if he could keep the hurt in her gaze from touching him. But she was already in his heart, like a forbidden jewel that he could never claim. It was hopeless, and to think he could keep any of it, any of her, was nothing more than a doomed man's dreams.

He opened his eyes. "I told you. You must go. I cannot be held accountable if you stay."

"You're accountable for everything. Who brought you that food? Is that why the gamekeeper was here?"

He dug his fingers deeper into his palms as anger flared. "You've been watching me. So why ask? You already know it wasn't Archer. Only Beacham and Mrs. Torbett provide for me. Archer just argues with me."

"Beacham? Mrs. Torbett? They lied to me, too?" The pain in Ellie's gaze sliced through his chest as she grasped her belly. "They know why you're here, but not me! Not your *wife*?" She was yelling now.

He wanted her to yell. He needed her angry, so she'd go away.

"You're not the man I married. I don't know who you are, and I don't want to know. Not anymore." She turned toward the door and opened it.

Even as she started to do what he'd asked, his heart constricted painfully and panic swept through him. "Wait, Ellie. I didn't mean..." Didn't mean that she should leave? Didn't mean to betray her trust?

She looked back and scowled at him before running down the path, leaving the door open to the cold, dark night.

Her expression broke him. So much pain and anger and disbelief in her eyes.

He stood frozen to the spot, unable to move, his heart cracking. He couldn't lose her, no matter what he'd done. If he lost her, there was no reason to continue his struggle.

He ran out the door. "Wait! Ellie! Ellie!" A pain sliced through his chest, making it impossible to breathe. *I love you.* He bent over trying to fill his lungs. As soon as air returned, he straightened. He had to catch her.

No, he'd make things worse. But she already thought the worst. He couldn't even remember what he'd said, too anxious to get her to leave. And now that she was gone, he needed her back. "Ellie!" He started to run after her. She couldn't be far. He had to explain. There was so much to explain. He needed her, but she had to know he wasn't worthy of her. That he could never be the husband she hoped for. He had to—

"Umph!" His foot hit something on the path and he started to fall.

Someone grabbed his arm. "Here you go now. No time to be eating the dirt."

Archer's voice had him yanking his arm from the man's grasp, barely staying upright in the process. "Let me go. I have to catch her."

Archer grabbed his arm again. "Who are you yelling at?"

Darius rounded on the gamekeeper. "My wife!"

"All the more reason not to go after her."

"Bloody hell! You don't understand. She found me. She knows I lied and that others also know I hide away in my cave like the monster I am. I have to explain."

"And what will you tell her? That you're a madman, a monster? Or will you tell her that you hope to one day follow in your selfish uncle's footsteps and make her a widow so she can marry another lord?"

At the thought of Ellie with another man, rage filled his gut. He pulled back his arm and punched Archer.

The man's head whipped to the side, but when he turned back, he was smiling. "Always hoped you'd do that one day."

That was the last thing Darius heard before darkness wiped away all thought, welcoming him to oblivion.

CHAPTER EIGHTEEN

December 23

ELLIE STOOD ON the steps waving as Rose and Georgie, in separate coaches, waved back until they were well down the drive. Luckily, she'd been able to explain away her weepiness at the fact that they were leaving, and by the time they were out the door, *everyone* was crying, but assurances were made that they would gather again at the Twelfth Night ball. If only she'd never sent out the invitations.

She finally dropped her arm and turned back to enter the house, where Sophie waited in the entryway. "What?" She let Beacham have her cloak.

Sophie clasped her hands before her. "Something is wrong. It's not because Rose and Georgie are gone."

Ellie glanced at Beacham, thankful that Sophie always spoke quietly. Unfortunately, Sophie was far too observant and wouldn't stop asking until she was satisfied. "Beacham, Lady Sophie and I will take tea in my glass terrace."

"Yes, my lady."

"Shall we?" Ellie held her arm out toward the grand staircase.

Sophie ascended beside her, not saying a word, the white skirts of her dress swishing as they climbed.

Her friend's loyalty and caring almost undid her, but Ellie managed to keep her wits about her until they entered the terrace. Then, as if being called to it, she walked to the wall of glass and stared out at the north wood…where Darius hid from her.

Sophie joined her but said nothing.

They stood there for at least fifteen minutes, Ellie not sure how she could explain her unhappiness.

At the sound of the door opening, she directed the footman to set the tea service on a small table she'd added to the space. Moving to it, she poured the tea, making sure that Sophie's had extra cream and no sugar, as she liked it.

Sophie lifted her cup and sipped, smiling at the taste, but not saying a word.

Ellie knew that her friend could go a whole day without uttering a sound and feel completely content. That, coupled with her patience, meant if Ellie didn't say something, there would be no further discussion. On the one hand, that was tempting, but the pain inside her needed to be released, and Sophie was such a good listener.

"He'd hiding from me."

"Your husband?"

"Yes." She turned her head to look out the glass, waving her hand toward it. "Out there in the north wood in an old bathhouse. He told me he had to travel and attend to business, but he's been there all this time. He's still there. Even after I found him last night."

Sophie touched the side of her jaw with two fingers. "Is it perhaps that he hides from your guests? Some people prefer not to interact with others very much. After all, there were three of us."

That hadn't occurred to Ellie. "He seemed to be fine when we went visiting."

"Yes, but that is not the same as having guests in your house, constantly underfoot." Sophie gave her a small smile.

She grimaced. "That's true. It could also be why he didn't wish to host a Twelfth Night ball. But if that were it, why could he not tell me? I would understand. He certainly didn't need to lie to me."

"It may be much like the reason you haven't told him about your tendency to knock into things. Or he may have thought you'd be insulted that he didn't wish to be around us."

Again, that was a plausible answer. Just as she began to feel a bit better, she remembered the first time he'd gone "on business." Was that *truly* business?

She shook her head. "It can't be that simple. When I discovered him, he kept telling me I had to leave and that he'd tell me why he was there when he returned to the house. He was frantic about it, and even yelled and cursed."

Sophie's green eyes widened. "Then it must be something extremely important. He does not appear a gentleman to put aside formality and appropriateness unless it's absolutely necessary."

Ellie blew out air between her closed lips. "He was a completely different person. He told me he had to protect me." She shook her head again, rising from her seat, the uncomfortable feeling starting in her belly again. "Why would he tell me that lying to me and sending me away was to *protect* me? It doesn't make sense. Something untoward is happening. And he's keeping it from me, his wife." She walked to the glass and stared at the north wood, the sun shining happily on the barren trees and dried grass, making everything slightly yellow.

"Many men keep things from their wives."

At Sophie's comment, Ellie turned. "I know. It's just that it didn't seem like he would. He even told me about his late wife and their unhappy marriage. What could be worse than that?"

Sophie looked away.

"No, it's not a mistress. I had thought that too. But the only person who was with him was the gamekeeper." Remembering that had Ellie growing angry again. "Others have known where he was hiding, when I, his wife, have not. If I hadn't seen the lights flickering in the trees last night while here using my telescope, I would still not know. Yet his servants know. I'm not sure I can forgive him for that. What do they think of me that they keep his secret from *me*?" Her voice was rising, but she couldn't help it.

Sophie rose from her chair and walked to her, placing a hand on her shoulder. "You're hurt."

Her eyes began to tear. "I am. He thought I was wonderful. No one has ever thought that." Sophie opened her mouth, but Ellie held up her hand. "Except for my dear classmates. He's even grateful I'm in his life. He said so. He *told* me that. But he couldn't tell me he was hiding? And why is he hiding from me?" She looked at her friend, wishing she could make the pain go away.

"You love him."

Sophie's soft words seemed to seep into Ellie's soul, and understanding came. She did love Darius. "I must, because his betrayal hurts here." She placed her hand on her chest and let her tears fall.

"Come sit." Sophie led her to a settee. "Here, take my handkerchief."

At the simple kindness, Ellie started crying harder. "I should have known it wasn't meant to be. I should never have hoped. Mother always said I'd be lucky to marry, and look, the only reason I did is because he didn't know me. To think that I could have a marriage like Elsbeth or Dory or Lissa was no more than a dream. It's my fault I'm hurt. I expected too much."

Sophie jumped to her feet. "Don't you say that. You're not the one who is wrong. He is. Eleanor Compton Taylour, he *lied* to you. Not only did he treat you kindly and made you trust him, but he broke that trust. He must not be the man you thought he was."

Since those had been her exact thoughts, she couldn't argue, even if a part of her still believed she should have somehow known. "But who is he, then?"

"I have a more important question, Ellie. Will you be able to forgive him?"

"I imagine it depends on why he did it." She tried to imagine a good reason for Darius to hide from her. "What if he lured someone out there to keep them from harming me? But then he would have rounded them up and not stayed over a week. Or what if he contracted scarlet fever and didn't wish me to see him fighting it? But he looked fine, though maybe a bit feverish. What if he owed a life debt to the gamekeeper and was forced to meet with him there? But he could certainly tell me that."

"It doesn't matter why he did it. Men, from what I've observed, will make decisions far different than women in the same set of circumstances. What may seem like the right decision to one feels like the worst decision to the other. So it really doesn't matter why he hid from you and lied about it. What *will* matter in the end is if you can forgive him."

Ellie's head understood what Sophie was saying, but her heart rebelled. "I don't know if I can."

Sophie sat next to her again. "I understand."

"You do?"

"No, not truly. I've never been in love. But I do know you, and you are a strong, capable, intelligent woman with a kind heart, who I'm honored to call my friend. I know that you will do what is best for you."

She hadn't realized how much Sophie's words meant to her until just that moment. "And you are my wise, kind, and very patient friend whom I will always support." She gave Sophie a hug, her friend's small frame comforting, then stood. "Now, as your strong, capable, intelligent friend, I plan to talk to both my butler and my housekeeper and discover what has been afoot."

"And so you should." Sophie nodded.

Ellie moved toward the tea service, intending to warm up her drink to settle her belly before calling her staff, but her hip caught the chair, which hit the table and sent the pot of tea crashing to the floor. Though it didn't break, the small carpet quickly turned dark brown. "Oh, no." She looked back at Sophie, whose brows rose in concern. "Maybe just strong and intelligent?"

Sophie stood once more. "No, you are very capable as well. You had to hit that chair at just the right angle to tip the table so the teapot would fall but nothing else. I call that quite capable." Then she crossed her arms, mimicking Ellie's usual stance.

Ellie grinned, then chuckled, then laughed loudly until new tears fell from her eyes. "Oh my... Just right...nothing else... Sophie..." She finally stifled her humor a bit and sniffed, wiping her eyes with the handkerchief her friend had lent her. "Thank you."

Sophie grinned. "You're welcome."

"I'm so glad I know you so well. I would not like to be on the opposing side of your mind."

"Thank you. Would you like help with confronting your servants?"

All humor vanished, but Ellie felt much more ready to tackle that situation. "No. I am capable of handling Mr. Beacham and Mrs. Torbett on my own. You can return to whichever book you've been reading, and I shall go to the parlor—no, the study, to talk to my servants."

"I look forward to hearing what you discover."

She gave her friend a nod before striding out of the room and downstairs. When Beacham appeared in the entryway, she halted. "I need you and Mrs. Torbett to attend to me in the study."

"The study? Yes, my lady." The butler quickly disappeared down the opposite corridor.

Ellie entered the study and settled herself behind Darius's desk. As she waited, she looked at the drawers and contemplated investigating. She never would have thought to do so before, as it was his desk, but now...

The doors to the study opened and Beacham and Mrs. Torbett hurried in.

Ellie rose. "Please, take a seat."

"If you're worried about the Christmas goose, my lady, rest assured it will arrive tomorrow, and we will have it prepared and ready for the oven by Christmas morning," Mrs. Torbett was quick to speak.

"I have no doubt at all about your ability to ensure we have a proper Christmas feast. Nor do I have any doubts about Mr. Beacham's ability to ensure all the staff will be present for their boxes the following day. What I do doubt is your loyalty to me."

"What?" Mrs. Torbett appeared duly shocked.

Beacham's eyes actually rounded. "I assure you, my lady, that we are absolutely dedicated to you."

"And, I must say, much happier to serve you than the late Lady Ferncroft. May she rest in peace." Mrs. Torbett made the sign of the cross.

Ellie crossed her arms over her chest. "Then why is it that you have both lied to me?"

Mrs. Torbett's brow furrowed, her confusion complete.

Beacham stared at Ellie for the longest time before something flickered in his gaze and he looked away. The man was astute.

"Beacham?"

He returned his gaze to hers, straightening his posture a bit more. "You must know, my lady, that our loyalty to you is only superseded by our loyalty to Lord Ferncroft."

Ah, so her butler *did* understand.

Mrs. Torbett nodded her head vigorously. "Absolutely. I swear on my dear grandmother's grave that—"

Beacham stopped Mrs. Torbett in mid-sentence with a squeeze to her forearm. "We are sworn to Lord Ferncroft."

Mrs. Torbett's eyes widened as she looked at him. She closed her mouth, pursing her lips as if it were the only way to avoid saying the wrong words.

Ellie studied them both. While she applauded their loyalty to Darius, she wanted answers. "So, what you are telling me is that he made you swear not to reveal to me that he is hiding even now in the bathhouse in the northern wood."

"Oh no, my lady." Mrs. Torbett faced her. "We swore not to tell anyone."

Beacham's shoulders slumped.

Ellie knew she shouldn't feel good that the two servants were miserable at the moment, caught between their lord and lady, but she was far too hurt to care. "As I now know, then perhaps you can tell me why he is there."

Mrs. Torbett appeared ready to explain, sitting up straight as if to launch into a dialogue that would be most edifying, but Beacham's hand on her arm still remained, and if Ellie guessed correctly, he squeezed again. The housekeeper sank back in her chair.

"So, I am to understand that neither of you will explain why my husband hides away for a week or longer once a month?"

There was a slight frown on Beacham's forehead for a moment before his face relaxed into his usual formal position.

"And you do both understand that with my husband supposedly away, it would be my decision which servants remain at Hawthorne Park and which are dismissed. I find I can no longer trust either of you."

Mrs. Torbett clasped her hands tightly in her lap, but Beacham remained as usual.

Ellie continued, becoming more frustrated. "I must admit to being angry at the moment at the lie perpetrated upon my person. But unlike the former lady of this house, I will not hide away and spread rumors among the neighbors and force the children to be hurt. One person doing that in this family is quite enough. Instead, all shall know the force of my will in the next few days. Now go. I cannot have you in my presence any longer." She flung her arm toward the door, knocking the quill from the ink, causing it to flip end over end across the desk to land on the floor.

"I'll have a maid clean that up right away." Mrs. Torbett rose.

"No! Leave it. Let it stain. Just go."

Beacham, who still held Mrs. Torbett's arm, guided her out of the room quickly.

Ellie watched them leave then turned her gaze to the inkwell. The need to tip it over on purpose was strong, her hurt and frustration growing. Instead, she curled her fingers into her palms. Despite what Sophie had said, she needed to know why Darius had lied. Her heart kept hoping for a reasonable explanation, even if her head said nothing would make the feeling of betrayal go away.

She slumped down in the chair, not sure where to turn next. Maybe the gamekeeper? But if it was dangerous, that wouldn't be a good tack. Back to Darius? Even at the thought of seeing him again, she felt her eyes itching with tears.

She would not cry any more over a man who would purposely lead her to falling in love with him only to betray her. No, crying accomplished nothing. She needed to learn the truth of the matter.

Surprised the top-right drawer of the desk was unlocked, she opened it and found the estate ledger. Quickly, she pulled the leather-bound book out and skimmed down the rows of neat penmanship. Was that Darius's writing or his steward's? The fact that she didn't know just proved that in the two months she'd been married, she'd learned very little about Lord Ferncroft.

The items appeared normal, and if there were any mistakes or glaring issues with the sums, she wouldn't know it. Her mathematical skills weren't up to par. She flipped through the pages to see if there were any other papers tucked away. Though she'd told Sophie there was no mistress, it was the only plausible explanation she could imagine, and she dreaded finding a love note buried in large volume.

When no perfumed paper could be found, she sighed with relief then checked the drawer to see if anything else resided there. Two extra quills sat at the back, but otherwise it was quite empty.

After returning the ledger, she turned to the top drawer on the left. It stuck a little, but as she pulled harder, it released. It was filled with blank paper and a few letters addressed to *The Marquess Ferncroft*, but one was addressed to *Darius Taylour*. That was odd and very out of character. Hesitantly, she lifted the folded paper with the broken seal, not completely comfortable reading her husband's correspondence—but since he'd already broken her trust in him, she unfolded the letter and read.

Dear brother.

Note I didn't write "dearest." As you know, I haven't decided which of my brothers I wish to ingratiate myself with the most. Though I will say that your appreciation for my recommendation of your current wife has gone a long way in moving you to the top…for now.

That you would agree to hosting such a fete as a Twelfth Night ball, given your proclivity for isolation, proves to me that you hold Lady Ferncroft in the highest of esteem. It also relieves me much that I haven't thrown an innocent miss to the lions, or lion, so to speak. My wish has always been that you, my eldest and most formal of brothers, could find some small amount of happiness.

To that end, I will gladly don any disguise you wish in order to pose as you if the need should arise, so that you may make your new bride happy. Having her know of such arrangements, again, if needed, will aid me tremendously in convincing those attending that I am you. I have perpetuated much more difficult disguises of people of whom I know much less of than you. I'm quite sure I can take on the utmost formality that is the essence of who you are, and a pair of extra-heeled boots will bring me easily to your height. Soot in my hair will hide my lighter strands, while the hooded cape will go a long way in hiding my bulk. The full domino face mask you suggest is an exceptional idea, though I do believe we have a similar jawline. Lissa is in agreement and willing to attend "without me" if necessary, though more for the happiness of her friend than for you in particular.

Of course, payment will be required, as usual, for such a significant favor. After all, it sounds as if your future wedded bliss depends upon my performance. That you have a chance at even a small bit of contentment gladdens me to no end. You deserve to be so. I promise to arrive days in advance. My wife is actually insisting that we do so, and since our investigation is almost complete, I see no impediments to being reunited with you once again.

Your ever-bothersome brother, Anthony.

Ellie blinked, not a little confused. Anthony was to pose as Darius at the ball? Why? Did it have to do with why Darius hid now? Did Anthony also know that Darius hid away for some reason and that was why he referred to his brother's proclivity for isolation? It had to be. What must Lissa think that her husband planned to *be* Darius?

She could feel a flush of embarrassment inching up her neck. What must Lissa think? Or had Anthony told her? Did everyone know except her? Maybe she should ask the children.

Even as the thought occurred, she shook her head. She would not involve them in any way. If they did know and their father had sworn them to secrecy, it would only cause hard feelings between them and her. And if they didn't know, it would cause them to ask questions they were better off not knowing the answers to. Because whatever it was, it was not pleasant.

As much as she wanted to read into Anthony's letter that Darius deserved happiness after Dinah, her instinct was telling her it was more than that. If that were true, it couldn't be a mistress, as men were quite happy with them, or they wouldn't have them. Was it something more sinister? Was he being blackmailed, or was he actually telling the truth about tending to business—only what he didn't say was that his business was with smugglers he met in the building in the north wood?

She had far too many questions and no answers…as of yet. But she would find them, even if she had to wait for Darius to return to the house.

She studied the letter again, noting it revealed the love and yet contention between the eldest and youngest Taylours. Her gaze fell upon a sentence she'd read but hadn't pondered.

That you would agree to hosting such a fete as a Twelfth Night ball, given your proclivity for isolation, proves to me that you hold Lady

Ferncroft in the highest of esteem.

He held her in the highest esteem? Darius himself had said he was protecting her. Had she indeed misinterpreted her discovery?

She finished folding the letter and returned it to the drawer. Now she didn't know what to think or how to feel. But she couldn't simply wait to find out the truth. She needed to act.

CHAPTER NINETEEN

D ARIUS BLINKED, HIS vision blurry, his head pounding. His mouth felt like he'd eaten cotton, and as he tried to focus, the light streaming in the windows sent shooting pain through head. He grabbed it with both hands as he closed his eyes. "The devil take me."

"Sorry, old chap. Even the devil doesn't want you."

He snapped his eyes open and then wished he hadn't, but forced himself to turn his head. Anthony stood by the fireplace in the converted bathhouse. "Bloody hell. What are you doing here? How did you find me? And why the hell does my head feel like I've been to hell and back?"

Anthony had the nerve to chuckle, but at least he did so softly. "You must be hurting if you use the word *hell* three times. Let me see if I can help clarify a few things for you. I'm here in this rather interesting billet because Archer sought me out and brought me here. I was on my way to spend Christmastide with you, as you had invited us. Lissa and I were at an inn a couple of towns away."

Darius frowned as he tried to remember Anthony arriving, which didn't help the pain, so he stopped. "And my head?"

"From what I understand, your wife discovered you here the night before last. When you went after her, you got into an argument with Archer and hit him. He hit you in return, only you fell back, and your head slammed against a rock. When you didn't wake up after a few hours, Archer grew concerned. He conferred with your butler, and it was determined they must seek me out, which is why I'm here."

Some of Darius's memory rushed back, causing him to moan with both emotional and physical pain. "I have to see my wife." He sat up, and the room started to spin.

"Whoa, there." Anthony's hand was suddenly on his shoulder. "You're not ready to move yet."

"Then you bloody well better get me a bucket if you don't want me to relieve myself on you."

His brother's hand immediately lifted, and in short order Darius was able to take care of his immediate bodily needs, which included tea and poached eggs with toast. He didn't eat a lot, as his stomach didn't seem to want much despite his unintended fast. But the tea seemed to lessen his head pains slightly.

He set his teacup down on the table next to the wingback chair Archer usually sat in. Since he couldn't remember why he'd hit the gamekeeper, he couldn't well blame the man. "I wish I could remember what happened."

Anthony, who now sat on the settee, leaned his elbows on his thighs. "Lissa said you have a concussion, so you may have some gaps in your memory, but it's only temporary until the swelling goes down."

Darius felt the back of his head and winced as he encountered a bump. "I remember Ellie coming here. I have no idea how she found me, but she thought I had a mistress. She kept wanting to know why I was here. I told her to leave, but when she did, I had to get her back." He started to shake his head then thought better of it. "I don't remember what happened after I ran out of here." His chest tightened at what he'd had and what he'd now lost. "All I know is I have to go to her. I can't have her despising me."

He rose. The room wobbled.

"Darius, no." Anthony stood too. "You were always frantic after a black mood, immediately wanting to fix things. I only saw them come upon you twice before you moved here to take over Hawthorne Park. Both times, after you became more yourself, you were anxious about everything."

"*Became more myself?* I don't even know who I am since these started." Darius sank back into the chair. "I'm not like you, confident in doing whatever you wish and not caring about what others think or even what your family thinks." He'd always looked down upon Anthony's penchant for flitting about—yet even after marrying, he and his wife continued to do secret investigations for various peers.

Anthony laughed. "Be like me? On no, brother. I thought I was expendable, being the fourth son. It was Mother who told me I had the freedom to do and be whatever and whoever I liked. Since I found gambling boring and horse breeding predictable, I had to search for what my life was meant for. It wasn't until I stepped in when a village lad was being beaten upon by a few Eton boys that I understood I was meant to help people. If you don't know who you are, then you can decide who you want to be. You're a tabula rasa."

Darius gripped the arms of the chair, needing to do something but having no direction. "I'm hardly that. I have to be the heir—I can't choose. My life is set before me. I have produced an heir and must have additional sons to ensure our line continues." And he wanted more than anything to continue the line with Ellie by his side, but how could he fix what he'd done?

Anthony finally sat again. "Then we know two things about you. You're not like Lord Durham, who is squandering away his inheritance frequenting the gaming hells. You're responsible. You care about those who depend upon you."

"Yes. And I need to get back to my wife and explain, or at least tell her *something*. I must make my children's first proper Christmastide a happy one." He stood quickly. This time the room tilted so much that he fell back into the chair. His stomach didn't like the feeling either, and he took deep breaths, hoping not to embarrass himself before his little brother by vomiting.

"You can't. Not yet. I don't know why you're cursed with these black moods and subsequent agitated periods, but Lissa thinks they may be due to a physical anomaly."

"Lissa thinks? What does she know about the body?" Darius paused. "And how does she know I have a concussion?" If she was wrong, he might be able to get to Ellie before dark.

"I forget that your most recent marriage did not follow the usual courtship." Anthony rose again before going to the sideboard and bringing back the teapot, refilling Darius's cup. "My wife, like yours, attended the Belinda School for Curious Ladies. There, as part of their first-year curriculum, they were educated on the human body and how to attend to illnesses, broken bones, diseases, and even sword and gunshot wounds. You see, the Duchess of Northwick has a strong and distinct dislike of physicians. The reason behind that is a far longer tale, but she ensures that all the ladies have these skills, and they are sworn to send for her if what they encounter is beyond their abilities. Under no scenario are they to send for a physician."

Even as Anthony explained, Darius remembered the confidence with which Ellie had attended to Peter not once, but twice, as well as her insistence that no physician be called, but Lady Northwick could be if needed. Still, it was such an unusual phenomenon that he couldn't help sharing his doubt. "And do we know if the duchess has any skill in this area? From my one meeting with her, it appears her interest was more of the intellectual pursuit as opposed to the practical application."

Anthony, who had returned the teapot to the sideboard, grinned. "Because she saved my life after I was shot and bleeding to death."

"What? You were shot? Where? When?" The fact that his brother, who was always too full of life for his own staid views, could have died had Darius's stomach clenching for a far more serious reason than standing.

"Not to worry. As you see, I am quite fine now, but it wasn't a sure thing. I was shot by a former soldier while attending my captain's wedding, or rather the Viscount of Blackmore's wedding. Her Grace is not only well studied but has applied her knowledge, so I am here to tell you today. That is to say, if my wife or your wife tell you what to do based on whatever malady you have, you should listen."

He was still imagining his life without Anthony and the agony that would be, when he realized he would never have married Ellie if not for the duchess's skills. "Then what you are saying is that no matter how strongly I feel that I must fix my marriage as best I'm able this very moment, I cannot do so now."

"Exactly." Anthony grinned.

"I understand. I am not happy this is the way it has to be, and come tomorrow—" Darius froze, frantic that he'd slept too long. "Tell me, is tomorrow Christmas Day?"

"It is."

That meant the yule log would be set afire and he would not be there. The house was even now being decorated with greenery. Did Ellie have the children helping? Was she with the children at all, or was she so furious with him that she had no desire to be in their company? At that thought, a memory of the hurt in her gaze resurfaced, and he groaned.

"What's wrong?"

He looked at his brother. "I hurt her. And then I didn't explain why. The mood was still upon me, and I tried so hard not to say the wrong thing, but I know she feels betrayed."

Anthony's blue gaze didn't leave him. "Why did you not tell her of your black moods? Surely you didn't think you could hide it from her for the rest of your life?"

"When you have these, you don't think your life will be very long. So yes, I thought to hide them from her until that time."

His brother's face paled considerably. "Then they have become worse."

Darius started to nod, then stopped. "Yes."

"I had feared so when you requested a wife. Now that she knows, will you tell her the truth?"

Would he? "I told Dinah, and it ended all communication I had with her. She called me a madman. I call myself a monster. I'm not sure I could bear what Ellie might call me." He paused, not sure he could communicate the depth of his feelings. "Anthony, having seen what life could be like with her, I'm not sure I could continue if I don't have her."

His brother audibly sucked in his breath. "You love her. I didn't expect that."

"Neither did I. But she's everything I could ever want in a wife. More than that, she's special, unique, and if it weren't for my damned black moods, we would fit together well, like a bow and arrow."

Anthony raised his brows. "Truly? I understand she may be lacking in a few areas, though she surpasses expectations in others."

Anger flashed through Darius so fast that he winced at the throbbing that started in his head. Closing his eyes, he tried to calm himself, but he was already in an agitated state. "She's perfect." He opened his eyes, daring his brother to deny it.

"I can see she's perfect for you. I understand. There aren't many women who would be perfect for me, but Lissa is. Since that is the case, then I suggest you be honest with your wife. From what Lissa tells me, no one has a more encompassing heart than Ellie." Anthony shrugged. "Who knows, she may have suggestions for helping your moods."

He'd seen the best physicians back when he still lived with his parents, and nothing had helped. He'd learned to lie to the men of science, so as not to be branded insane, his biggest fear. No, his biggest fear now was losing Ellie. "I will tell her. I can no longer lie, as it would hurt her too much to be lied to again. I only hope she will forgive me and not fear me, or worse."

"What could be worse than your wife fearing you?"

"The woman I love hating me." Saying it out loud felt like a prophecy of doom, but he refused to follow that train of thought. It was his black moods that had brought him to this, and now, out of their clutches, he was anxious to fight for Ellie, even if she no longer wanted him.

Anthony walked back over to the sideboard and poured two drinks. He returned and handed Darius a brandy.

Darius raised an eyebrow in question.

His younger brother sat on the settee and took a sip from his glass. "We need to strategize your approach, and I think better with a drink."

Strategize? As he took a cautious sip, Darius felt the anxiousness to fix his problems immediately dull a bit. "I welcome any suggestions."

Anthony put down his glass. "Lissa told me that your wife used to mother the ladies at their school. Has she taken to your children?"

At the thought of Ellie with Peter and Maggie, he smiled. "She loves them, and they love her. I couldn't have asked for a better mother for them."

"Perfect." Anthony grinned again, an impish light in his blue gaze. "When you return to the house, visit your children first, especially as it will be Christmas Day. While there, send for your wife. If she sees you first while you are with your children, she won't be able to yell." He lifted his glass again. "And if you're lucky, it will mellow her mood a bit." He took another sip.

Darius pulled his head back, not a little surprised by his brother's idea. Then again, he couldn't deny the fact that the man had some valid points, and right now, he was willing to do anything to win Ellie back.

CHAPTER TWENTY

December 25, Christmas Day

ELLIE ALLOWED BEACHAM to take her cloak, her relationship with her butler reduced to short orders and minimal responses. She turned to Lissa, who had arrived the day before, shortly after Sophie left. Ellie had cried watching Sophie leave, feeling so absolutely alone, so when Lissa and Anthony arrived, she'd cried again, though with happiness.

It was obvious to her, as it had been to Sophie, that she was very emotional since her encounter with Darius. She felt as if something terrible was about to occur, and even jumped in church when the vicar had dropped his spectacles. Unfortunately, Lissa had noticed, and the coach ride home had involved Ellie revealing her disappointment in her husband, which had been rather awkward in front of his brother. But Anthony hadn't made a single comment.

"My lady, the nursemaid has requested your presence in the nursery."

At Beecham's statement, she frowned since she'd spent the early morning hours with the children. Why would Anna make such a request when she was well aware they had guests.

Lissa waved her off. "Go ahead. I'm going to settle in the parlor and discuss my observations on the sermon with my husband."

Anthony stepped behind his wife. "In other words, she's

going to tell me what everyone's behavior told her and see if I concur. Then she'll hound me about which investigation I've decided to accept next." The man sighed as if Lissa's questions were tiresome.

She slapped Anthony's arm. "Don't listen to him. He loves debating which investigation we should pursue."

"True. But I'm so much more sympathetic when it appears I'm persistently being nagged."

Ellie put her hand on her hip. "Do remember, my dear Lord Bellamore, that I know your wife quite well, and never would I believe she has nagged you. Held a dagger to your throat, perhaps, but never nagged."

At Lissa's laughter, Anthony smiled. "I forget you two are dear friends. And please, call me Anthony. We are family now."

A pang of longing hit Ellie's heart hard, and she moved her hand from her hip to her chest. "Thank you. That is most gracious of you."

"Come on, husband, we have much to discuss." Lissa took Anthony's hand and pulled him toward the parlor.

Ellie stood alone for a moment in the entry, Beacham having disappeared. The silence as she stared up at the grand staircase seemed to intensify her loneliness. Going to church had been difficult without Darius, as many had asked about him. She'd simply given them the same excuse he'd given her, not willing to share her agony with those she barely knew.

Giving herself a mental shake, she started up the stairs. She wasn't alone. She had two wonderful children who, she was quite sure, loved her almost as much as she loved them. She'd never leave Maggie and Peter, no matter how difficult her marriage became.

When she came to the nursery door, she listened for a moment. She couldn't hear anyone talking, so the children could be sleeping. She wouldn't be surprised after how excited they'd been earlier in the morning.

She smiled at the thought and softly turned the knob—then

peeked her head in and froze at the tableau before her.

Darius sat at the children's table drawing something. Maggie stood at his shoulder, while Peter sat on his lap. Both children seemed fascinated by the sweeping movements of his pastel crayon. Ellie's heart thundered in her chest with pleasure that the children had become more comfortable with their father, but on the heels of that thought was another, much sadder scenario, where Darius and she would have separate times with them.

Deciding that Anna could wait, she started to close the door when Maggie spotted her.

"Mother! Come look!" The little girl ran to her and took her hand, pulling her in. "Father is going to build us a zoo."

"A zoo?" Ellie didn't remember telling the children about zoos.

Darius stopped drawing and turned his head to look at her.

Her breath caught at the black and blue skin beneath his eye. What had happened?

He pointed to the paper on the table. "It won't have live animals. We shall have wooden ones that Peter and Maggie can play with."

Peter, who'd still been gazing at the paper, reluctantly turned his head. "Papa is building me a big elephant."

Ellie forced a smile. "An elephant? That's very exciting. What other animals will you have?"

Maggie let go of her hand as they reached the table, and pointed. "This is the giraffe, and over here will be the hippa...*hippamatamas*, and here will be the lion."

Ellie followed Maggie's finger to avoid looking at Darius. The drawing was not excellent, but the images made it clear what they were. "And what is that next to the lion?"

Peter piped up. "That's a *rino-sorceress*. They're mean and have a big horn."

She nodded. "Yes, they can be dangerous. Will there be zebras?"

Maggie's finger immediately moved. "Right here. And father

said we need to add a dragon and call it Draco."

Ellie's heart hitched at Darius's thoughtfulness. "Where will he be?"

"I wanted to have you choose his placement." Darius's voice slid through her. It wasn't angry or contrite, just controlled, formal.

"I'll have to think about it."

He looked first at Peter than Maggie. "I want to talk more about the zoo with your mother. You two can decide what other animals you would like."

"Yes!" Peter hopped off Darius's lap. "Maggie, where's the book?"

Immediately, Maggie ran to a bookshelf and grabbed a book from it before plopping down on the floor as Peter hobbled over on his crutch.

Darius rose, forcing her to look at him. "Shall we?" He held his arm out toward the door.

She gave a short nod and strode forward. Now that he was back inside the house, she didn't know how to feel. She was angry and hurt, but also curious. Anthony's letter to Darius still confused her. She'd planned to ask Anthony about it at dinner, but now she had Darius at hand.

They continued down the hall in silence until he stopped at the first door to her glass terrace and opened it.

She stepped through before him and strolled to the settee where they'd first made love. He hadn't been in the room since then. If he thought to seduce her, he wouldn't succeed. She was far too angry with him and just hoped she could keep from yelling.

Settling her hands on the top of the settee, she controlled her voice. "Did you come home just for Christmas, or will you be staying for a while?"

He'd been walking toward her but halted at her question. "I would stay here every day for the rest of my life, if I could."

"And are you going to tell me why you can't stay here with

your family? I mean, tell me the *truth* about why you hide away in a single-room building in the middle of the north wood?" She waved her arm toward the window where her telescope was still set up, since she'd continued to watch the building at night. Though it had been lit, she'd seen little movement except Mr. Archer entering and exiting, along with Beacham.

Darius looked to the window and ambled over to the telescope. He set his eye to it then stood again. "This is how you found me."

"I had hoped to discover a new star cluster, but instead, I discovered you on this very property, when you said you were traveling. Why were you there?" Her voice had risen, her anger taking over her hurt. "I want to know what could pull you from your family and yet be so near."

"The answer to that is me. It's me that forces our separation. I do not wish it."

"By Jupiter, don't talk to me in riddles! I'm not your brother. I don't like mysteries. Tell me plainly or don't tell me anything and just get out!" She pointed toward the door, her patience gone, her heartache resurfacing.

He took a step toward her then stopped. "I beg your forgiveness for being so cryptic. I've only told a few people why I must retreat to the north wood, and only one of them knew all."

She crossed her arms at the reminder that others knew but she had been left in the dark. She'd always enjoyed the dark, but not when it meant a lack of knowledge. It just hurt. "Anthony?"

Darius raised his right brow. "My brother? No. He only knows what he saw when we were younger. No, the one person I truly shared my secret with was Dinah."

She didn't think the pain of betrayal could be worse, but hearing that he'd shared something of great importance with his first wife but kept it from her had her gripping the back of the settee until her knuckles turned white. "I see. You felt comfortable confiding in her." She couldn't look at him, the softer feelings she'd held for him shrinking even more. Once again, she wasn't quite good enough. "I understand. Then there is no need to share with me what you shared with her. I would not presume to impose on such a sacred trust."

She forced herself to let go of the settee and turn toward the door.

Darius snorted. "Hardly a sacred trust."

His words brought tears to her eyes. She wasn't even worthy of learning a secret that wasn't important? She didn't turn back toward him, not willing for him see how close she'd come to loving him, but that tiny flame she'd kept going after reading Anthony's letter extinguished itself. "I should not have intruded on your privacy. I shall not bother you again about it...or anything." She walked to the door.

"Ellie, wait."

She didn't. She closed her hand around the knob and turned it. Just as she started to open the door, it was slammed shut, the knob slipping out of her grasp, Darius's hand firmly on the wood.

"We have not finished our conversation."

His voice had grown cold, which made it so much easier for her. "Was there something else we need to discuss?"

"Yes."

Though he stood just to the side of her, his hand still on the closed door, she didn't turn to face him. Instead, she turned away and strode toward the closest wingback chair. Unfortunately, she bumped into the table next to it, toppling it. Instead of feeling embarrassed, she felt vindicated. Satisfaction filled her, and she continued past the chair and purposely tipped over another small table. Again, a small feeling of ugly pleasure flew through her.

Then her gaze landed on the telescope. She headed for it, the thought of throwing it through the glass windows filling her with an odd sort of anticipation. But two steps away from it, Darius yanked it out of the way.

"No. If you're angry at me, then hit me, not some innocent inanimate object."

She rounded on him. "That telescope is far from innocent. It was *your* gift to me to make me think you were thoughtful. To make me think I was worthy of being your wife. And then, like you, it betrayed me and revealed to me your perfidy. It showed me the truth of what you thought of me—not nearly as worthy as Dinah."

He stepped back, setting the telescope behind him to protect it. "That's what you think? You're twenty times as worthy as Dinah."

She crossed her arms over her chest, tired of the conversation. "You said you had something else you wished to discuss?"

Darius closed his eyes for a moment then opened them. "Yes. I wish to tell you why I had to leave the house and stay in the old bathhouse alone."

She raised her brows. "But that's a secret. One I'm not supposed to know."

"I was wrong not to tell you. I didn't wish you to feel betrayed." His hands formed fists. "Now I see I only made you hate me sooner."

She started at his use of the word *hate*. *Did* she hate him?

"What I should have told you is that I hide away in the north wood because I suffer from bouts of melancholia. And when that happens, I am not in full control of my thoughts, feelings, or, most importantly, my words. Rather than inflict my mercurial presence on others, act and say things that would destroy my relationships, I stay away from everyone. No one wants a monster in the house."

Despite her need for revenge, a drop of sympathy sizzled against the fiery anger in her heart. "And that is the only way for you to cure this? Hide from everyone...alone?" She let her doubt that what he spoke was the truth seep into her tone.

"I have tried all avenues. My parents brought in the best physicians to cure me when I wasn't yet sixteen. After numerous purgatives, bloodlettings, special foods, cold baths, and one session of blistering, I overheard a physician suggesting to my father that they take me to a private madhouse. After that, I pretended to get better, always hiding this malady I have, which my uncle, who was the marquess before me, also had. He drowned himself in the north pond."

She stared in horror, not just at the suicide, but at what Darius must have endured. Everything he described was part of why the Duchess of Northwick had insisted on educating them all on how to treat the unwell. To be so set upon by the medical community and then threatened with a madhouse had to have been terrifying for such a young man.

Her anger dissipated, and she was unable to do much but empathize—but that still left behind the raw hurt, which was far worse. "Why could you not tell me this?"

He cocked his head slightly. "When I was married before, I could not live with the guilt of lying to my wife, so I told her. After that, she wanted nothing to do with me. She called me a madman and insisted on leaving me, but I couldn't let her. I couldn't allow her to tell others, and I still needed another son." He moved to face the windows of the terrace. "My hope was that if I eventually succumbed to my black moods, my wife would be here for my children until they were grown. I wanted them to have the love of at least one parent, and not the formal relationship many children have today with their mother or father. I was raised with loving parents and wanted that for my own children, but I cannot know how long I will be here."

He turned and faced her. "I didn't want to tell you because I feared the same rejection." He took a step forward. "And rejection from you would truly end any reason for living."

She sucked in a breath at the sincerity in his eyes. "Why?"

"Because I have come to love you. I married you for my children, but I now know you are as important to me as you are to them. Your presence in our lives has made us whole, a family." He looked away. "I cannot be whole." He returned his gaze to hers. "Yet with you, I wish it so with all of my being. I want to be the husband you need, the one you can depend upon, your protector and your champion. Ellie, please forgive me."

Her throat closed with emotion at his impassioned plea. She blinked away the tears in her eyes. He wanted to be everything she'd always dreamed of but never expected.

Yet a niggling doubt remained. She swallowed hard, needing to ask. "But how could you think that I would act like Dinah?"

He shook his head. "I don't know. Though I've constantly thought about how different you are from her, I feared having life return to how it had been with her. And after understanding how perfect you are, I became more worried, because you make everyone's life better by being a part of it, and I couldn't lose that." He took another step closer. "I still can't."

Perfect? He thought her *perfect*? She was far from—

Maybe she was perfect for *him*?

Darius took two more steps toward her before going down on one knee. "I am no more than a monster and don't deserve your forgiveness, yet I kneel here before you, asking for it anyway, because there is nothing else I can do. Nothing I wish to do without you…my wife."

Ellie's chest tightened, warming as her love for her husband rushed back into her heart like the Great Comet of 1811. Tears fell down her cheeks and she knelt to join him. "Oh, my love. I do forgive you. You've been through so much, alone, fighting to survive. I can help. I could never let you continue alone now that I know the truth."

"Ellie…" he whispered before pulling her to him.

She wrapped her arms around his neck, holding on to him as his sweet kiss healed her heart.

He pulled his head back and gazed at her, love clear in his eyes. "My Ellie. I love you and will until the stars fail to shine."

She smiled. "You do realize that depends on which star."

He chuckled. "All of them."

She widened her eyes. "That's forever."

"Exactly." He kissed her again, a sweet, gentle promise that he meant every word.

When he broke the kiss, she raised her brows. "And you

promise to never lie to me again."

"I—I do, but I reserve the right to lie about any happy surprise I may be preparing for you, such as a present."

She pretended to ponder his caveat. "That is fair, as long as that applies to me as well."

"I agree."

An inkling of guilt tainted her perfect happiness. She needed to take Sophie's advice. "I must also tell you something that, while I have not lied about it, I have not been forthcoming about either."

"Truly? Then please, tell me."

She blew air out from between her closed lips, her need to tell him fighting against her willingness to do so. "I tend to knock things over." She watched his reaction, bracing for his surprise or questions, but mostly for his disappointment.

He smiled gently. "I know."

"What? How?"

"My dear wife, we all know, except the children. Why do you think the flower vases are on the top shelf of a bookcase in my study?"

She frowned. "You said you disliked them."

"Indeed, I do. Immensely. But I had them moved up there because I didn't wish you to feel guilty for knocking one over, which you would have eventually, based on where they had been."

Her surprise was complete, even if her heart melted at his thoughtfulness. Could he really still feel she was perfect for him? "You must know, I won't ever be able to stop. I've tried. Mother had me take classes in walking, but I always failed. I'll always be"—she swallowed hard at the word her mother always said—"*clumsy.*"

He brushed a stray hair from her face with gentle fingers. "And I'll always have these bouts of melancholia. They will never go away. Can you still care for me despite that?"

Though his tone was light, she sensed the tension in his body as he held her. "Not only can I care for you, but I love you and I can accept that because it's a part of you."

His gray eyes shone with pleasure at her words. "You love me? Then I am more than content."

"I might even be able to help you with your malady." As she said the words, a treatise she'd read came to mind.

"You don't have to help. I just need to know that you will be here when I come home, and *want* me to be here."

"I do want you, always."

He smiled slyly. "I want you always, and especially now."

He lowered his head, and this time when he kissed her, his tongue begged entrance, and she opened her mouth to welcome him in.

CHAPTER TWENTY-ONE

Darius felt as if he were tasting his wife for the first time. Everything he'd thought he'd lost was once again in his arms, and he needed to show her exactly how much he loved her. Barely holding back his need to take her, he unpinned her hair from the back of her head and brushed his fingers through the long red strands, even as his tongue sparred with hers.

She tasted better than he remembered, and her unique, tantalizing scent filled his nostrils. It was her and a light fruit that he still couldn't identify. Suddenly, it came to him, and he broke their kiss. "Apricot!"

Her eyes fluttered open. "Apricot?"

He grinned, very pleased with himself. "Your scent. It's apricot, is it not?"

She broke into a wide smile. "It is! No one has ever identified it before. You have a most impressive nose." She punctuated her statement by touching his nose with her index finger.

Immediately, he snatched her finger with his mouth and sucked.

"Oh." Her eyes widened.

He slowly released her finger. "I wish to taste every part of you."

She stared at her finger for a moment before a sly smile tilted her lips. "Not yet. I want to taste you first." Her gaze moved downward between them.

A spike of need ran through his sac, causing him to harden beneath his pantaloons. "Why would you want to do that?"

She pulled from his arms and sat back on her heels. "Because I want to give you a Christmas gift, and I know you will like it."

Doubt niggled its way into his contentment. "How do you know I will like it?"

Her chin lifted with pride, her smile rather smug. "I'm very well read."

He raised his right eyebrow. Yes, she was intelligent and learned, but on such a subject? "You've read about how to provide *fellatus?*"

"I have indeed. Of course, the duchess doesn't know that we ladies found a particular book that is very educational in this area, and none of us plan to tell her. So, you must also keep our secret. For how would it be if Sophie or Georgie or Rose, or any of the other Curious Ladies, were to go to their marriage ignorant of the pleasures of the flesh?"

He pulled his head back, not a little shocked, even as his body reacted to her words, making his pantaloons downright uncomfortable.

"Now, if you will be so kind as to sit back, I will be happy to release you." She laid her hand on his erection beneath his clothing.

He barely kept from pressing her hand against him. Beyond pleased that she would wish to taste him, yet still in shock, he found himself unable to move.

Luckily, that didn't stop his determined wife as she moved her hand to the buttons of his fall. Recognizing her intent, he did as she asked and sat on the floor, his back up against the chair behind him. He gritted his teeth as she unbuttoned him, brushing her hand against his erection, but as the material loosened, he was able to breathe a little easier.

That lasted but a moment before Ellie expertly cradled him in her hand and set her mouth to his tip. Her tongue encircled his head, licking at the top before stroking the underside from the base to the rim.

He sucked in his breath as hot pleasure filled him. Then her lips encircled him, and she sucked him into her mouth. He fisted his hands at the exquisite feel of her moist mouth upon him. As she pulled up and moved down again, he ground his teeth, trying to stay in control of his release. Not only did he need her, but his need to act immediately was still with him, despite his holding off a day to come home, which now drove him to take her *hard*. He couldn't do that with his wife.

She continued with slow strokes before her gaze found his as she held him in her mouth.

He swallowed hard at her look. "Elle, you need to stop now."

Her brow furrowed and she released him. "Why? Don't you like it?"

He cupped her head in his hands. "I love it. So much so that I'm going to release in your beautiful mouth."

She grinned. "I'd like that." Her thumb continued to stroke him as she still held him in her hand.

He barely held back a groan. She may have read about what to expect, but he was quite sure the taste would be a surprise. "But my need for you is riding me hard, and I want to give you pleasure as well."

Her eyes rounded. "Are you saying if I keep touching you that you will take me fast?"

He dropped his hands from her head, shocked by the hope in her eyes. "You wish to be taken in such a way?"

Instead of answering him, she lowered her head and sucked him into her mouth as far as he would go, then, as she pulled her head up, she dragged her teeth lightly along his skin.

It was too much. He pulled her atop him and rolled her over.

She squealed with laughter.

Her delight fueled his need, and he lifted himself to bunch her skirts to her waist. Quickly, he moved his hand between her thighs. Finding her ready for him, he positioned himself, still trying to hold on to some civility.

She grinned, then reached into the neckline of her dress and pulled her breasts out above it. "You can taste me too."

He couldn't have resisted if he'd tried. Bracing himself, he lowered his mouth to one luscious nipple and sucked.

She arched into his mouth, pressing her breast into his face. "More."

He sucked harder as her moans of pleasure filled his ears, but his own control slipped away. Unable to resist, he plunged into her wet depths.

Her hands came down on his arse and she pulled him against her.

Somewhere in his brain was the fact that this was his wife and he should be gentler, but his body didn't care what he thought. Unable to hold back, he let go of her nipple and moved to the other as he pulled out. As he thrust back into her, he sucked hard.

She grabbed his hair and pulled his head even closer as her hips met his, sending a wave of exquisite pleasure through his whole body.

He let go of her breast and lowered himself to capture her lips, sweeping his tongue inside to fully taste Ellie as he thrust into her.

She grasped his back, and her booted feet pressed against his arse, pushing him into her as fast as he pulled out.

Suddenly, she tightened around him, and he couldn't hold back any longer. His release was powerful and long. Every fiber of his being filled with a bliss he'd never experienced as he spent himself deep inside the woman he loved.

She broke their frantic kiss, and her scream of rapture echoed around him, filling his heart with pure joy.

He wasn't quite sure when he stopped moving, their bodies were so in rhythm with each other, but he did notice that she ran her hands lightly over the back of his head and shoulders. Lifting his head, he gazed into her bright-blue gaze. "I love you, Ellie."

Her hands moved to each side of his head and her gaze

turned soft. "I love you too. You make me feel wanted just as I am. Thank you for showing me how much." Tears gathered in her eyes.

Concerned, he rose up on his elbows. "I do want you. I want you like this. I want your heavenly body. But I also want your thoughts and kind actions, your laughter and your wise counsel. I love everything about you. Tell me why you cry, and I will fix it."

She sniffed. "Oh, Darius. My tears are not of sadness but of joy. You make me happier than I ever thought possible, more than I thought I deserved."

His heart constricted at her words. "You deserve a better husband than I, but I promise to try to make you happy every day."

"You already do. I'm beginning to think that we are perfect for each other."

He nodded. "I do believe you're right. If this is the case, then—"

A loud knocking on the door interrupted him, and he froze.

Ellie's brows rose.

"My lord! Is anything wrong? The maid said she heard a scream coming from this room!"

Ellie touched the chair near her head and grinned.

Darius gave her a nod. "Everything is fine, Beacham. I was just moving furniture. Lady Ferncroft isn't sure which way she likes it."

Ellie giggled, and for some reason it had him growing hard inside her. Surprised, he almost forgot his butler. Almost.

"Would you like me to send up a footman to assist you?"

"Beacham, this kind of furniture moving is strictly between me and my wife."

Ellie clapped a hand over her mouth, even as her silent laughter vibrated around him, making it even more difficult to remember that the door might open at any moment.

He wished Beacham gone, but he didn't hear footsteps. What was the man waiting for? After what seemed like an interminable time but was probably less than a minute, the butler responded.

"I do hope my lady finds an arrangement that she enjoys."

She let out a bark of laughter at that. It appeared the butler had finally realized what they were doing, yet instead of turning red with embarrassment, Ellie grinned. "Don't worry, Beacham. I'm sure there are numerous arrangements I will like." She laughed outright, which just made Darius harder.

As footsteps finally moved away from the door, he shook his head at his wife. "I will never be able to say the word 'furniture' again."

"That won't be a problem. I'll be happy to bring it up when appropriate. For instance, now."

"Now?"

"Yes. While I like this arrangement. I believe I would like to be on top, but this time with you on this piece of 'furniture.'" She wrapped her hand around the leg of the chair near her head, much like she'd wrapped her hand around him.

His body immediately responded, and he growled low in his throat. "I can make those arrangements, but only if we completely strip the furniture."

It took them a long while to fully undress. He couldn't stop kissing her, whether it was her neck, elbow, or back, but eventually they were unclothed, and he was seated in the chair. He held his hand out to her. "I am at your service."

"So you are." She stared at his erection, which jerked at her look. Then, instead of taking his hand, she walked behind him and hugged him around the neck, placing a kiss on his head. "I suppose we'll have to keep Beacham now that he knows our secret."

He frowned. "Keep Beacham? Why? Was he leaving?" He didn't want to train a new butler, especially one entrusted with his secret.

Her hands moved to his shoulders. "It was a possibility. I did threaten to dismiss him and Mrs. Torbett."

"What? Why?"

Ellie moved to stand in front of him and set her hands on her hips. "They refused to tell me why you were in the wood. That is highly unacceptable."

It had never occurred to him what a position he'd put his servants in. Beacham hadn't said anything to him about it when delivering food at the old bathhouse after Ellie had found him. That the butler was loyal to both of them proved how trustworthy he was. "I understand your concern, but I believe that now we can rest assured Beacham will continue his loyalty to both of us."

"I know. That he was so loyal to you to keep your secret means a great deal. And now we must hope he keeps this secret as well." She held her arms out.

At the sight of her fully naked body standing before him, he gazed his fill. From her long red hair to her large breasts and full hips, he couldn't believe she was his. "My love for you will never be a secret, whether from the servants, our neighbors, or our children. I want everyone to know that I love you and am the luckiest of men that you love me in return." He held his hand out once again.

Her eyes shimmered. "You make me so happy, Darius."

"Then allow me to make you even happier." He patted his thigh with his free hand.

She gave him another sly smile. "I don't doubt that at all."

His wife straddled him and slowly lowered herself until she was fully impaled. "Oh, I think I'm going to like this arrangement *very* much."

With her nipples before him, he grinned before looking up at her. "I know you will." Then he latched on to a nipple and gently nibbled.

She grabbed his shoulders and started to rock.

As the friction built and their pleasure grew, a contented feeling settled deep in his soul. Though he would take her to the stars, he would always come back into orbit about her. She was the center of his universe, now and forever.

EPILOGUE

January 5, 1818
Twelfth Night

E LLIE COULDN'T STOP smiling. The ballroom was filled with everyone she'd invited, and they were having a wonderful evening. But the best part was that her husband stood at her side. As she'd predicted, his black mood had not arrived yet. Though she hadn't told him of her theory, she was quite sure that the full moon was a significant determinant of when it occurred. She'd also done some research that might mitigate his symptoms a little when the time came.

But for now, he was with her and happy to be so, and he made an excellent black hole with his black clothing and cape when next to her universe costume. He'd opted for no mask and allowed her to place a ring of sliver stars about his head, which made him appear the king of the dark. She'd also forgone a mask, since as hostess, everyone would need to know her, even if her red hair made it clear anyway. Her own blue gown with silver stars sewn all around it—along with a comet, two nebulae, and seven planets—sparkled in the lamplight. Darius had called her a "heavenly body" when he first saw her in it. The memory of the other time he called her that had her blushing.

Darius squeezed her hand before leaning in. "Is that not your friend Lady Georgina dancing with Lord Ashfield?"

She looked to the dance floor. Since she and Darius knew all her friends' costumes, it was easy to figure out who was who for her, despite the masquerade. Georgie wore an emerald-green gown with colorful feathers sewn into it. Even her mask sported red and orange feathers on the sides, and her hairpiece had an array of brightly colored feathers. The man dancing with her wore a king costume, though he didn't appear to be any particular king. "If the man dressed as a king is Lord Ashfield, then yes, it is."

"She is quite energetic, is she not?"

"Yes, she enjoys dancing. It's always amazed me that she is so quick in her movements, yet when she's bird-watching, she's absolutely still."

"An interesting observation. Perhaps her frequent inactivity is why she is so active at other times."

Ellie turned to Darius. "What an astute observation."

He lifted her hand from his arm and kissed it. "Your praise is welcome."

Though his actions appeared simple, his finger stroking her palm was anything but. "Darius, we have a house full of guests. We must wait."

He grinned. "I know, but teasing you is so enjoyable."

His gaze dipped to her bosom, and she pulled out her fan to cool herself. Since Christmas, she'd kept discovering other sides to the man she had married. All of them were intriguing.

"Ellie, I'm so proud of you." The Duchess of Northwick approached with her husband. "Your first hosted ball is a true success."

"It is because of you, Joanna, that it is so. Your acceptance of my invitation made it *the* ball to attend."

The duchess waved off her comment. "Not at all. James and I were excited to see one of our students so well established and successful. I can't tell you how pleased I am that you won't be hiring a governess and tutor. Your education far exceeds anything they could offer."

Ellie felt her cheeks heating at such lavish praise. "Like you, I have a husband who understands what it is to have an educated wife." She looked to Darius.

"And very glad I am at that." Darius gave an arrogant nod to punctuate his statement.

The duke nodded as well. "It's good to meet another enlightened man. Hopefully, more will come to appreciate our students."

The musicians cued up a waltz and the duchess turned to her husband. Without a word between them, the Duke of Northwick gave Ellie and Darius a short nod. "If you will excuse us?"

Ellie grinned as the couple took their place on the dance floor. She turned to her own husband. "They love to waltz, and do so beautifully. Just watch them."

"I'd rather watch you."

That Darius felt so strongly for her had her feeling sorry for her classmates who had yet to find their own love. Scanning the room for her friends, she searched for Sophie, who wore a white shepherdess costume. Unfortunately, there were at least nine women dressed similarly. But as Ellie's gaze fell on a short monk, she sucked in her breath. What was Rose thinking to be speaking to the three gentlemen by the punch table? "I must go save Rose. She'll ruin her reputation."

Darius did not release her arm. "That is no longer your concern. Does she not have a chaperone tonight?"

He was right, of course. Quickly, she spotted Lord Sommerset and Lord Harewood by the terrace doors, but Lady Sommerset and Dory seemed to have vanished. "Lord Harewood is her brother and chaperone, and he's standing by the terrace doors. He's the one in a musketeer costume speaking to the other monk we have tonight."

"Then let us make our way there."

Her husband expertly led her through the crush. They had almost reached their goal when Darius's parents intercepted them. Despite her concern over Rose, Ellie felt her heart warm that she'd been able to convince Darius's parents to attend the ball.

Lady Roxburgh, in a full mask and long Grecian toga, held her hands out. "My dear, thank you so much for inviting us. We are having a marvelous time."

Ellie took the duchess's hand as Her Grace leaned in closer. "No one knows they have another duke among them, so we are truly enjoying ourselves."

Darius's father—dressed as a pirate, also masked and complete with real pegleg—chuckled. "Son, we would be happy to travel south every year for this wonderful event."

"I have my wife to thank for your enjoyment. It is a rare pleasure to see you both out and about in a social setting."

Lord Roxburgh looked at Ellie. "Actually, I have *you* to thank for making my son happy."

She blushed at the compliment. "It is a mutual feeling, Your Grace."

Lady Roxburgh squeezed Ellie's hands and let go. "We will not keep you from attending to others. We just wished to tell you of our appreciation before the night ends."

As the two wound their way through the crowd, Darius took her arm once again. "I don't know what you wrote in your letter to convince them to change their mind, but I thank you for giving them this night."

She wasn't sure she deserved so many accolades. "I only explained that since they could wear masks, no one would know them, so there was no reason to forgo our ball. I put forth the situation logically and hoped they could see past their natural emotional response to social gatherings."

"Ellie, what seems so simple to you is often complicated for others. It is part of why I love you."

She met his gaze and felt another wave of love for him. "And I appreciate that you supported my whim to host this ball, for none of the festivities would have happened without you. And I'm particularly happy I didn't have to be escorted by Anthony." She grimaced, having dreaded such a charade.

"Speaking of my brother, he appears to have cornered Lord

Harewood and Lord Sommerset by the punch table, but I don't see Lady Rose now."

Ellie did a quick scan of the ballroom. He was right. "I also don't see Sophie, and I am her chaperone. Perhaps we should split up and tackle both tasks at once."

"I prefer not to, but I understand your concern. Very well, I will talk with the lords about the strangely absent Lady Rose, and you search out Lady Sophie."

As they parted, Ellie made a note where every shepherdess was and began a methodical search. It didn't take long to be sure it was indeed Sophie who was missing, though she did get pulled away for a moment or two by Lady Saunders and Lady Chelton, who seemed to forget they were friends in their anxiousness to invite her to tea. Once away from them again, she counted shepherdesses. There were only eight, which could mean that Sophie had left for the ladies' retiring room.

Seeing that her husband was no longer in the room, she hesitated to leave. One of them should be present. They were the hosts. Impatiently, she strode toward the table with the punch and took a glass, absently sipping it. Soon dinner would be called, and it would be difficult to find anyone in the crush.

Finally, her husband reentered the ballroom and made his way to her.

"Where is Rose? Tell me her brother did not send her to her room."

Darius shook his head, his lips twitching. "No. It seems your classmate was challenged to a game of billiards. Lord Harewood found her in the middle of the game and, since she was winning, thought it best not to expose her. He's waiting to escort her back to the ball. Lord Sommerset found his brother Christopher there as well, and expressly, though quietly, commanded him to return to the ballroom as soon as his card game was complete."

Relieved that Rose was safely chaperoned, she smiled. "I'm pleased that one lady is well attended, but now I must find Sophie."

Her husband's right eyebrow rose. "You didn't find her?"

"No. I plan to check the—" Someone bumped into her. Though her husband caught her arm, as she turned, her punch spilled all over the shepherdess dress of Sophie. "Oh, Sophie."

Sophie, usually so calm and reflective, appeared a bit wild-eyed as she looked about before gazing down at her ruined costume. She raised her head. "It was my fault. I'd best change."

She turned to leave, and Ellie grabbed her hand. Something was wrong. "Come to my room. I have a simple domino cape in my chest that you can wear."

Sophie hesitated, still scanning the room. Finally, she nodded.

Ellie looked up at Darius. "I'll return shortly."

He glanced at Sophie and also nodded. That he understood something was amiss relieved her. Quickly, she looped her arm through Sophie's and guided her out. In the entryway, she felt Sophie tense before she almost pulled Ellie up the stairs.

Concern wormed its way into Ellie's heart as she guided Sophie to her room. Once there, her friend seemed to return to her usual calm. In the lamplight, Ellie noticed that Sophie's hair was a bit messy and her cap was askew. "Come, let us get you out of your costume."

That Sophie didn't say anything as Ellie pulled the outer costume from her was not particularly unusual. Sophie didn't talk much unless with the Curious Ladies, and even then, it was only when she had something significant to say.

"Come sit at my dressing table so I can remove the cap." Sophie did as requested. Sometimes she reminded Ellie of a bird that might fly away at any moment. Other times, she was like a flower that reached its face to the sun, quietly living and thriving. "Did something happen downstairs? I couldn't find you."

Since Sophie always told the truth, Ellie waited patiently for an answer as she unpinned the shepherdess cap and brushed out her friend's brown hair. It was the color of coffee and cream, and was so soft, it didn't wish to stay where she wound it.

"I went to the ladies' retiring room with Rose and Georgie,

but forgot my crook. I sent them on ahead while I searched for it. On my way back to the ballroom, I lost my way."

"I'm sorry." Ellie added the last pin and set down the brush, pleased she'd been able to play lady's maid to Sophie.

"I thought I knew where it was, but when I left, I got turned around. I…"

She put her hands on Sophie's shoulders. "You can tell me."

Sophie's green gaze met hers in the mirror. "I encountered a man in the corridor."

"Oh, you poor dear. I wish I could have been there with you. I could tell you were rattled about something. Did you say anything to him?"

Sophie shook her head.

"Then all is well. It's not as if you had a conversation with him without a chaperone present. Besides, now that you will be in a different costume, he won't even know who you are. Come, I believe I have a different mask as well."

Ellie turned away and moved to the chest at the end of her bed. Opening it, she pulled out the domino she'd originally planned to wear to match her husband before Darius insisted that she dress as the universe to "eclipse all others," as he had so phrased it. She rose and laid it out on the bed to examine any wrinkles. Blowing air from between her closed lips, she wished she'd hung it in her armoire, as there were quite a few.

"What's this?"

She looked toward her chest to see Sophie holding the book Ellie had learned so much from. She smiled, not surprised Sophie would find the only book in the room. Her friend studied literature at the Belinda School and could always be found reading. "That's the book Lissa spoke about. You should take it now. I believe it's good luck."

Sophie's eyes lit with excitement. "Thank you. I will put this in my room before returning to the ball." She started for the door.

"Wait. You need your costume."

Sophie gave an apologetic smile. "Of course."

In no time Ellie had Sophie in her domino, now looking quite mysterious with the hood pulled up. The black mask, so different from the white one she wore earlier, made her appear a completely different person. "You must look at yourself."

She pulled Sophie by the hand to the mirror at the dressing table and tilted it.

"Merciful heavens." Sophie's whispered words pleased Ellie.

"I told you."

Sophie turned and took her hands. "Thank you. You are such a good friend. I'm going to miss you so much." Then, without warning, Sophie hugged her.

Ellie could feel tears gathering as she hugged her friend back. "I'll miss you. But I promise we will visit each other. Besides, it's still days before we must part, and the night is yet young. Come, let us deliver that book to your room and join the crowd. If I'm not mistaken, dinner will be rung for at any moment."

Sophie nodded, wiping her own eyes. "Yes."

No sooner had they reentered the ballroom and joined Darius, than Georgie came looking for Sophie, exclaiming over her new costume.

Darius leaned down. "I had Beacham hold the bell until you returned."

Ellie leaned into him. "Thank you."

As if the butler had heard her husband, he stepped forward and rang the bell.

She smiled at their guests as they moved through the open double doors toward the dining room, where multiple small tables and a buffet awaited them. "Mrs. Torbett has proved herself invaluable with my many Christmastide activities. I'm very glad I didn't dismiss her."

Darius smiled. "You have a forgiving heart, for which I'm grateful. And now that all our guests are busy enjoying Cook's meal, can I interest you in a short walk in the moonlight?"

"Truly?" To have a bit of time with him after their hectic day seemed like heaven.

"Yes." He held his arm out, and she wrapped hers around his. They strolled to the terrace doors, which a footman opened.

The chilly night air wasn't nearly as cold as it had been, and the moon was but a sliver in the night sky.

Darius brought her to the edge of the terrace before pulling her into his arms. "Elle, I have a confession."

She rested her hand against his cheek. "I will always listen to you. You know that."

"I do. But what I have to say may surprise you."

"No matter what it is, I am here." Her heart beat harder in her chest at the seriousness in his tone.

"Then I confess that I cannot wait for all these blasted people to leave so we can truly begin living our lives together."

The growl in his voice sent her over the edge. Laughter, pure and joyful, burst forth, and she let it be as loud as it needed to be.

He smiled at her with love, not censure, his happiness with her filling her soul.

She calmed and looped her arms around his neck. "Then I must confess something as well."

"I am listening."

"I am very glad I don't have to plan anything else until next Christmastide. I just want to enjoy being your wife and a mother to your children."

"*Our* children."

She smiled. "Yes, *our* children."

"And, my lady wife, would you be amenable to more children in the very near future?" Darius lowered his head, his lips barely a breath away.

"Oh, yes."

His lips touched hers and she found herself swept away in his love. A love that surpassed all earthly bonds and took her beyond the moon to the stars, wrapped in his arms.

The End

About the Author

Lexi Post is a New York Times and USA Today best-selling author of romance inspired by the classics. She spent years in higher education taking and teaching courses about the classical literature she loved. From Edgar Allan Poe's short story "The Masque of the Red Death" to Tolstoy's *War and Peace*, she's read, studied, and taught wonderful classics.

But Lexi's first love is romance novels so she married her two first loves, romance and the classics. Whether it's dashing dukes, hot immortals, sizzling cowboys, or hunks from out of this world, Lexi provides a sensuous experience with a "whole lotta story."

Lexi is living her own happily ever after with her husband and her two cats in Florida. She makes her own ice cream every weekend, loves bright colors, and you'll never see her without a hat.

Website: lexipostbooks.com
Lexi Post Updates: app.mailerlite.com/webforms/landing/c1w1g3
Facebook: facebook.com/lexipostbooks
Twitter: @LexiPost
Instagram: instagram.com/lexipostbooks
Amazon Author Page: http://amzn.to/1IEL2cc
BookBub: bookbub.com/authors/lexi-post
D2D: books2read.com/author/lexi-post/subscribe/1/16171
Goodreads: goodreads.com/goodreadscomLexiPost
Instagram: instagram.com/lexipostbooks
Blog: happilyeverafterthoughts.com
Pinterest: pinterest.com/lexipost77
Email: lexi@lexipostbooks.com